The Time for Healing

Ramona K. Cecil

The Time for Healing
COPYRIGHT 2020 by Ramona K. Cecil

Contact Information: titleadmin@pelicanbookgroup.com

All scripture quotations, unless otherwise indicated, are taken from the Holy Bible, New International Version(R), NIV(R), Copyright 1973, 1978, 1984, 2011 by Biblica, Inc.™ Used by permission of Zondervan. All rights reserved worldwide. www.zondervan.com

Cover Art by *Nicola Martinez*

White Rose Publishing, a division of Pelican Ventures, LLC
www.pelicanbookgroup.com PO Box 1738 *Aztec, NM * 87410

White Rose Publishing Circle and Rosebud logo is a trademark of Pelican Ventures, LLC

Publishing History
First White Rose Edition, 2020
Paperback Edition ISBN 978-1-5223-0232-2
Electronic Edition ISBN 978-1-5223-0258-2
Published in the United States of America

Dedication

Dedicated to Mary Jane and Randy Smith, whom I miss every day as I treasure the memory of our friendship.

A time to kill, and a time to heal;
A time to break down and a time to build up;
Ecclesiastes 3:3 (KJV)

1

Shawnee village, southern Missouri, 1824

"Life will change for you soon, Daughter."

At her mother's quiet words, anger rumbled through Red Fawn like the low howl of the autumn wind outside their wigwam. She knelt and tugged the shaggy buffalo robe closer under her mother's swollen chin. Their tribe had moved twice since they buried her father where the Pigeon Creek flows into *Spelewathiipi*, the big river the white man called Ohio. She hated the thought of moving again before the time of the Spring Bread Dance. And she hated the whites who would force that move.

"Life will change for all of us when the white man makes new laws that will force us to move west again."

Would Mother even survive another move? Red Fawn's heart quaked at the thought.

"No, Daughter." Mother shook her head as she rose onto one elbow and coughed. Her raven braids streaked with silver shook with her convulsive movements. Red Fawn snatched a scrap of cloth from a nearby basket and handed it to her mother, who pressed it to her mouth. Despite Red Fawn's efforts, her mother grew weaker.

When her coughing had subsided, Mother grasped Red Fawn's hand. The comparison of her own freckled skin against the smooth brown hue of Mother's jarred Red Fawn anew, reminding her that she hadn't been born a Shawnee.

"No, Daughter," Mother insisted through a wheezy breath. Her grip tightened and her dark gaze grew intense. "You will not be going west. You will go east. The Great Spirit has told me in a dream."

Red Fawn's heart clenched. She eased her hand from her mother's and stepped toward the fire pit at the center of the wigwam. Normally, she wouldn't question her mother's visions. Everyone in their tribe knew that, along with Falling Leaf's gift of healing, the Great Spirit had given her a special gift of prophesy. But lately, Mother's visions had become disturbing.

Frowning, Red Fawn crouched beside the circle of stones that surrounded the shallow fire pit. Tugging at the blanket draped around her shoulders, she wrapped herself tighter in its warm folds and gazed into the orange flames and the plumes of pale-gray smoke that wafted up through the wigwam's vent hole.

The tin kettle resting on a bed of hot stones near the fire rumbled and began spewing foggy vapor from its spout. Gingerly grasping the kettle's doeskin-wrapped handle, she poured some of the boiling water over crushed herbs she'd sprinkled into a cup.

"The white man will never allow us to move back east." Red Fawn returned to her mother's bedside and handed her the cup of steaming liquid. "I fear the jimson weed seeds I mixed with the herbs to help you sleep are clouding the true visions the Great Spirit is trying to send you."

In the shadowy confines of the wigwam, the firelight burnished Mother's coppery profile. "My visions do not come from the jimson weed." Her voice held an unusually sharp edge. Cradling the earthen cup in both hands, she inhaled the aromatic vapors spiraling from it and turned a distant gaze toward the hide flap covering their home's doorway. With a whispered *thwap-thwap*, it billowed and collapsed against the buffeting winds.

"The Great Spirit has shown me two horses, one light and one dark." With each word Mother's voice grew stronger—stronger than Red Fawn had heard it sound for many days.

"I saw you take the reins of the dark horse," Mother said, "but it turned and moved away and would not allow you to mount it. It pulled you to the light horse." She paused to draw in a deep, ragged breath.

Red Fawn wished Mother would save her energy, but the urgency in Mother's tone stopped the words of caution before they left Red Fawn's tongue.

"You mounted the light horse, but you kept the reins of the dark horse in your hand, so it followed you as you rode east into the morning sun. Into a new day. A new world."

Red Fawn lowered herself against the curved bark

wall beside her mother's bed and pulled her knees up to her chest. She wrapped her arms around her doeskin-clad legs covered by her black skirt. "You know very well that I have never been fond of riding horses of any color."

Mother drained the last of her drink and handed the empty cup to Red Fawn. Instead of softening the severe lines around Mother's mouth and eyes as Red Fawn had hoped, her light remark seemed to have etched them deeper.

"If you are to be a healer, Daughter, you must never brush away the Great Spirit's guidance as you would an insect from your nose. And you cannot hide from what is meant to be, like the turtle that pulls his head into his shell."

"I am sorry, Mother." Contrition dragged down Red Fawn's voice. "I will pray the Great Spirit will bless me with words and visions to guide me as He has guided you."

She could not find the courage to tell her mother that she, too, had experienced visions. But hers were not glimpses of the future. They were scenes of an odd dream-life that had haunted her since childhood. Like rays of the sun caught in a turning glass they flashed in her mind and then vanished, leaving her feeling unsettled.

Fighting the worry gnawing at her chest, she tucked the buffalo robe more snuggly around her mother. Though she'd lived eighteen winters, fear and sadness gripped her at the thought of facing the future without her only remaining parent.

At a cold gust of wind, Red Fawn turned around. The wrinkled face of Spotted Bird poked through the hide flap covering the doorway.

"I have news." The old woman's eyes popped wide and a tremor of excitement warbled through her voice.

Red Fawn nodded toward the cooking fire. "Come. Warm yourself and tell us what you know." Old Spotted Bird loved nothing better than bringing news to her fellow villagers.

The old woman bustled in. The bright ribbons edging her black skirt flashed as they caught the firelight.

"Two white men have come to our village and are asking permission to enter." Spotted Bird reached her hands toward the fire and the many copper bangles on her arms tinkled merrily.

"We have little to trade, Spotted Bird." Falling Leaf's voice sounded strained from her cot across the floor. "But if they have the cloth they call flannel, we could exchange Red Fawn's woven baskets for enough cloth to make new winter underskirts."

"These men are not traders." Spotted Bird turned her back to the fire. "They have come with the book the white man says holds the words of the Great Spirit." She gave a snort that ended with a chuckle. "As if there could be such a book."

"Has the council decided if the men should be allowed to enter the village?" Mother's voice sounded serious, as if she considered the decision one of great importance.

Red Fawn brushed a stray strand of hair from her mother's face. "Surely a council is not needed for such a decision. Such men have come to our village before, and Chief Great Hawk sits and talks with them and then sends them away."

Spotted Bird came and crouched near Falling

Leaf's bed. "Not this time. Chief Great Hawk has asked for all the elders to come to the council house. And as you are the head of the women's council, Falling Leaf—"

"You know my mother is not well." Red Fawn did not try to blunt the sharp edge of her words as she frowned at Spotted Bird. "I have just given her a hot drink to help her sleep. I will not allow her to get up from her bed and go out into the cold."

"You must go in my stead, Daughter." The words crawled slowly from Mother's lips, and her eyelids fluttered as if fighting sleep. "The time has come for you to take your place at the council. And you speak the words of the white man better than I do. Even better than Chief Great Hawk."

"I will do as you say." The sooner the council met, made their decision, and sent the men on their way, the sooner she could get back to her mother. "Rest. I will be back soon." Red Fawn followed Spotted Bird out of the wigwam.

"The time has come."

Red Fawn barely caught her mother's parting words as she emerged into the gray, blustery afternoon. But the finality of her tone chilled her more than the north wind slapping her in the face.

She glanced across the village to where two white men stood beside their horses—one animal dark and the other pale. Her mother's prophetic words rang in her ears and shot fear through her heart.

The older of the two men fixed her with a piercing gaze. Suddenly, the vision of a face much like this man's flashed before her mind's eye. In the vision, she'd looked down upon the laughing, whiskered man as if he'd picked her up and held her above him.

A great shiver shuddered through Red Fawn. She hurried toward the council house with Spotted Bird puffing behind her. The sooner they sent these men on their way, the better.

~*~

Jeremiah Dunbar blew on his frigid fingers and crossed his arms over his chest to tuck his hands into the warmth of his armpits. He stomped his feet to get the blood circulating through his frozen legs and made a quarter turn to keep the slicing wind at his back.

He gazed over the little Indian village dotted with dome-shaped wigwams. Covered with slabs of bark, they looked like large inverted baskets laid out in haphazard fashion.

With each passing minute, his patience seeped away with his body's warmth. He wished Zeb didn't have his mind so set on preaching to these Shawnee.

Over the past weeks, he and Zeb had shared God's Word with settlers, keelboat river men, and the occasional band of Delaware and Miami Indians they'd happened across on their journey. In most instances their efforts had been met with respect if not enthusiasm. Jeremiah rejoiced that several of the encounters had resulted in souls won for Christ.

It had been for the specific purpose of bringing the Scriptures to these Missouri Shawnee that they'd traveled westward for the better part of a month. But having reached their destination, he saw no advantage in freezing to death while waiting for permission to enter the Indians' village.

"How long do you think they'll make us stand here?" Jeremiah could not keep the aggravation from his voice.

"Reckon they'll need to talk it over a might 'fore they let us come any farther," Zeb said as his horse neighed and shifted its dark bulk.

A shiver shook Jeremiah. Earlier today, they'd ridden through an icy drizzle, and the sore throat he'd awoken with this morning had become a searing pain. With each swallow, it felt as if someone were ramming a hot poker down his throat. For support and warmth, he leaned against the smooth coat of his cream-colored mare as he tried to push the pain, fatigue, and biting cold from his mind.

But aside from his physical discomforts, he most wished he could rid himself of the disquiet burrowing deep in his chest. Just as uncomfortable as the inclement weather and his weakening constitution, this emotion seemed stubbornly entrenched and far more troublesome. He knew its name.

Resentment.

Even now, twelve years later, the word Shawnee still conjured frightful memories of being besieged in Fort Deux Fleuves at the age of twelve. The horrific attack on Pigeon Roost Settlement by a band of Shawnee had resulted in terrifying nightmares that had plagued his boyhood dreams.

He wasn't convinced that a people capable of such acts of cruelty would be receptive to notions like God's love and mercy and Christ's salvation. He wondered how Zeb could be so sure. Zeb's brother, sister-in-law, and baby nephew had been among those slaughtered at Pigeon Roost, and his little niece had vanished, presumably taken by the marauding Indians. How could Zeb be so zealous to take the gospel to the very people who'd visited such atrocities on his family?

Jeremiah scrunched his head between his shoulders so his hat's wide brim blocked November's icy gusts from nipping at the back of his neck. "We've been here a good half hour. You'd think by now they'd either allow us in or send us packin'." He gave a little snort, beyond caring that his tone had turned downright petulant. "Maybe they think if we get cold enough, we'll just leave."

The aroma of roasted meat wafting from the village teased Jeremiah's nose and made his stomach grind, reminding him that he hadn't eaten for many hours. From the top of each wigwam, a thin finger of gray smoke curled toward the pewter sky as if taunting him with the knowledge of warmth and shelter within reach, but denied to him and Zeb.

"If we are to win their respect, we must, in turn, respect their ways. I'm sure it will not be much longer—"

At the abrupt halt in Zeb's voice Jeremiah's gaze slid over to him. Zeb's narrowed eyes seemed fixed on a couple of black-skirted Indian women crossing the village toward the longhouse.

"Did you see what I saw?" An uncharacteristic tremor shook Zeb's voice.

"You mean the two Shawnee women?" Jeremiah saw nothing remarkable about them.

"One had red hair. I caught sight of it just before she covered her head with her blanket." Zeb's voice sounded more awestruck than curious.

"Probably some kind of adornment." With every muscle of his half-frozen body aching, his stomach growling with hunger, and his throat on fire, Jeremiah didn't give a whit if the woman's hair were grass-green.

At that moment a lanky Indian draped in a blanket and wearing a spiky headdress of dyed red animal hair ambled toward them with a bandy-legged gait. A half-grown boy followed close behind him.

"You may come to the council house," the older Indian said without emotion. "Chief Great Hawk wants to hear of the white man's book that holds the words of the Great Spirit."

Without waiting for a reply, the man turned and headed toward the oblong structure the other Indians had entered.

"Praise be to God." The prayer puffed from Jeremiah's lips on a relieved sigh.

The boy took hold of their horses' reins, and Jeremiah and Zeb followed the other Indian across the village. Jeremiah shot a parting glance over his shoulder at their mounts, wondering at the wisdom of leaving their possessions in the Shawnee's care.

At the longhouse, the Indian pushed aside the buckskin flap covering the opening, and Jeremiah and Zeb ducked into the dim, smoky structure. The scents of sassafras, wood smoke, and tanned leather blended with a mixture of other pleasant, but less familiar aromas. A fire burned in a rock-lined pit in the center of the space, welcoming them with the warmth Jeremiah had craved.

A man of about forty-five years of age sat on the far side of the fire. The moving flames raked him in alternating light and shadows, so he appeared apparition-like. He sat with his deerskin-clad legs crossed in front of him at the ankles, his knees pointing outward. A woolen blanket hung about his shoulders, while copper rings dangled from his ears and a small ring hung from his nose.

"Sit." The Indian punctuated the one-word command with a sharp nod.

They obeyed. Mimicking the chief's posture, they faced him across the fire pit. As Jeremiah lowered himself to a woven mat on the hard-packed dirt floor, the room tilted before his eyes. He fought the dizziness gripping him. It wouldn't be prudent to show weakness to this Shawnee.

Though dimly aware of the intense gazes trained on him and Zeb by the many villagers lining the longhouse walls, Jeremiah focused on the man before him.

"I am Great Hawk, a chief among my people." The Indian's voice sounded distant in Jeremiah's ears. "You are not the first to bring to the Shawnee this book that holds the words of the Great Spirit. I have heard that its medicine is strong."

Zeb's head bobbed in agreement.

Great Hawk glanced at the Bible Zeb clutched in his hands. "Tell me, does the new white chief in Washington believe what is in this book?"

Zeb took a deep breath. "To my understanding, President Monroe is a Christian man. But I am not privy to the depth of his faith."

Great Hawk looked at Jeremiah. "Do you believe that this book holds the words of the Great Spirit and has strong medicine?"

Jeremiah licked his parched lips. They felt as stiff and cracked as strips of leather that had dried for days in the sun. He prayed he could form an intelligible reply.

"Yes." Though his voice sounded hoarse, the word rang with the strength of his conviction. "I believe it with all my heart."

A hint of a smile lifted the corner of Great Hawk's mouth. "In my life I have heard the voice of the Great Spirit in the wind, the rushing waters of the rivers and streams, and in the cry of my brother hawk, my clan totem. I have learned that the Great Spirit can speak in many ways. Great Hawk and his people are willing to listen to the words of your book. We will decide for ourselves if they are truly the words of the Great Spirit."

During the chief's soliloquy, a sudden chill shuddered through Jeremiah. He gripped his knees in an effort to still his body's convulsive movement, while praying Great Hawk didn't notice. He swallowed and tried not to grimace at the pain it caused him. This wasn't a good time to fall ill, but he couldn't remember when he'd felt worse.

Great Hawk looked sharply at Jeremiah. His lowered brows above his long, noble nose reminded Jeremiah very much of the bird for which the chief was named.

"We will talk again tomorrow. The owl calls, and the shadows grow long. You will sleep here in the council house tonight. Our women will bring you food and blankets."

Great Hawk rose, and Zeb followed. Somehow Jeremiah managed to push himself up on unsteady legs while the chief beckoned to several of the women.

Jeremiah's attention shifted from Great Hawk to the women who came forward to take the chief's directions. One of them—the youngest, it appeared—had red hair twisted into two braids that draped over her shoulders. This must be the girl Zeb had seen earlier.

The woolen blanket draped around her blue calico

blouse and black skirt could not hide her appealing form. As he admired her profile, the gentle curve of her pale cheek reminded him of a rose petal. Long lashes, a shade more golden than her hair, fringed large, wide-set, blue-green eyes. This girl couldn't have been born a Shawnee.

A sudden movement to his right accompanied by a guttural grunt wrenched Jeremiah's gaze from the beguiling vision. He turned to find Zeb on his knees, tears streaming from his wide eyes down his ashen face as he gazed at the girl.

Zeb raised his hands above his head. "Dear Lord in heaven, praise Your holy name!"

The Indians fell silent as they turned toward the spectacle Zeb presented.

"Ginny girl, do you know me? It's your Uncle Zeb." His voice shook with the heart-rending plea. "I declare, you are your ma made over."

The scene before Jeremiah began to swirl. The Indians' mutterings became like the roar of a distant waterfall in his ears. He sensed the villagers rushing toward him and Zeb as blackness descended.

2

Red Fawn crouched beside the council house fire. Glad for something to do, she reached unsteady hands into a skin bag, pulled out a fistful of dogwood bark shavings, and dumped them into an earthen cup. The bearded man named Zeb had shifted his attention from her to the other white man, now rousing from a fever-faint. But the name he'd called her echoed like ghost whisperings in her ears.

Ginny. The word had haunted her dreams as far back as she could remember. And now this stranger had called her by it, as if it were her name.

The sputtering of the kettle heating over the fire drew her back to the work at hand. She poured the steaming water into the cup she'd prepared, covering the bark.

Glancing at the younger white man, now sitting up and rebuffing the ministrations of his friend, her conscience chafed. She should feel no gladness at the man's illness, even though it had interrupted the unsettling words his friend had uttered. Hadn't

Mother taught her that to be a true healer she must have a compassionate heart for every living thing that suffered an affliction?

Sniffing the steam rising from the cup, Red Fawn surmised that the bark's healing properties had sufficiently leached into the hot water. She rose, cradling the warm vessel in her hands, and carried it to the sick man.

"Drink," she said, using the English she'd known as far back as she could remember. "This will take away your fever." As she transferred the cup to his hands, their fingers touched, sending a pleasant tingle up her arm.

A look of gratitude shined from his blue eyes, glassy with fever. As she watched him lift the cup to his cracked lips, she had to admit she found him pleasing to look upon. His hair, the tawny color of cornstalks in autumn, fell across his wide, tanned forehead. Sandy stubble covered a square jaw that gave him a strong, determined look.

He grimaced as his throat moved with his swallow, and Red Fawn made a mental note to cook a syrup of horehound honey, the best sore-throat remedy she knew.

"Thank you." He handed the cup back to her and smiled, sending warmth spiraling through her.

Red Fawn reached down for one of the blankets the women had brought, hoping her face hadn't betrayed her reaction to his smile. "You sleep now," she said, handing him the blanket with barely a glance at his face. "I will bring you more medicine tomorrow."

As she stood, she noticed the man called Zeb staring at her. Her insides squirmed like a nest of snakes. She turned, eager to return to her wigwam.

But before she could step away, her patient captured her hand. "What is your name?" The earnest look he gave her, as well as his strong, warm fingers wrapping around hers, compelled her to answer.

"Red Fawn," she murmured, wishing she didn't like the feel of his hand holding hers.

"I'm Jeremiah Dunbar." The smile that split his upturned face did uncomfortable things to her belly, and she slipped her hand from his.

"Do you not remember the name your ma and pa gave you, Ginny?" the older man's impassioned voice intruded.

She turned to him. The tears glistening in his gray eyes clawed at her heart. Once again, the image of a face flashed in her mind. She saw the same gray eyes, and heard laughter as he swung her up into the air.

"Ginny girl, do you remember nothing?"

She wanted to deny his question. But suddenly another face appeared in her mind—the stern face of her father, Painted Buck, admonishing her for telling a falsehood. *Speak only the truth, my daughter, for the Great Spirit frowns upon a lying tongue.*

She nodded. "Yes, I do remember. In my dream-life I am called Ginny. Ginny McLain."

A tear slipped from Uncle Zeb's eye to his bushy black-and-gray beard.

Uncle Zeb? *Yes, and Aunt Ruth.* The names popped into her mind and attached themselves to each other as easily as two pieces of wood carved to fit together.

"Do you remember me?" He peered into her eyes as if trying to see into her mind.

"I—I think so." The smiling image of a woman with walnut-colored hair vied with a sterner visage of a yellow-haired woman. One must be the woman called Aunt Ruth. The other? She'd rather not speculate.

"We thought you dead, child." Uncle Zeb grasped her shoulders and shook his head as if in wonder. "Me an' your Aunt Ruth's been mournin' you 'long with your ma, pa, and baby brother, Joseph, for lo these twelve years past."

Red Fawn stiffened and pulled away from his grasp. Her mind recoiled from thoughts of the people who belonged to her dream life—the people with whom she associated piercing screams that had terrorized her dreams since childhood.

"My mother, Falling Leaf, lies sleeping in our wigwam," she said, skewering him with her glare. "Three winters have passed since white trappers killed my father, Painted Buck, in the time of the Pawpaw Moon. He is buried beyond the Wabash River where the Pigeon Creek flows into Spelewathiipi. I have no brother."

Red Fawn hastened from the council house. Outside, she quickened her steps through the wind-driven snow. An urgent need to put distance between herself and the white men spurred her on.

She ducked into her wigwam, aching to run to the safety of her mother's arms like she'd done as a child when the frightening dreams became too real. She longed to speak to her about the troubling things that had transpired. But Mother's soft snoring told her Falling Leaf now traversed a dream journey of her own, and Red Fawn could not bring herself to call her from it.

From her mother's baskets of herbs, she gathered walnut and cherry bark and dried sumac berries and then found the earthen bowl of horehound honey. If she healed the man called Jeremiah, perhaps the two would leave.

She poured water from a skin pouch into the kettle, a knot of dread tightening in her stomach. As sure as a red evening sky and upturned leaves signaled a coming storm, she sensed that the arrival of the two white men heralded the changes Mother had foreseen. And she feared no herbal concoction could fend off those changes.

~*~

A soft, moist touch against his lips jerked Jeremiah awake. At the sight of the white Indian girl kneeling over him, myriad emotions darted around his chest like a bevy of barn swallows. *Surely she had not…*

Red Fawn dipped her finger into a little wooden bowl then touched it to his lips, moistening them with an oily salve. "I am sorry to wake you, but the sun is rising in the sky, and your friend asked me to bring you medicines."

Jeremiah pushed up to a sitting position on his woolen-blanket cot. Heat suffused his neck and face at his initial mistaken impression of her actions. He poked out the tip of his tongue to taste the oil she'd spread over his cracked lips. The sweet, light taste told him it must be either plant or mineral based.

"It is sweet birch oil," she said, answering his silent question. "It will heal your lips and make the skin soft again." Her smile transformed her features from comely to breathtakingly beautiful.

"You speak English well." He found it surprising that she hadn't lost the language of her childhood during her years with the Shawnee.

She set the bowl aside. "My father wanted me to keep the white man's language and to teach it to him and my mother. He said it would be good for our family and our tribe when dealing with the whites, so we spoke it often in our home."

"Where is Zeb?" Jeremiah cleared his burning throat and glanced around the longhouse. He needed to direct his thoughts away from this girl who made his heart hammer like a woodpecker's beak on a dead log.

"He has gone to Chief Great Hawk's lodge to tell him what is written in the book you brought," she said, her voice turning harder. She walked to the fire, bent over a steaming iron pot, and stirred its contents with a shaved stick.

She spoke as if the Bible was new to her, but Zeb said the Shawnee had taken her at the age of six. Jeremiah recalled his own sixth year vividly. That year, his family had traveled from Kentucky to Indiana, and his mother gave birth to his brother Joel in the Conestoga along the way. He and his seven-year-old sister, Dorcas, had kept three-year-old Lydia occupied by fishing for crawdads on a creek bank during Mother's travails. It seemed inconceivable that this girl, who remembered her given name as Ginny McLain, had no memory of her parents or Zeb and his wife, Ruth, setting her on their laps and telling her stories from the Scriptures.

"Surely, you remember the Bible. I remember the Bible stories my ma and pa told me and my sisters when I was six."

She stopped stirring the sweet-smelling contents of the pot and became still. At her silence, hope leapt in

Jeremiah that perhaps he'd jogged a long-buried memory in her.

Without answering him, she grasped the pot handle with a scrap of wool material to protect her hand, lifted the pot from the fire, and set it on a flat rock. She dipped an earthen bowl into the pot and then carried the vessel to him. She set the bowl on the ground in front of him. "When it is cool enough, drink it. It will heal your sore throat."

As she walked out of the longhouse, an ache not associated with his illness throbbed in Jeremiah's chest. Regret filled him. God had given him an opportunity to share Christ with Red Fawn, and he had squandered it.

He opened his mouth to call her back but then closed it. She'd doubtless gone beyond earshot of his voice. But even if he could summon her, he couldn't think of anything to say that wouldn't irritate her further.

At another painful swallow he picked up the bowl she'd left in front of him and took a sip. Though slightly bitter, the sweet taste of honey rendered the concoction palatable. The warm liquid trickled down his throat, soothing as it went. The bittersweet taste of the medicine fit his conflicted emotions exactly.

As he polished off the last of the drink, a new resolve filled him like the warm liquid filling his belly. He knew he'd not draw another contented breath until he convinced the lovely girl called Red Fawn to open her heart to Christ's salvation.

Stifling a shiver that shook his frame, Jeremiah lay back down on his pallet and pulled the wool blanket snug beneath his chin. He prayed that Red Fawn's medicine worked quickly. The Lord had granted him strength of purpose. Now he needed renewed strength of body to carry it out.

3

Red Fawn strode toward the circle of villagers who sat listening to the words of Zeb McLain. She struggled to push down the dismay rising inside her at the sight of Mother's straight back among the group. Despite the midday sun warming her shoulders, she feared that sitting on the damp ground might bring a recurrence of Mother's cough.

Reining in her frustration, she moved to her mother's side. Old Spotted Bird grunted and inched away to make room. Red Fawn nodded her thanks. In truth, she wanted to grasp her mother by the arm and tow her back to their wigwam. But that would show disrespect, and she would not embarrass her mother in front of their tribe members or the white man called McLain.

Falling Leaf turned a knowing smile on Red Fawn. The knowledge that her mother understood her concern and displeasure stoked the fire of Red Fawn's smoldering temper. But Father had always rebuked Red Fawn when her temper flared, saying, "Anger is like a young colt. It only becomes useful when it is tamed and controlled. Otherwise its power is unpredictable and dangerous."

Red Fawn managed a quick, tight smile before turning her attention to Zeb McLain, who stood in the center of the circle, the Bible laid open across his outstretched arm. In the week since their arrival, she'd avoided the unsettling white men as much as possible. She couldn't determine which made her more uncomfortable: Zeb, who seemed to feel he had some kind of claim on her, or Jeremiah, whose presence made her senses crackle like summer lightning.

"The Son of the Great Spirit interceded for man. He took the punishment meant for us for all the things we have done or ever will do that displease the Great Spirit." Zeb's voice boomed from his spot in the midst of the people. As he spoke, he turned slowly so that each person listening could feel that his words were directed at him or her.

His impassioned voice captured Red Fawn's attention, and despite herself, she found his words stirring her interest in this Son of the Great Spirit.

Over the past few days, while she'd plied Jeremiah with medicines to heal his fever, cough, and sore throat, he too had spoken to her of this being whom he claimed was both man and spirit. But talk of Jesus always evoked troubling flashes of memory for Red Fawn. So with her mother's renewed strength, Red Fawn had refrained from treating the young white man's sickness, allowing her mother to take over much of Jeremiah's care. And when she *had* taken him medicines, she'd been careful to add herbs like dried blossoms of the hop tree to the concoctions so he'd quickly fall into a deep sleep, and she wouldn't have to listen to his strange talk.

Jesus. The name that Zeb McLain uttered in a tone of reverence and wonder echoed in Red Fawn's mind as if reverberating from the depths of a dark, narrow cave. When she first heard the word from Jeremiah's lips, it had ignited a flash of memory. But when said in Zeb's voice, the memory blazed like a fire fed with dry cedar branches.

Jesus Christ, the same yesterday, and today, and forever.

An instant after those words formed in her mind, they flew from Zeb McLain's mouth. "Jesus Christ, the same yesterday, and today, and forever."

Red Fawn shivered. She knew the words before he said them!

She fidgeted, wanting to leave. But she'd come to remind Mother that she needed to take her tea of hawthorn bark to strengthen her heart.

"Jesus wants to make you His brothers and sisters—true children of the Great Spirit." Zeb read from the book. "'And this is His commandment, that we should believe on the name of his Son Jesus Christ and love one another, as He gave us commandment.'" He lifted his face and looked directly at Red Fawn, his gray eyes burrowing into hers.

With difficulty, Red Fawn yanked her gaze from his. Irritation prickled down her spine like sand burs. She wished this man, with his grizzled whiskers and piercing gray eyes, would stop acting like she belonged to him.

Eager to leave, she leaned toward her mother and whispered, "It is time for your medicine."

"Patience, Daughter," Mother murmured as she took her hand in hers.

At her mother's touch, Red Fawn relaxed. She listened in rapt attention while the white man told stories about the man named Jesus. As he spoke, she realized she knew the details of each story before Zeb uttered them.

At length, Zeb closed the book and bowed his head. "Dear heavenly Father, be with all these precious souls who have gathered to hear Your Word…"

Red Fawn stopped listening and focused on the squawking of two blue birds arguing in a nearby oak tree. She didn't want to hear him say more words and know what he was going to say next.

When Zeb stopped talking, Chief Great Hawk and several of the villagers surrounded him, asking questions. Relief flooded Red Fawn. Perhaps now she could coax Mother back to their wigwam. She understood her people's curiosity about the white men, and she had to admit the stories Zeb told were entertaining. But she'd be glad when the men left their village and life returned to normal.

Linking her arm with her mother's, she pulled her away from the group. "You should rest by the fire, and take hawthorn tea to strengthen your heart."

"The sunshine and fresh air will strengthen me as well as the tea." Mother glanced into the blue sky decorated with clouds that looked like mounds of fluffy milkweed fibers. "The Great Spirit has sent us a beautiful day. I should not dishonor Him by hiding away from it."

Red Fawn also preferred to stay outside and enjoy the warm autumn day…as long as Mother felt well and they stayed away from the white men. She glanced back to assure herself that Zeb McLain remained occupied talking to Chief Great Hawk.

"Come, Mother; let us walk beside the river." Red Fawn smiled and started in the direction of the wide stream behind the village, but Mother stopped, halting her.

She looked intently into Red Fawn's face. "Why do the white men frighten you so?"

"Because a white man killed Father," she blurted.

"I know when you are not being truthful, Daughter." The gentle chide in Mother's voice caused tears to spring into Red Fawn's eyes.

Her arm still linked with her mother's Red Fawn began walking, but toward their wigwam, not the river, and Mother fell into step beside her.

"I—I believe the Great Spirit has been sending me prophetic visions." She glanced at her mother's face, curious how she would react to her words.

Mother's eyes showed no emotion. "And what does this have to do with the white men and their Bible?"

"When they tell stories from the book, or talk about the man they call Jesus, who, they say, is the Son of the Great Spirit, I...I..."

"You feel as if you have heard these things before." Mother's quiet words held no hint of question, but Red Fawn felt relief in answering.

"Yes."

They came to the front of their wigwam and stopped.

Mother's shoulders rose and fell as she heaved a deep sigh. "I do not think you are seeing what is to be, but what has been." Her eyes squinted to dark slits. "Do you remember when your father found you?"

"Some," Red Fawn murmured. She'd resisted any memory that nudged too near her frightening dream-life.

"Twelve cycles of the moon have passed since your father came upon you and a Shawnee warrior in the forest. The man was full of the white man's fiery drink and hitting you with a stripped willow branch. The harder you cried, the harder the man hit you."

Red Fawn glanced at the scar on her forearm just above her wrist and shivered. She'd had the scar for as long as she could remember—or wanted to remember. But she had no memory of the incident that caused it. Her earliest memory of her true life as a Shawnee was of being carried in her father's arms and then handed to her mother, who'd cradled her.

"For many cycles of the moon, your father and I prayed to the Creator for a child, but no child came. Your father said he loved you the moment he saw you and he knew the Creator had finally sent us a child of our own." Mother smiled. "He traded the hide of a buck deer for you."

"Why do you tell me this?" The wind gusted, sending a shiver slithering through Red Fawn. Rubbing her arms, she stepped out of the shadow of a tall cedar and into the sunlight.

"I wanted you to know that it was not your father who took you from the ones who gave you life."

The tinge of guilt in Mother's voice and the pain in her eyes squeezed Red Fawn's heart. She wrapped her arms around Mother in a warm embrace. "I have only good memories of my father...and of you."

"You have no memory of your white mother and father?"

"I—I do not know. Maybe. I see flashes of people who seem familiar, yet are strangers." Their talk had taken a turn down a path Red Fawn did not care to explore. "They belong to my dream-life. They mean nothing to me."

"And the man named Zeb McLain?" Mother's voice softened. "Do you remember him?"

"Maybe. I cannot tell for certain." Irritation honed a sharp edge on Red Fawn's voice. "I do not wish to speak of the white men. I will be glad when they leave our village."

"Both of them?" The hint of a tease in Mother's voice did nothing to soothe Red Fawn's bristling nerves. "The one named Jeremiah keeps asking to see you."

"He is better, then?" Red Fawn's heartbeat quickened. By turning his care over to Mother, she'd hoped to scour all thoughts of Jeremiah Dunbar from her mind. It hadn't worked.

"His fever has broken, and he says his throat feels much better. He needs only to regain his strength." Mother gave her a mischievous grin. "I told him the turkey broth you will bring him today will help restore his strength."

Something akin to panic leapt in Red Fawn's chest, cinching it tight. "Can't you or Spotted Bird take it to him? I know she cooked a turkey yesterday."

"And she was kind enough to give us some of the broth." Mother chuckled. "Jeremiah does not want an old woman like Spotted Bird or me to bring him broth."

Mother stooped to enter the wigwam, but Red Fawn grasped her arm, stopping her. She wouldn't defy Mother's wishes, but if she could make her understand how uneasy the white men's presence made her, perhaps Mother wouldn't force the errand upon her.

"I would rather stay away from the white men."

Mother shook her head. "You need to get used to them. You will take broth to the man Jeremiah."

At Mother's words a wad of fear knotted in her belly. "Why do I have to get used to them? They will be leaving in a few days."

"Yes. And when they go, we will be going with them."

4

Jeremiah quickened his steps toward the wigwam where Red Fawn stood beside Falling Leaf. Having awakened feeling more robust than he had in days, his first thoughts had turned to the beautiful girl whose medicines had restored his vigor.

The image of the girl Zeb insisted was his niece had emblazoned itself on Jeremiah's heart. Soon, he and Zeb would need to head back to Indiana in order to arrive home before winter set in. The thought of leaving Red Fawn behind saddened him. So when Zeb told him that Falling Leaf had requested that he and Zeb take her and her daughter back to Indiana with them, his heart had soared.

Though Red Fawn continued to show little interest in the scriptures Zeb shared daily with the Shawnee villagers, Falling Leaf often joined those who gathered to hear the gospel message. Jeremiah prayed that through her mother's influence, Red Fawn, too, would eventually open her heart to Christ's offer of salvation.

"Red Fawn. Falling Leaf. Halloo there!" He waved

toward the two as he approached.

Falling Leaf ducked into the wigwam and, for a moment, he thought the women hadn't heard him calling to them.

He opened his mouth preparing to repeat his salutation when Red Fawn, who hadn't moved, slowly turned and faced him. Her lovely blue-green eyes wide, she fixed him with a stunned look.

His heart bucked at her beauty. But at her surprised and somewhat distracted expression, he couldn't help grinning. Perhaps she hadn't expected him to live. Did she have such little faith in her medicines? But as he stepped nearer, both his grin and lighthearted mood left him.

Along with surprise, anger and fear shone from Red Fawn's tear-filled eyes. A slight trembling of her delicate chin compelled him to reach out and take her hand.

"Red Fawn, what is the matter? Are you ill?" It pained him to think his presence disturbed her so.

She looked down at her hand in his and yanked it away as if his touch might burn her.

"I am well." Her barbed tone along with the tremor in her voice belied her words. She took a half-step backward, and her gaze that had pierced him a moment ago now skittered away like a frightened rabbit. Her reticent attitude gouged at his heart. Did she find him distasteful or the mission that had brought him and Zeb to this village? Both thoughts filled him with sorrow.

If she didn't want to speak to him, why hadn't she followed her mother into the wigwam? He should simply thank her for the care she and her mother gave him during his illness and return to the longhouse where Zeb sat discussing the scriptures with Chief Great Hawk. But reluctant to leave her company, he lingered, pressing the toe of his boot into the soft dirt and carving out half-moon impressions. When he finally spoke, she did, too, their voices clashing.

"Red Fawn."

"Jeremiah."

They both laughed, their gazes meeting. He couldn't remember when he'd heard such a lovely, melodious sound. Her red-gold lashes swept down to kiss her cheeks, extra rosy now beneath their whimsical sprinkling of freckles.

This time he sensed that shyness, not disdain, had chased her look from his. At the thought, his spirit lifted with a burgeoning hope. Maybe it wasn't his presence after all that had caused her earlier show of distress.

"You first," he murmured with a nod, praising God that he'd actually managed to push the words through his tightening throat.

She toyed with an orange ribbon that decorated the length of her skirt. "Mother said the fever has left you, but you should not be up. The sickness could come upon you again."

Her concern squeezed his heart. He longed to reach for her hand again, but fearing the action might upset her, he clasped his hands behind him to ease the temptation.

"I woke feeling considerably better this morning. I've grown weary of lying down and couldn't resist coming out into the sunshine." He glanced up at the crystal blue sky. "I wanted to thank you and…your mother for the fine care you gave me." Hopefully she hadn't noticed how he'd stumbled over the word mother. To him, Zeb's dead sister-in-law, Carolyn McLain, remained Red Fawn's mother.

"Have you had anything to eat today?" Again, her gaze slid shyly away from Jeremiah's, sending his heart into a gallop. It took him a second to recover sufficient breath to answer.

"No, and to tell you the truth, I am a might hungry." Grinning, he rubbed his stomach that rumbled beneath his hand at the thought of food.

Her roving look assessed him, making him painfully aware of how his clothes hung on his gaunt frame. "You are not strong enough yet for a heavy meal, but turkey broth and ash cakes will give you strength and fill your belly. Come."

With that, she ducked into the little wigwam and he followed. Although about a quarter the size of the longhouse, the wigwam's interior mimicked the larger structure in many ways. Baskets of various sizes and shapes sat scattered about the place. Bunches of dried herbs hung from the wigwam's support poles and filled the room with a pleasing aroma. Two low beds covered with wool blankets took up a quarter of the space.

Falling Leaf squatted beside the rock-lined fire pit situated in the center of the room, where she tended a steaming pot suspended above a small flame. The smell of rich meat broth wafting from the pot started Jeremiah's mouth-watering and his stomach to rumbling again.

The hint of a smile touched Falling Leaf's lips as she looked up and nodded a greeting. "It is good to see you well, Jeremiah Dunbar. Sit." She cocked her graying head toward a woven mat near the fire pit.

Jeremiah obeyed while Red Fawn busied herself

patting what looked like a thick cornmeal mush into thin cakes, which she gingerly slapped onto a flat rock near the fire.

He returned Falling Leaf's smile. "I thank you, Falling Leaf, for the care you and Red Fawn gave me. Your tonics are strong medicine."

Falling Leaf nodded. She didn't smile, but her placid countenance suggested his words pleased her. For the first time, Jeremiah noticed the woman's sunken cheeks and the sallow skin. Though he had little medical experience, it didn't take a doctor to see that she wasn't well. Concern pricked him, and he wondered what ailed her.

Red Fawn glanced at him, her face full of pride. "Mother is one of the finest healers among our people. The people of our village depend upon her knowledge of healing herbs." Her voice turned strained as she deftly snagged one of the johnnycakes with two fingers and turned it over on the hot rock. "One day I, too, hope to be a great healer among my people."

She patted another johnnycake from palm to palm in a harder motion than Jeremiah would have thought necessary. The way her lips pressed in a thin, tight line suggested barely contained anger. Something had put her out of sorts. At the glint of aggravation in her eyes when she glanced at her mother, he wondered if the two had quarreled.

Falling Leaf dipped a hollowed-out gourd into the pot of steaming broth and ladled the soup into a waiting earthen bowl.

"My daughter should know that the gift of healing is from the Great Spirit," she said, handing Jeremiah the bowl of broth. "It is meant to be used for all people."

Her words and terse tone confirmed Jeremiah's suspicion that he'd stepped into the midst of an argument between the two women. He wished he could gracefully leave, but both decorum and his empty belly forbade any exit.

"Speaking of the Great Spirit," he ventured, "I would like to thank Him for the meal you have prepared."

Falling Leaf nodded, and Jeremiah bowed his head and offered a short prayer of thanks.

Red Fawn, who'd remained quiet following her mother's gentle but stern chide, passed the fritters she called ash cakes to her mother and Jeremiah.

For several minutes the three ate in silence. When the stillness became oppressive, Jeremiah turned to Falling Leaf. "Zeb tells me you and Red Fawn will be traveling with us back to Indiana," he said brightly, hoping to ease the tense atmosphere.

Jeremiah wouldn't have imagined the room could get quieter. He immediately sensed that he'd said exactly the wrong thing. His throat tightened around the bite of corn cake he'd just swallowed, causing him to cough and requiring him to take a big swig of broth to clear his throat.

"My father used to say that both food and decisions need to be chewed well." Red Fawn's voice sounded as flat and hard as the stone on which she'd baked the corn cakes.

Jeremiah coughed again to better clear his throat. "Your father must have been a wise man." He prayed the girl would find nothing offensive in his statement.

"Your words are true." Falling Leaf answered for her daughter. Unlike Red Fawn, the older woman's expression and tone exhibited no hint of rancor.

Indeed, her gaze that touched gently on her daughter before returning to Jeremiah held only patience and fond indulgence. "My husband, Painted Buck, was a wise and good man. He is buried near the place where the river called Wabash flows into the great Spelewathiipi.

"Ohio," Red Fawn translated at Jeremiah's puzzled look.

"I am sorry," Jeremiah uttered, his unease building.

Without acknowledging his cursory sentiment, Falling Leaf continued. "When his spirit walked beyond the sunset into the hunting grounds of the Great Spirit, the place became sacred to me." Tears welled in her dark eyes. "When our people were driven from the land beside the Wabash, I prayed that the Great Spirit would let me see the place once more before my spirit leaves my body." She thumped her finger against her chest. "The peace in my heart tells me my prayer will soon be answered. When you and Zeb McLain came to our village, I knew it was *ka-tet*, the work of the Great Spirit."

Jeremiah stopped nibbling his corn cake. "But if you want to visit your husband's grave, why doesn't Chief Great Hawk just have someone from the village take you back there?"

Falling Leaf shook her head. "Chief Great Hawk says when our people signed the treaty of St. Mary's, we turned our back on the land you call Indiana. He…" She turned to Red Fawn and spoke in Shawnee. Red Fawn nodded and looked at Jeremiah.

"Mother says to tell you that Chief Great Hawk does not want to be seen breaking a treaty, so he will not allow anyone from our village to travel past the great river called the Mississippi."

"But traveling with white men would not break the treaty," Falling Leaf added before taking a sip of her broth.

"Mother." Red Fawn dropped her corn cake into her lap and faced Falling Leaf, worry lines knitting her brows together. "We are nearing the time of *kini kiishthwa*, the Long Moon. You are not strong, and the weather will make traveling difficult." When her gaze touched Jeremiah, he knew the warmth in his belly could not be attributed to the turkey broth. "We cannot ask Jeremiah and Zeb to take us to Father's burial site and then bring us back to our village. By the time they would have to travel back to their homes *Pepoonwi*, grandfather of the North, would be blowing his coldest breath upon the land."

Jeremiah opened his mouth to correct Red Fawn's mistaken impression. According to Zeb, they wouldn't be returning here to the Shawnee village, but the four of them would travel on together to Zeb's home in Underwood, Indiana. But before he could speak, Falling Leaf spoke up.

"When we leave this place, Daughter, we will not return." Falling Leaf's soft voice held a note of finality.

Red Fawn's jaw fell slack. The fear and anger Jeremiah had seen in her face earlier in front of the wigwam returned full force. But if Falling Leaf took note of her daughter's agitation, she showed no sign of it. Instead, she calmly lifted her cup and sipped the steaming broth.

Red Fawn sprung to her feet and yanked the blanket that draped her shoulders more tightly around her. Jeremiah sensed it wasn't for warmth that she pulled the wrap closer, but to help still her trembling form. "Mother, you cannot mean the words you say. You are not strong enough for such a journey."

Jeremiah agreed with Red Fawn. Though he looked forward to Red Fawn's company on the trip back home, Falling Leaf looked too frail to travel across country on horseback in mid-November. Watching Red Fawn's lovely eyes fill with tears and her delicate chin quiver, he longed to rise and comfort her. But Falling Leaf would undoubtedly view such an act with disfavor. And he also doubted she would appreciate his interjecting himself into the debate.

Falling Leaf continued to munch her corn cake, outwardly unfazed by her daughter's volatile demeanor. "We will talk of this later, Daughter." Her voice dismissive, she set her corn cake aside.

Taking Falling Leaf's words as a signal to leave, Jeremiah quaffed the remainder of his broth and then stood and dipped a quick bow toward the two women.

"Thank you for the meal, Falling Leaf. Red Fawn. Your hospitality is as warm as your medicine is strong. Together they have revived both my spirit and my constitution."

Falling Leaf answered with a nod and a pleased sounding grunt, while Red Fawn's frown smote his heart like a Shawnee war club.

Jeremiah left the wigwam slump-shouldered. Red Fawn was right. For Falling Leaf to attempt the trip to Indiana wouldn't be wise. But according to Zeb, sometime next year, the tribe would be required to move further west. While he didn't doubt Falling Leaf's desire to visit her husband's grave, he couldn't help wondering if, at the same time, she also saw the trip as a way to return Red Fawn to her blood kin.

"Jeremiah." Red Fawn's voice stopped his trek

back to the longhouse.

Turning, he saw that she carried a small earthen jar.

"Mother says you must drink the rest of the turkey broth."

"Tell your mother I thank her." Jeremiah took the jar, making sure his hands touched hers in the transfer.

Their eyes met, and he sensed she felt the same warm tingle he did at the touch. But the next instant she snatched her hands away from his and hid them in the folds of her skirt.

He stifled a sigh. The girl sent his senses spinning. One moment she seemed to return his interest only to shrink from it an instant later. Perhaps his attention frightened her. He would need to cultivate patience if he were to have any chance of winning her heart to him as well as to Christ.

Jeremiah reached out for her hand. "I am glad you and your mother will be returning to Indiana with me and Zeb. He is very excited about bringing you back home to your Aunt Ruth."

She ignored his proffered hand, keeping hers hidden. Her expression changed from tentative to stormy and green lightning flashed from her eyes.

"I am not glad to be leaving my tribe! And you tell Zeb McLain that I have no family but my mother, and I will do all in my power to convince her that we should stay here."

5

The pungent scent of decaying leaves met Red Fawn's nose as she crouched beside the river. The morning sun peered over the treetops, warming her head and shoulders and painting streaks of rose and gold on the river's surface.

She paused for a moment while clutching the skin bag she'd brought to collect water and gazed across the sun-dappled stream that drifted lazily southward. An eddy swirled against the wide, flat rock beneath her feet, pushing the water up to lap playfully at the toes of her moccasins. Across the river's gurgling expanse, the forest line hugged the sandy bank. Bare limbs of willow, sycamore, elm, and maple trees seemed to weave together like the side of a large basket. When the time of the Spring Bread Dance came, the trees would grow green again with new leaves. Many of the forest's trees and bushes would celebrate by wearing showy blossoms in their hair.

A sigh puffed from her lips. She would not be here to see it. At the thought, sadness stabbed at her chest, accompanied by a twinge of fear. In the two days since Jeremiah's visit to their wigwam, she and Mother had spoken often about the two of them leaving the village with the white men. Red Fawn continued arguing against the wisdom of such a trip. But Mother hadn't budged from her decision.

That Mother insisted Red Fawn should abandon her tribe and rejoin the people of her dream-life still astonished—and pained—Red Fawn. It hurt to think that Mother wanted to give her back. Back to people she did not know and into a life she did not want.

Falling Leaf insisted that her decision for them to leave had come at the Great Spirit's direction. Although Mother believed this to be so, Red Fawn had her doubts. It bothered her that Mother, along with many others of the tribe, went each day to listen to Zeb's words, something Red Fawn diligently resisted. She worried that Zeb McLain, not the Great Spirit, had convinced Falling Leaf that she and Red Fawn should travel back with him and Jeremiah to Indiana.

She plunged the skin sack into the water and pressed the floating bladder under the river's surface. The vessel's narrow opening spit out bubbles as the sack filled. The icy stream nipped at her hands, but they quickly numbed to the cold. As a Shawnee, she'd learned early not to flinch at discomfort.

Shawnee.

How could she think of herself as anything but Shawnee?

She pulled the sack full of water from the river and yanked the leather strings at the neck, drawing it tightly closed.

Peering into the stream, she waited until the troubled surface became more placid again and then studied her reflection. Her hair the color of flame and her eyes that mimicked the blue-green of the river had always set her apart from her parents and other tribe members. The sun that browned her skin to a hue a shade lighter than her mother's had also deepened the freckles that mottled her face and arms.

She rose slowly and slung the water bag's leather strap over her shoulder.

You are your ma made over.

Remembering the words Zeb McLain had said when he first saw her in the longhouse, her chest cinched as tightly as the neck of the water sack.

Even if she looked like the white people from her dream-life, that didn't make her any less Shawnee on the inside. A ball of determination formed in her middle and hardened like a lump of clay baked in a fiery furnace. She would not let anyone—not Zeb McLain and his wife called Ruth, or Jeremiah Dunbar—change that.

Jeremiah.

At the thought of him, butterflies took flight in her belly. She could not deny the unsettling effect he had on her. And the thought of traveling alongside him for many days made her stomach quiver as much as the idea of having to live in the white man's world.

Across the river, a doe stepped from the shadows of the forest to the water's edge. With her tawny front legs planted widely apart, she bent her graceful neck and poked out her long pink and gray tongue to lap the clear water. Suddenly, the animal lifted her head and stood alert. She turned her big brown eyes toward Red Fawn. For a long moment, the doe watched her. Then she dipped her head as if in greeting and went back to drink again from the river.

Calm settled over Red Fawn like the buffalo skin mantle embracing her shoulders. Surely, the Great Spirit had sent the deer, her family's totem as a *manito*—a spirit guide to assure her she would always be Red Fawn, proud Shawnee daughter of Painted Buck and Falling Leaf.

She turned from the river and began climbing the well-worn path that twisted up the steep bank toward the village, dry leaves crunching softly beneath her moccasins. She needed to get back and help Mother with their morning meal. Perhaps she could convince Mother to stay in the wigwam today, away from the white men's influence. She would tell her of the deer and suggest that the Great Spirit had sent the deer as a sign that she should not return to the white world.

At the sound of a voice, she stopped her trek. At first, she heard only bits of sound, softly spoken words snatched away by the wind. But as she rounded a bend in the path, the words took shape. English words.

Through an opening in a leafless thicket she saw the figure of a man. Jeremiah stood on a jagged rock outcropping that jutted from the leaf-strewn hillside. He faced the river, his head bowed and his eyes closed.

"Forgive my weak faith and selfish heart, dear Lord," he intoned. "Please give me the words that will win her heart for You. Help me and Zeb preach Your word in a way that will bring every soul within hearing into Your fold."

At the sight of him, Red Fawn's heart jumped like a frightened rabbit. How strange to feel both drawn to someone yet, at the same time, uneasy near him.

She stood still, her unease growing stronger by the second. Without a doubt, his words were petitions to the Great Spirit. Years ago, Mother and Father had taught her to respect another person's prayer time with the Great Spirit as a sacred moment not be intruded upon.

But as if rooted to the spot, her feet refused to move. The way the morning sun's rays touched his pale hair, making it shine like polished brass held her gaze captive. Caught in the bright sunrise, the stubble covering his angled jaw glinted like flecks of gold. The sight stole her breath away and set her heart beating like the wings of a great bird.

Was Red Fawn the "she" of whom he spoke? Her rabbit heart jumped again. Remembering the angry words she'd said to him the last time they talked, stinging briers raked across her conscience.

His strong fingers curled around the brim of his black hat that dangled at his thigh. "Dear Lord, give me a humble heart, and the opportunity—"

A small rock shifted beneath Red Fawn's foot, making a grating sound, and Jeremiah stopped his prayer.

As he stepped toward the bush that shielded her from view, Red Fawn's thudding heart leapt to her throat as if trying to escape her chest. Would he think she'd deliberately hid to listen to his prayers?

"Red Fawn."

Surprise widened his blue eyes, but Red Fawn detected no anger in his pleasant smile.

"I—I went to get water." Red Fawn's voice stumbled. With fingers that felt as thick and awkward as paw-paws, she tugged at the water sack's strap on her shoulder.

The weight of the water yanked the sack from her grasp and it hit the ground with a splat. A stream of water gurgled from the sack's opened neck and trickled down the dirt path, turning the dust covering the packed earth to mud.

Feeling as deflated as the skin sack, Red Fawn reached down to retrieve it at the same moment Jeremiah did, causing their heads to collide.

"Ouch!"

"*Aiee!*"

They uttered the words in near unison as they popped up, rubbing their heads.

At Jeremiah's widening eyes, slack jaw, and the red spot appearing near his hairline Red Fawn burst into laughter.

"I'm so sorry, Red Fawn." A look of horror filled his wide eyes. He reached tentatively toward the spot on her forehead that still stung and, she assumed, matched his injury. "Are you all right?"

"Yes." She managed to work the word between her giggles. "Are you injured?"

"No." The little red bump rising on his forehead answered to the contrary. "But I'm afraid I've caused you to spill your water."

Again, he bent and picked up the skin bag, and this time she remained standing. "The least I can do is to fill it for you."

Red Fawn followed him down the trail, scolding her silly heart that sang like the blue songbird perched on the leafless branch of a nearby maple tree.

At the river's edge, he knelt and plunged the skin bag into the ice cold water, enduring the discomfort for her. The kind gesture scratched again at Red Fawn's conscience. Two days ago, she'd left him with angry words, and just now, he'd caught her listening to his prayer. Yet without hesitation, he'd performed a task most Shawnee men would consider strictly women's work.

The thought flowing from her heart spilled from her mouth. "I am sorry."

He pulled the dripping bag from the water and rose, grinning. "You have nothing to be sorry about. I'm sure the accident was my fault." He cinched the sack's neck shut and held it out to her.

"No. I am sorry for what I said to you when you left my mother's wigwam." She took the bloated sack but couldn't quite make her eyes meet his. "My father taught me that anger, like an arrow, should be aimed at the right target. I forgot his teaching. I was angry because I do not want to leave my village, but my mother says we must go, and I must obey her."

"Apology accepted." He smiled as they headed back up the path, but his smile soon disappeared. He focused on the path in front of him, his forehead puckered as if deep in thought.

At a steep, rocky stretch of the path, he grasped her elbow to help steady her, and Red Fawn couldn't help smiling. If he knew how many times, in all kinds of weather, she'd made this daily trek to fetch water without help, he'd realize she didn't need his assistance. Her feet knew every rock, dip, and turn in this path her moccasins had helped to form. But while she didn't need the assistance, she very much liked the feel of Jeremiah's strong hand on her arm.

The thought occurred to Red Fawn that she might enlist Jeremiah as an ally in her quest to stay in the village.

She stopped and grasped his arm, compelling him to face her. "Jeremiah, Mother is ill. Too ill to travel. Please, you must talk to Zeb. I fear she will not change her mind about leaving unless Zeb refuses to take us."

A look of pain flickered in the blue depths of his eyes. He reached out and grasped both her hands in his as a great sigh heaved his broad shoulders.

"Red Fawn, I have already spoken to Zeb of Falling Leaf's ill health and, he, too, is concerned. As much as he and Ruth would like to have you back with them, he would not put your mother in jeopardy." He shook his head. "But when Zeb tried to convince your mother she shouldn't attempt the trip, she wouldn't hear of it. She insisted that it is the will of the Great Spirit that you both return to Indiana, and that the Great Spirit will grant her the strength to make the trip."

Hope ebbed in Red Fawn, but surged with her next thought. She gripped Jeremiah's hands tighter. "Jeremiah, you and Zeb say you were sent by the Great Spirit. Every day Mother listens to Zeb talk of what is in the heart of the Great Spirit. If Zeb would tell Mother that the Great Spirit does not wish us to leave our village, perhaps Mother would listen."

He slipped his hands from hers and a furrow cleft between his brows. "To my knowledge, Zeb has not received such a revelation, and he would never tell a falsehood."

Shame sizzled in Red Fawn's chest. What she'd suggested would bring dishonor to her mother and to the memory of her father. She tried not to think of her father frowning down upon her from the land beyond the sunset. But somehow, she must convey her desperation to keep both herself and Mother here in their village.

"Jeremiah." She stepped toward him and grasped his hand, hoping he could read in her face her need for him to understand. "Then I must beg you and Zeb to leave in the night without me and Mother. Please—"

"Red Fawn!"

At the sound of her name barked from a distance, Red Fawn sprung away from Jeremiah. She turned to face the chief's son, Flying Hawk. Her face grew hot, its color, she suspected, matching the smudges of red streaking the eastern sky.

A couple years older than Red Fawn, Flying Hawk had made clear his interest in her. After the Fall Bread Dance, he'd spoken of his disappointment at her refusal to partner him in any of the celebration's dances. And lately, he'd begun bringing gifts to her and Mother's wigwam as a show of his intent to court Red Fawn. But to Red Fawn's relief, Mother had refused to accept the gifts, thus indicating her unwillingness to sanction the courtship.

Mother had never spoken of it, but Red Fawn suspected she shared Red Fawn's misgivings about the young brave. Though handsome, brave, and one of the village's best hunters, Flying Hawk had acquired a taste for the white man's whiskey. Red Fawn had observed that when full of the evil drink the naturally surly Flying Hawk became especially loud and cruel.

Flying Hawk's gaze seared Red Fawn and Jeremiah. Displeasure honed the angles of his face to the sharpness of knapped flint. Anger smoldered from the dark slits of his eyes.

At length, Flying Hawk slid his focus to Red Fawn's face as if to dismiss Jeremiah's presence.

"My father wishes to speak to you." His icy tone formed a wad of dread in Red Fawn's belly.

6

Red Fawn followed Flying Hawk into Chief Great Hawk's lodge. A keen awareness of Jeremiah's presence behind her helped calm her jumpy nerves.

Mother sat beside Zeb at the council fire. As usual, her expression remained unreadable. Zeb, too, wore his familiar placid look, but as he glanced toward her and Jeremiah, Red Fawn thought she glimpsed apprehension in the preacher's gray eyes.

"Sit." Great Hawk accompanied his command with a nod toward the two already seated. Red Fawn and Jeremiah joined them on mats beside the fire, Red Fawn beside her mother and Jeremiah beside Zeb. Flying Hawk sat across the fire next to his father.

The chief waited until all were settled in their spots. While only the crackling fire filled the silence, Red Fawn fought to keep her features unaffected by the tempest roiling inside her. Several scenarios of why Great Hawk had requested their presence vied for dominance, but none offered ease from the invisible hand knotting her insides.

At length, the chief directed his gaze toward Mother. "Falling Leaf, I have learned that you and your daughter plan to return with McLain and Dunbar to the land above Spelewathiipi, the river called Ohio."

Mother nodded. "Yes. The Great Spirit has told me in dreams that it should be so." She angled her face toward Red Fawn. "I was told that before I journey to the land beyond the sunset, I should visit the place where my husband, Painted Buck, began his journey to the hunting lands of the Great Spirit."

Perhaps Great Hawk had called them here to convince Mother not to leave the village. Hope bloomed in Red Fawn's chest. She searched the chief's face for a hint of his thoughts, but his stony features gave away nothing. Although she knew the chief held Mother in high esteem, regarding her as a great medicine woman and spiritual leader with special gifts of prophesy, he may not agree that Zeb and Jeremiah should play a part in this prophesy.

Great Hawk's gaze slid to Zeb and Jeremiah. "Has the Great Spirit instructed you to make this journey with these men?"

"No." Mother's voice held a touch of hesitancy. "But it was to the family of Zeb McLain that Creator first sent my daughter, Red Fawn. We believe that the Great Spirit does nothing by chance, that all His actions are deliberate." She looked directly at Zeb and Jeremiah. "Is that not the same as is written in your book of the Great Spirit?"

"It is." The hint of a smile lifted a corner of Zeb's mouth.

Mother turned back to Great Hawk. "The Great Spirit has told me that Red Fawn must come to know the people the Creator first gave her to."

"And you, Red Fawn, do you desire to return to the alien whites of your birth?" Great Hawk's dark piercing gaze seemed to search the depths of Red Fawn's mind as if to deny her thoughts any crevice to which they might escape detection.

Unable to bear the scrutiny, Red Fawn dropped her gaze to her hands balled in her lap. "I will do as my mother wishes." She barely managed to coax her voice above a whisper.

"Red Fawn does not wish to go!" Flying Hawk's angry voice intruded, causing Red Fawn to jerk her face upward. He bent forward, glaring at her across the fire, the flames dancing in the smoldering depths of his dark eyes. "Twice I have heard her arguing with Falling Leaf about leaving our village."

The urge to demand why the chief's son lurked outside her mother's wigwam rose in Red Fawn's throat, but she forced it back down. Such a challenge might well take the conversation down a path to a wasp nest she'd best not prod. Many nights since the Fall Bread Dance, she'd heard the plaintive tones of a courting flute near her wigwam; doubtless, it was Flying Hawk continuing his attempts to woo her.

"Is it true what my son says, Red Fawn? Do you wish to remain here with our people?" Great Hawk's voice turned as gentle as if he were speaking to a child.

All eyes turned toward Red Fawn. The slight smile on Mother's serene face conveyed her love and understanding. The silent permission for Red Fawn to freely speak her mind squeezed Red Fawn's heart until hot tears stung her eyes and nose. Zeb stirred as if uncomfortable, but his face, too, displayed peaceful acceptance.

Patient interest settled over Great Hawk's visage

while his son's brow cleft in an angry V above eyes narrowed to accusatory slits. But the indefinable look in Jeremiah's light eyes most affected Red Fawn. It shook her heart, jarring the breath from her lungs. Her heart pounding, she wrenched her gaze from his and swung it back to Chief Great Hawk.

"What I wish matters not. I am my mother's daughter. I honor her and will accept her decision and abide by her wishes."

Thoughtful wrinkles snaked across Great Hawk's wide brow as he heaved a sigh and shifted his gaze to the fire pit's flames. For long moments he stared into the bright, upward-licking tongues as if he might find the Great Spirit's will amid the flickering orange light.

At last, he looked up, his gaze sweeping those before him. "Falling Leaf. Red Fawn. I cannot forbid you to go with these men." He focused on Falling Leaf. "I have much respect for you, but in this, I fear you are not understanding the will of the Great Spirit. Four days I will smoke my pipe and pray to the Great Spirit. If His will is as you say, I will be given the same vision you say he has given you." His gaze took in the group again. "When the number of days that are sacred to our people have passed, we will sit together again, and I will tell you what the Great Spirit desires should be done about this."

Chief Great Hawk rose as a sign of dismissal, and everyone followed his lead. Red Fawn followed her mother out of the wigwam with Jeremiah and Zeb trailing her.

Outside the wigwam, Mother slipped the water bag's strap from Red Fawn's shoulder, her face showing no sign of concern about what had transpired inside the chief's wigwam. "Daughter, I will begin our breakfast," she said in Shawnee as she shouldered the bag. "I think today we shall have honey with our corn cakes." She sauntered off toward their wigwam.

Looking after her, Red Fawn marveled at Mother's ability to tame her emotions and wondered if she'd ever learn to tame her own emotions as well.

"Red Fawn."

At the sound of Jeremiah's voice, her heart became a hopping rabbit again, and she turned to face him. Wonder, along with emotions she couldn't define, shined from his broad face.

"Your mother has reason to be very proud of you, Red Fawn. You do her great honor. In the Bible, God says we should honor our fathers and mothers and that those who obey this teaching will have a good and long life."

For an unguarded moment, Red Fawn allowed herself to bask in his praise. But to reject the white man's world meant she must reject Jeremiah's friendship as well. At the thought, sorrow twanged hard in her chest. But when a basket is dumped, all within it is discarded at once.

Lifting her chin, she fought the impulse to return his warm smile as she met his look. "The Shawnee believe the same, but though the Great Spirit may grant me many days in this life, they will only be good if I can live them among my people."

Four days later, that sentiment still dominated Red Fawn's thoughts as she and her mother made their way back toward Chief Great Hawk's lodge.

Red Fawn slowed her steps to better match her mother's halting gait and wished the chief's lodge wasn't so far across the village. She gripped Mother's elbow swathed in a wool blanket against the biting

November wind. "Do you need to rest, Mother? Spotted Bird would be glad to let us warm ourselves at her fire."

"No." Mother shook her head. "The wind is too cold for us to stand still. Besides, walking will help make me stronger for the journey ahead of us."

Red Fawn doubted there'd be any journey for them—at least she hoped there would not be. She couldn't begin to guess what directions the Great Spirit might have given Great Hawk in the past days, but she doubted that in the end the chief would sanction her and Mother leaving with the white men. Over the years, she'd observed how the chief doted on his only son, spoiling the boy in ways most Shawnee fathers would not have done. Rarely had she witnessed Great Hawk deny Flying Hawk anything he wanted. And judging by the sound of Flying Hawk's courting flute outside her wigwam, which each night grew nearer and more haunting, he presently wanted Red Fawn.

But in truth, the persistent attentions of her would-be suitor bothered her little more than a pesky insect. Flying Hawk would doubtless soon tire of her rejection and pride would turn his interests elsewhere. But knowing the chief would be reluctant to allow the object of his beloved son's affection to leave without objection gave Red Fawn hope that she and Mother would be staying in the village.

As they approached the chief's lodge, Zeb and Jeremiah appeared from behind a nearby wigwam. The two men removed their hats as they greeted Red Fawn and her mother. The strange white man custom never failed to amuse Red Fawn.

Zeb offered her a nod and scant smile before turning his attention to Mother. Taking Mother's arm, he assisted her into the chief's lodge. Red Fawn appreciated that he no longer tried to prod her memory or treat her as if she were a member of his family.

Jeremiah's bright smile sent Red Fawn's heart into a wild-horse gallop. The touch of his hand on her back, guiding her ahead of him as they entered the chief's wigwam spread waves of comforting warmth radiating across her back. While she still looked forward to the men's leaving and life returning to normal for her and Mother, she couldn't deny she'd miss Jeremiah's presence when he and Zeb left their village.

As the four entered the wigwam Chief Great Hawk and Flying Hawk offered them welcoming nods from where they stood beside the fire pit. A fog of pleasantly scented wood smoke and tobacco swirled about them.

Red Fawn tried to ignore Flying Hawk's piercing gaze that seemed to follow her every movement and managed to nod a return greeting. As before, she took her place with the others across the fire from the chief and his son. The somber look that chiseled hard lines on Great Hawk's face along with the knowing grin spreading across Flying Hawk's reinforced Red Fawn's suspicions of the chief's verdict.

Although the chief could not actually forbid them to leave, to ignore his wishes would be considered a great insult, and something she doubted Mother would do. She began composing and tucking away in her heart words of comfort to help salve the disappointment Chief Great Hawk's decision would surely inflict on Mother.

When all were seated and quiet, Great Hawk, with

his arms folded across his chest focused his eyes across the fire pit at Red Fawn and her mother. Although she respected the tradition that forbad the chief from hurrying his answer, Red Fawn wished he'd speak soon and relieve the tightness in her chest.

"In the past days—a day for each of the sacred four directions—I have smoked my pipe and communed with the Great Spirit." Great Hawk's deep voice filled the wigwam, his breath moving the orange flames that flitted heavenward. His gaze swung from Red Fawn and her mother to Zeb and Jeremiah and back again. "Falling Leaf, the Great Spirit has sent me many visions and directed me in how I should guide you concerning whether you and your daughter should leave our village."

Mother remained respectfully quiet although Red Fawn sensed her mother's body tense at the chief's words.

"I was told," the chief continued, "that if you and your daughter leave our village alone with these men you must never return." His voice softened, taking on a kinder tone. "But I understand the pain in your heart to visit the sacred burial place of your husband, Painted Buck. The Great Spirit has told me He would smile upon such a journey."

Confused, Red Fawn felt the small hairs at the back of her neck stand up like they often did before a storm.

Great Hawk's voice turned stern as his narrowed gaze swept the group before him. "But if Falling Leaf and Red Fawn go on this journey, the Great Spirit has warned that only in this way may they return to our village: that Flying Hawk and his cousin, Yellow Feather, join you on the journey; and when you come to the place where the Wabash River flows into the Spelewathiipi, McLain and Dunbar must part with you and return to their homes. For four days you will remain at the burial site of Painted Buck and honor his memory."

His piercing gaze shifted between Red Fawn and her mother. "After four days you must return to our village with Flying Hawk and Yellow Feather and begin preparations for the marriage of Red Fawn to Flying Hawk."

7

Red Fawn stared at Great Hawk in disbelief. Her insides went as cold as if she'd gulped great quantities of icy water. Surely, Great Hawk could not do this. Mother had never sanctioned any courtship between Red Fawn and Flying Hawk. But regardless of how she might feel in her heart, Mother would never outwardly question the chief's ability to accurately interpret the will of the Great Spirit.

Red Fawn's breath caught painfully in her throat as she awaited Mother's answer—an answer that would determine the direction of the rest of Red Fawn's life. The thought sent her heart slamming against her ribs.

Furious at Great Hawk for forcing her mother into such an impossible decision, Red Fawn reached for her mother's hand in a show of support for whatever decision Mother chose. Mother's fingers closed warmly around Red Fawn's, whose own hands felt as cold and damp as if she'd come in from a chilly rain.

Mother lifted an unflinching gaze to Great Hawk. "It is for my daughter to say."

At Mother's words, Red Fawn stifled a gasp, and for a long moment, her heart seemed to stand still in her chest. A wave of relief washed over her as she realized Mother had gifted her with the decision that would define her future. But the airy feeling of relief quickly vanished, replaced by the weighty burden of responsibility for her mother's happiness as well as for her own. Great Hawk had left no good options for either her or her mother.

Red Fawn searched her mother's face for direction, but Mother's smile conveyed only a confidence in Red Fawn that Red Fawn didn't share.

She remembered Mother's words when Jeremiah had visited their wigwam. *When we leave this place, Daughter, we will not return.*

She looked at the two men seated beyond Mother. Zeb's sad face hung between his slumped shoulders making her wonder if he was praying. Jeremiah's blue-eyed gaze that latched onto Red Fawn's held an unspoken plea she couldn't interpret, and his throat moved with a hard swallow.

A trickle of cold sweat slithered down her back. She glanced up at Flying Hawk, and rage boiled in her belly at the self-assured grin curling the corner of his mouth.

Her hand slid down to the stone encased in doeskin that dangled from her belt. She itched to employ her woman's button, the Shawnee woman's weapon against unwanted advances from ardent suitors. How she'd love to bop Flying Hawk on the head with her woman's button to change his mind about wanting her for his wife and at the same time wipe the haughty grin from his face. But in truth, he'd made no forceful move toward her, and any such action by her would only embarrass Mother.

Perhaps, as her mother had prophesied, it was ka-tet—the will of the Great Spirit—that she and Mother leave the village. But she couldn't believe that the Great Spirit wished her to marry such a cruel and arrogant man as Flying Hawk. More likely, that part of the directive came not from the Great Spirit but rather had been contrived by Chief Great Hawk to satisfy the will of his spoiled son.

Red Fawn met Chief Great Hawk's smug look with an unflinching glare. How dare he try to force her to choose between disappointing her mother and marrying his son? Willing her voice not to tremble, she flung at him the only weapon he'd left to her, and the one thing she knew would wipe the smirk from his son's face as effectively as a woman's button.

"I will honor my mother's wishes and the Great Spirit's directions as He has sent them to her. Falling Leaf and I will return alone to Indiana with Zeb and Jeremiah."

Beyond the crackling of the fire, the *whoosh* of an exhaled breath came from Jeremiah's direction, and then silence filled the wigwam. Zeb remained quiet, but sat straight up. Beside her, Red Fawn sensed Mother's tense posture, relax.

Flying Hawk stared at her, his face turning first the pale color of river sand and then the purple of the thistle flower. His mouth gaped like a fish just pulled from the river. At his comical look, satisfaction swelled in Red Fawn's chest, and she fought to stifle a laugh. But the mirth rising in her throat died at the sight of Chief Great Hawk's face.

The chief's eyes that had popped wide at Red Fawn's utterance now narrowed with a searing anger that seemed to burn into her face. The muscles of his clenched jaw worked in and out, and Red Fawn thought she could detect a throbbing movement in his thick, muscular neck.

For the first time since entering the chief's wigwam, Red Fawn felt truly afraid. Would Great Hawk honor her decision, or would he violate the Shawnee tradition of freedom to choose one's life-mate and demand that she marry his son?

When the chief finally spoke, his voice reminded her more of the growl of an angry wolf than the voice of a man. "Then you must prepare to leave our village tomorrow." His angry glare raked the four people in front of him. Both he and Flying Hawk sprung to their feet, showing that both the meeting and their hospitality had come to an end.

Everyone else stood as well, and with respectful nods toward Chief Great Hawk, Red Fawn and her mother headed for the doorway. Behind her, Red Fawn heard Great Hawk say, "McLain and Dunbar, you stay."

Outside the chief's lodge, Red Fawn pulled her blanket tightly around her trembling body as the realization of what she'd done seeped into her consciousness. A combination of fear, anger and sadness vied for dominance in her chest. Because of the chief's treachery, she must forever leave behind the home and life she loved.

A sour taste filled her mouth and her stomach flopped like a fish on land. She felt thankful she'd drunk only a cup of tea for breakfast. If she'd eaten more, her stomach would surely expel it.

Mother laid her hand on Red Fawn's arm. The pride shining from her eyes helped to soothe the raging tumult inside Red Fawn.

"My heart swells with pride for you, Daughter. You have honored me and the memory of your father."

The smile Red Fawn tried to return to mother, withered. "Chief Great Hawk left me no choice, Mother."

Mother grasped Red Fawn's arm and began walking with her in the direction of their wigwam. "There are always choices, my daughter. You do not know it, but you are learning to obey the voice of the Great Spirit when He whispers to your heart."

Red Fawn started to say that she didn't believe the Great Spirit willed that she leave her people, but Jeremiah came trotting alongside them.

"Red Fawn." He paused to catch his breath which, in the chilly air, puffed from his lips in misty clouds. "We will need two more horses for you and your mother. Great Hawk tells me a man named Moni— Moni Wa—"

"Moni Waakoce'thi—Silver Fox," Red Fawn didn't try to keep the annoyance from her voice as she translated the Shawnee name to English. She hated how her heart leapt at the sight of this tall white man with hair the color of fine cornmeal. If not for him and Zeb coming to their village, she wouldn't be leaving behind the only life she knew. Yet her renegade heart danced whenever he came near.

"The chief says this man has horses he may trade." The wide smile splitting Jeremiah's face heaped fuel on the aggravation sparking in Red Fawn's belly. She wondered if his joy came from the thought of leaving the village, or because she and Mother would be traveling with him and McLain?

Mother nodded in agreement. "Silver Fox has

many horses, but he will want much in trade for them. You must be...*le-pi-do-wa* so he not *wan-ni-kee*," Mother said, her words of warning lapsing into Shawnee.

"My mother says you must be wise when dealing with Silver Fox," Red Fawn said at Jeremiah's puzzled look. "When dealing with white men, Silver Fox is not always honest, and you must be careful that he does not cheat you."

Her words wiped the smile from Jeremiah's face, a sight that should have pleased Red Fawn. But it didn't. "Great Hawk tells me the man speaks little English. I was hoping you could translate for me, Red Fawn. From what you and your mother say about the man, I fear that without your help I'll not be able to get us the best horses."

Red Fawn's world had just turned upside-down like a turtle flipped on its back. Her shaky heart didn't need to spend time in the presence of this man who made it jump like a scared rabbit.

"I—I cannot. I must get my mother back into our wigwam and out of the cold." She tugged on Mother's arm, but her mother refused to move.

Mother laughed. "We are only a few steps from our home, Daughter, and like the howling wolf that has gone to sleep, the wind has become quiet now." She smiled up at Jeremiah. "My daughter will help you make a good trade with Moni Waakoce'thi. And if you do not have enough in trade, tell him I will have many things to trade that we cannot take on our journey."

Red Fawn wished she could think of another reason to refuse Jeremiah's request, but she couldn't. Besides, she and Mother would need good strong, gentle horses for the long journey ahead, and she didn't trust Silver Fox to provide such horses out of a caring heart.

She watched to make sure that Mother made her way safely into their wigwam. Then with a defeated sigh, she turned and walked with Jeremiah toward the place where Silver Fox kept a corral of horses. She prayed Mother was right and the hand of the Great Spirit guided her life, for Red Fawn had lost all control.

~*~

The motliest assortment of horseflesh Jeremiah had ever seen grazed within a crude corral constructed of sapling poles. At least half of the dozen or so horses looked past their prime, some showing rib bones. A couple of the mares appeared swollen and ready to foal. Only a handful of horses seemed worthy of inspection for serious consideration.

"From where does Silver Fox acquire his horses?" The moment the question left Jeremiah's mouth, he wished he hadn't asked. If the horses for which he ended up bartering had been acquired by less than honest means, he'd rather not know it.

Red Fawn shrugged. "Who can say? Silver Fox trades with both white men and Indians."

She'd said nothing during their walk to the corral. The distant, almost hostile quality in her flat tone hurt worse than he'd like to admit. He didn't blame her for being angry at him. He could see how she might feel that he and Zeb were as much to blame as Great Hawk for her having to leave her home, never to return.

He'd noticed that as they walked, her gaze seemed to rove over her village as if she were trying to memorize its every detail. Her eyes held the same melancholy look now as she gazed beyond the corral toward the river, visible through a gap in the trees that bordered it.

Jeremiah's heart rent. Put in the same situation, he doubted he'd react as well. The courage and selfless sacrifice she displayed today in the face of Great Hawk's treachery had won Jeremiah's full-hearted admiration.

He still seethed with anger at Great Hawk for the anguish the chief had caused Red Fawn and Falling Leaf. Jeremiah could have happily pummeled the man and his son if it wouldn't have put all their lives in danger. He would also like to tell Great Hawk that he considered him a liar and a fraud. To make false claims concerning hearing and obeying the Lord's will—which he believed the chief's so-called visions amounted to—must be among the basest of sins. And using his power to force Red Fawn to marry his arrogant, selfish clod of a son compounded that sin.

As he gazed at Red Fawn's lovely profile deep, tender emotions filled him. How he wanted to take her in his arms, comfort her, and promise her that her future held nothing to fear. But he couldn't. Only God knew what lay ahead.

Gripping the sapling pole that served as the top fence rail, Jeremiah prayed that God might allow him to be Red Fawn's champion and protector.

"There is Silver Fox."

Red Fawn's declaration jerked Jeremiah from his prayerful reverie.

Following her gaze, Jeremiah looked down the right side of the corral to see a rather skinny, slump-shouldered Indian sauntering toward them and leading a couple of sorry-looking bays. Jeremiah's heart plummeted. Obviously, Chief Great Hawk, whose treachery seemed to know no bounds, had alerted Silver Fox in advance. Red Fawn and Falling Leaf would need horses capable of covering at least a hundred miles of hills and valleys between them and Evansville, where they could take a steamboat up the Ohio River to Charlestown, Indiana. He doubted these horses would last twenty-five miles.

8

Jeremiah scowled and shook his head at Silver Fox. He remembered Falling Leaf's warning concerning the man's trading practices. "No, these horses will not do."

Answering with a string of Shawnee that Jeremiah didn't understand, Silver Fox shrugged and gave him a puzzled look. At which time, Red Fawn turned to the horse trader and began speaking in no-nonsense-toned Shawnee.

Over the next several minutes, Jeremiah watched in amazement as Red Fawn and Silver Fox engaged in some of the liveliest horse trading Jeremiah had ever seen. Amid a hailstorm of fast-spoken Shawnee, emphatic head shakes and nods on both sides, as well as wild hand motions that he'd given up trying to decipher, Silver Fox finally gave an exasperated huff.

The horse trader removed the rope harnesses from the two nags and slumped to the far end of the corral. After a few moments, he emerged from the hodgepodge herd leading a sleek chestnut sorrel gelding and sturdy young dappled gray mare with gentle brown eyes.

After a few more words in Shawnee and some nodding, Silver Fox gave both Red Fawn and Jeremiah a quick, one-pump handshake and then handed the horses' rope leads to Red Fawn.

When Silver Fox sauntered away, Jeremiah shook his head at Red Fawn in wonder. "I don't know what you said, but it looks like you got us the best of the bunch."

Red Fawn stroked the side of the gray's head and smiled up at him.

Jeremiah's insides melted like butter beneath the sun. He drank in the smile—the first she'd given him in over a week—like a thirsty man guzzles water.

Her smile quirked up into a dimpled grin that made him wonder what that lovely, soft indention might feel like beneath his lips. "I reminded Silver Fox of a time when my father carried him from the forest after a snake bit his leg, and how my mother cured him with a snakeroot poultice. I also offered him everything my mother and I have that we cannot take with us, including our wigwam."

Jeremiah shook his head again in wonder, and his voice fell to a whisper. "You are a remarkable woman, Red Fawn." As he looked into her beautiful hazel eyes, Jeremiah couldn't help himself from clasping her free hand in his. "What I have seen in you today reminds me of the qualities of a virtuous woman, written about in the Bible in a book called Proverbs. 'Who can find a virtuous woman? For her price is far above rubies.'" He caressed the soft skin of her hand with his thumb. "I believe I have found a virtuous woman today. Chapter thirty-one of Proverbs is full of beautiful verses that I think describe you exactly, and I'd like to read it to you sometime."

She snatched her hand from his, anger lines marring her lovely features. "*Lenawe nilla*! I am Shawnee! I will always be a Shawnee. Wherever I live, I will live and worship the Great Spirit as a Shawnee. And I do not care what is written in your Bible book!"

~*~

I do not care what is written in your Bible book!

The next morning as Jeremiah stood in the longhouse and packed for the trip home, Red Fawn's parting words yesterday still stung. He blinked away the wetness that sprung into his eyes and tucked into a saddlebag the precious Bible Ma and Pa had bought for him when he decided to follow Pa into the ministry. How could someone with a heart as caring and beautiful as Red Fawn's reject God's Word?

A firm hand clapped onto his shoulder. He turned around and met Zeb's sad smile. "Pull your chin up off the ground, son. I know it's always hard to leave a place when we've made friends, but we're leavin' them with the Word of God and the hope of salvation."

Jeremiah expelled a frustrated sigh. "I just wish we'd convinced more to accept Christ. Like the chief and his son, and even...your Ginny." He stumbled at Red Fawn's birth name by which, Zeb insisted on calling his niece.

Zeb smiled, but his eyes held a look of sadness. "Several here have already accepted Christ's salvation. As for the others, we've sown the seed. Perhaps it is God's will that others come behind us and water that seed and for someone else to come along behind them and harvest the field we've sown. As for Ginny…"

He gave a little chuckle that both surprised and irritated Jeremiah. How could the man laugh when they were speaking of his blood kin's immortal soul?

Zeb raked the back of his curled fingers across his graying beard. "When you told me how Ginny outwitted the chief, I recognized the pluck and quick wit of her grandmother." He grinned, his gaze turning distant. "My ma was one of the most stubborn women to ever draw breath, but she had a heart as soft and sweet as puddin', a wit as sharp as a skinnin' knife, and more common sense than the Mississippi has water."

With a twinkle in his eye, Zeb turned a knowing smile to Jeremiah that sent heat marching up his neck to his face. It didn't surprise Jeremiah that the sharp-eyed preacher had noticed Jeremiah's interest in Red Fawn.

"Don't you worry none about Ginny, son. She got her pretty face from her ma, but that red hair and disposition came from her grandma. It may take some patience, but God's Word will eventually sprout in our Ginny's heart."

Jeremiah prayed Zeb was right. He also wondered if Zeb's use of the word "our" referred to Zeb and Zeb's wife, Ruth, or if it included Jeremiah.

The sound of running feet interrupted his pondering.

His heart took a quick leap into his throat as Chief Great Hawk, followed by his son, Flying Hawk, and several Indians he recognized as council members, burst into the longhouse.

A scowl ploughed furrows across the chief's forehead, but his expression held more curiosity than anger. Flying Hawk's features, however, seethed with anger. He stepped from behind his father and speared Jeremiah with his glare. Purple rage transfigured his handsome features into a grotesque mask of hate, while unbridled bloodlust sparked from his coal black eyes.

The Indian pointed an accusatory finger at Jeremiah, and he spat his words through clenched teeth.

"My father welcomed you into our village. From the rising of the Wilted Moon to the rising of the Long Moon, our people have given you shelter and food. We have listened to the words of your book, and our healers have even healed you of your sickness. Yet you repay us by stealing from us?" His dark glare burned into Jeremiah's eyes while his hand twitched over the deer antler handle of the skinning knife tucked in his hide belt.

Jeremiah's mind raced as he tried to think of any action he'd taken that the crazed man might have considered a theft. He sensed that were it not for the chief's presence, Jeremiah would, this moment, be struggling to prevent Flying Hawk from plunging his knife into Jeremiah's heart.

Zeb stepped toward Chief Great Hawk, his voice apologetic. "I assure you, neither Jeremiah nor I have taken anything that wasn't freely given to us."

Flying Hawk snorted. "They claim to speak the words of the Great Spirit. The words of truth. But they lie." His voice became a menacing snarl as he directed his words at Jeremiah. "It is not enough that you take our women. You must take our property as well?"

The young Shawnee glanced at his father and then swung his narrowed glare back to Jeremiah. "This morning while I hunted and you smoked your pipe in the wigwam of Green Corn, Laughing Crow saw this one take from our wigwam my pipe tomahawk carved with our family totem."

Great Hawk turned to a skinny, half-gown boy, whose shifting gaze never touched on either Zeb or Jeremiah.

"Laughing Crow." At the chief's booming voice, the lad jerked. The boy visibly trembled as the chief shot a string of Shawnee words at him in a questioning tone.

Laughing Crow, who looked more apt to cry than laugh, glanced at Flying Hawk's piercing glare. A swallow moved the boy's skinny neck, and he gave an emphatic nod.

Fury swirled like a growing cyclone in Jeremiah's chest. The despicable Flying Hawk not only bore false witness against him, but had obviously bullied the young lad into joining him in the duplicity.

With clenched jaw and fists, Jeremiah took a warning step toward Flying Hawk. How he'd love to take his wrath out on this lying vainglorious twit and pound his arrogant, up-tilted nose to a bloody mess. Once again, he thanked God that he and Zeb would be taking Red Fawn far away from this miscreant.

Bringing his face within inches of the Indian's nose, Jeremiah abandoned any pretense of diplomacy. "Listen here, Flying Hawk. I don't steal, and I certainly never took your tomahawk!" He jerked his head toward the blankets and saddlebags they'd packed up for the trip. "You can look through our things if you wish. But I can tell you that you will not find any property of yours."

Flying Hawk strode to the pile of bundled blankets

and saddlebags. After kicking aside a couple of saddlebags, he picked up a rolled-up brown sleeping blanket. With a sly, knowing smirk he unrolled the blanket and, to Jeremiah's stunned horror, out fell a magnificent pipe and tomahawk combination with an intricately carved dark walnut handle.

A sick feeling roiled in Jeremiah's gut. This morning after breakfast, he and Zeb had packed their belongings and rolled up their sleeping blankets before conducting a final sermon and worship service. Obviously Flying Hawk had placed the tomahawk in the blanket while he and Zeb were at the service.

Turning a triumphant face to his father, Flying Hawk folded his arms across his puffed-up chest. "See, it is as Laughing Crow said. Is it not our law, Father, that one who has been wronged by such an act is given the right say what punishment the guilty one should suffer?"

Chief Great Hawk, whose scowl had deepened, bobbed a nod. "It is as you say, my son."

A malicious sneer twisted on Flying Hawk's lips as he fastened his glare back on Jeremiah. "It is clear the man, Dunbar, likes tomahawks. So I challenge Dunbar to a contest. We will see who can throw my tomahawk truer. If Dunbar wins, he may have the tomahawk, and he and McLain may leave with Falling Leaf and Red Fawn. But if I win, Falling Leaf and Red Fawn stay in our village and Dunbar and McLain die."

9

"Falling Leaf. Red Fawn. Have you heard? There is to be a contest!" Spotted Bird bustled uninvited into Falling Leaf's and Red Fawn's wigwam, her eyes wide in her dried plum face.

Red Fawn looked up from packing cooking utensils into leather bags in preparation for the trip she dreaded. "What sort of contest?" Her curiosity piqued, she ignored her initial irritation at the old woman's lapse in manners. Contests were almost exclusively held during festivals, and there would be no more festivals until the Spring Bread Dance.

Mother stopped gathering medicinal plants for the trip. She put aside a little bundle of white ash bark and gave the woman a welcoming nod. "Sit and tell us of this contest, Spotted Bird."

Spotted Bird flounced out the folds of her black skirt and lowered herself with a grunt to one of the reed mats beside the fire. Spying the little pot of hominy and dried cherries sitting on the baking stone near the fire to keep warm, she craned her neck and sniffed.

Mother shot Red Fawn a knowing grin as she picked up the bundle of bark again and tied it together with a vine. "My daughter and I have had our breakfast, Spotted Bird. You are welcome to what is left." With only a grandson of fourteen moon-cycles to see to her needs, Spotted Bird regularly depended upon the kindness of other villagers to supplement her meals.

The old woman licked her lips. "Thank you, Falling Leaf. The hominy that you and Red Fawn make is some of the best I have had."

Red Fawn dipped the remainder of the sweetened hominy into a wooden bowl and handed it to Spotted Bird. Though curious about the contest of which the woman spoke, she knew Spotted Bird would say no more until she'd satisfied her hunger.

When Spotted Bird finished the last spoonful of hominy and took a long drink of sassafras tea, Red Fawn gathered the eating utensils for washing. The contented look on Spotted Bird's face as she swiped the back of her hand across her mouth suggested she'd forgotten the initial reason she'd stopped by.

"So what is this contest you speak of, Spotted Bird?" Red Fawn dumped the dirty bowl and spoon into a large gourd basin filled with warm water.

The old woman gave Red Fawn a momentary blank look, and then remembrance registered on her face.

"It is a contest of skill—throwing the tomahawk—and is to be between Flying Hawk and the young white man called Jeremiah." Spotted Bird returned to sipping her tea.

A fear she didn't understand curled in Red Fawn's

chest. Crouched at the basin, she pivoted to face Spotted Bird. What the woman said made no sense. Perhaps at her advanced age, she'd confused a dream with reality.

Red Fawn shook her head. "Jeremiah will be leaving here today. You know that Mother and I will be going with him and Zeb. Surely you have heard wrong. It makes no sense that he would agree to a contest with Flying Hawk."

Spotted Bird's head swiveled back and forth. "No. The contest is not of his choosing. It is the punishment Flying Hawk chose for him for stealing his tomahawk."

Red Fawn and her mother exchanged puzzled looks.

Mother's expression turned stern as she faced Spotted Bird. "You must be mistaken. I do not believe that Zeb or Jeremiah would steal. They have both spoken about the laws that are written in their book of the Great Spirit. They have said that stealing is against those laws."

Spotted Bird shrugged. "I just know what my grandson, Little Owl, heard. After the meeting where the white men read from their Bible book and prayed to the Great Spirit, Little Owl was passing the longhouse. He heard angry voices and stopped to see who was arguing." Having gained Red Fawn's and Falling Leaf's full attention, Spotted Bird paused to sip her tea before saying more.

The fear growing in Red Fawn's chest begat impatience. "Flying Hawk accused Jeremiah of stealing?"

Spotted Bird nodded. "Little Owl said when Flying Hawk looked inside the white man's blanket, he found his tomahawk." She drained her cup of tea. "Flying Hawk asked his father for the right to choose a punishment for the white man and Great Hawk granted it."

"And he chose a contest for punishment?" Red Fawn's heart raced. The loser of this contest would undoubtedly be required to pay a penalty. And rarely had anyone in their village bested Flying Hawk in a tomahawk throwing competition.

Spotted Bird nodded. Then, giving a grunt that mingled with the jingling sounds of the copper bangles adorning her arms, she slowly rose. She gazed in turn at Falling Leaf and Red Fawn, her eyes becoming sad. "I hope Flying Hawk wins the contest so you will stay in our village. I will miss you very much if you go."

Red Fawn rose and exchanged another look with her mother and found alarm in her mother's eyes. She grasped Spotted Bird's arm to stop her from leaving. "What do you mean?"

"Did I not say?" Spotted Bird laughed and grabbed her head. "My thinking is not so clear these days. Little Owl said that Flying Hawk declared that if he wins the contest, you and Falling Leaf will stay in our village and the two white men would die." She gave her head a sad shake. "It is too bad. I liked the stories the white men read from their Bible book."

After Spotted Bird left, Red Fawn stood frozen in place. Her heart felt like a rock in her chest. When her heart began beating again and sufficient breath returned to her lungs to give her voice, she turned toward her mother who now stood as well.

"Mother, we must do something to stop this contest." She grasped her mother's arms as much for her own comfort as to gain her mother's full attention.

"I do not believe Jeremiah stole Flying Hawk's tomahawk. Flying Hawk has done this to keep me here. Now Jeremiah and Zeb will die so Flying Hawk can get what he wants. You must talk to Great Hawk, Mother. He respects you."

Mother shook her head. "We cannot stop this, Daughter." Anger glinted in her eyes. "From the moment of Flying Hawk's birth and his mother, Sweet Grass, returned to the Creator, Great Hawk began spoiling his son. His ears are closed to anyone who would speak against Flying Hawk."

The image of Jeremiah's handsome face smiling up at her as he filled her waterskin played before Red Fawn's eyes, making her heart quake. Remorse gouged at her chest. She shouldn't have reacted so angrily yesterday when he complimented her on her dealings with Silver Fox.

Perhaps Mother could do nothing to stop this, but Red Fawn could. She strode to the foot of her bed, snatched up a blanket, and threw it around her shoulders. "Then I will go to Flying Hawk. If I accept Chief Great Hawk's offer and agree to marry Flying Hawk and allow him and Yellow Feather to ride with us to Father's gravesite, maybe there will be no contest and Flying Hawk will allow Jeremiah and Zeb to leave unharmed."

Mother picked up her own blanket and followed Red Fawn out of the wigwam. "Wait, Daughter."

Though desperation strained at Red Fawn's every nerve, she waited on Mother and gazed across the village. Many people made their way toward the open area in front of the longhouse. "Please, Mother, we must hurry. I must talk to Flying Hawk!"

Mother grasped her arm and held her back. "No,

Daughter. I know your heart holds no love for Flying Hawk. I do not approve of him for your husband, and I know your father would not approve of him." She cupped the side of Red Fawn's face. "Trust the Great Spirit, my child. What happens now is in the hands of the Creator. If Flying Hawk has acted dishonorably, the Great Spirit will not smile on him in this contest." She patted Red Fawn's cheek. "We will go and watch this contest and pray that the Great Spirit will smile upon Jeremiah."

Red Fawn's heart wilted. Though she knew she must obey her mother, she couldn't imagine Jeremiah ever winning such a contest with Flying Hawk.

Gripping her mother's arm, Red Fawn crossed the village on legs that threatened to fold beneath her.

Many people, including Spotted Bird and her grandson, Little Owl, gathered before the longhouse, talking and laughing. A festival atmosphere filled the chilled air.

On a birch tree several strides away, someone had peeled off a large section of bark and painted a red spot the size of a large man's hand. *About the size of Jeremiah's hand.* At the thought, Red Fawn remembered the first time she'd noticed the size of Jeremiah's hands. That first day after she'd treated his fever, he'd grasped her hand and asked her name. She remembered thinking how gentle his hands were for being so large.

The sight of Jeremiah and Flying Hawk emerging from the longhouse jerked Red Fawn from her muse. Her heart shot up to her throat, and she slipped her arm around her mother's waist and held tight.

Like Flying Hawk, Jeremiah wore no coat over his brown calico shirt, the sleeves of which he'd rolled up above his elbows. Neither man glanced at the crowd, but focused their full attention on the birch tree with the painted spot.

The sun that had hidden behind the pewter clouds crowding the sky now peeked out as if to watch the proceedings. It sent a shaft of light down onto the spot where Great Hawk, carrying a pipe tomahawk, joined his son and Jeremiah. The sunlight glinted off the shiny black hawk feather that dangled from the chief's scalplock...and the bead of sweat trailing down Jeremiah's temple.

"Two times you will each throw the tomahawk at the red mark." Great Hawk's voice boomed over the scattered laughter and mumbled conversation spreading through the crowd, stilling it. "The one who puts the blade closest to the center of the red mark wins."

The talking resumed, sounding like a flock of birds chattering in the trees. Red Fawn heard snatches of wagers being transacted in favor of Flying Hawk and her stomach rolled, threatening to expel her breakfast of hominy.

Feeling as if the breath had been squeezed from her lungs, she pressed her hand to her throat where her pulse throbbed wildly. If not for her mother's arm securely circling her waist, she would have flung herself at Flying Hawk and begged him to stop the competition.

Great Hawk handed Jeremiah the tomahawk. "Dunbar, you will throw first."

Jeremiah nodded and grasped the weapon's handle with an apparent calm that amazed Red Fawn.

She wished she'd had time to offer up proper prayers to the Great Spirit for Jeremiah's success. But there'd been no time for her and Mother to sit around their fire and burn tobacco to get the Creator's attention. So her heart cried out in silence, sending up petitions for the Great Spirit's favor as Jeremiah widened his stance, and with his arm muscles bulging, lifted the tomahawk over his head.

Red Fawn's heart stood still as the weapon left his hands and a rapid *whoosh, whoosh, whoosh* sounded as it flew end over end, finally burying its blade just inside the red spot on the far right edge of the target.

Red Fawn sagged against her mother in relief while grumbles sounded around the crowd.

Great Hawk held up his hand for silence.

Flying Hawk accepted the retrieved tomahawk with a look of impatient confidence and cast a sidelong smirk toward Jeremiah.

Red Fawn's heart lodged in her throat as Flying Hawk raised the weapon. Afraid to watch, she covered her eyes with her hand. But curiosity pried her fingers open in time for her to peek between and see him let the tomahawk fly. Time seemed to slow to the pace of a turtle's crawl as the hatchet tumbled through the air toward the target. The blade hit the wood with a thud, and Red Fawn's body jerked.

Gasps rippled through the throng of villagers. They mixed with Red Fawn's own sharp intake of breath as she gazed unbelieving at the skinned birch. The tomahawk's blade had come to rest just outside the red circle.

She offered up a silent prayer of thanks to the Great Spirit, and for the first time, allowed hope to bloom in her chest that Jeremiah and Zeb might live after all.

Spotted Bird's grandson, Little Owl, pulled the

tomahawk from the tree and loped to Jeremiah. But Flying Hawk stepped to his father. After father and son exchanged words Red Fawn couldn't catch, Great Hawk nodded, took the weapon from the boy, and handed it to his son.

Indignation sizzled in Red Fawn's belly. Having gotten a feel for his target, Flying Hawk obviously thought his chances of hitting the mark were better now than if he waited for Jeremiah to throw. The man had no honor. She vowed that whatever happened, she'd rather forfeit her life than wed the selfish, mean-spirited Flying Hawk.

With an ugly scowl marring his handsome features, Flying Hawk hoisted the weapon and sent it whirling through the air once more. It landed left of center, but safely inside the red spot.

Jeremiah rubbed his palms down his thighs and terror gripped Red Fawn's chest like the teeth of a bear. The tomahawk's handle could easily slip in sweaty hands, sending it far off course.

For the first time, she glanced at Zeb who stood in the shadows near the longhouse. He and Jeremiah seemed to locked gazes. Zeb gave Jeremiah a smile and a nod then dragged off his hat and bowed his head.

The preacher doubtless petitioned the Great Spirit to guide the tomahawk. Red Fawn joined her own prayers with Zeb's as she gripped her mother tighter.

Jeremiah's face suddenly swung toward Red Fawn. For a long moment, his blue gaze smoldered into hers, causing her heart to throb with a deep ache. A corner of his mouth curled up with the hint of a smile. Then he turned his focus back to his target, and the smile left him. His lips pressed in a thin, bloodless line as he lifted the tomahawk for the throw that would determine both their futures.

10

The tomahawk bit deeply into the target's heart, and a hush fell over the village.

With his arms still extended in front of him, Jeremiah gazed in wonder at what had just happened, the broader meaning slowly sinking into his consciousness.

"Thank You, Jesus!" His arms fell to his sides as the whispered words rushed from his lips on a puff of breath he hadn't realized he'd been holding. A moment ago, he'd prepared his heart to accept whatever outcome the Lord delivered. But now, the pent-up anxiety that had built inside his chest over the past tortuous moments threatened to explode in a celebratory release. Such an outburst, however, might be taken as unsportsmanlike by the surrounding Shawnee, so he kept quiet.

He thought of his brother Joel forever hounding him to compare tomahawk-throwing skills. Jeremiah's determination not to allow his younger brother to best him in anything had saved both him and Zeb today. A grin tugged at his mouth as he realized God had used his own pride to prepare him for this moment.

His face turned unbidden toward the spot in the crowd of villagers where earlier he'd seen Red Fawn and her mother. A ball of unease wadded in his chest. If he'd lost, she'd have gotten her wish; she and her mother would be staying in the village. Would Red Fawn be disappointed in the outcome?

He searched the milling crowd, many of whom exchanged wampum beads and other trade items. Only a happy few would have wagered against the chief's son.

The thought made him smile the same moment his gaze found Red Fawn's. The return smile blooming on her face sent his heart rearing rampant, thundering against his chest. Could she be happy that he'd won?

"The Great Spirit has found favor with you today, Dunbar." Great Hawk's voice at his shoulder dragged Jeremiah's attention away from Red Fawn's smiling face.

A look he hadn't expected to find flickered in the chief's eyes. Respect.

"I pray I find His favor every day." Emboldened by his victory, Jeremiah squared his shoulders as he met the chief's gaze. "But Great Hawk's words are true. The Great Spirit has blessed me with victory today."

The chief glanced at the angry figure of his son striding away, pushing aside any hapless person in his path. A pained look flashed across Great Hawk's features before he turned back to Jeremiah.

"With your victory, the Great Spirit has declared your innocence." Great Hawk extended his hand and Jeremiah accepted it. The chief gave his hand a firm, quick shake—an Algonquin custom Jeremiah had become familiar with over the past weeks. "You and McLain may leave with the women, Falling Leaf and Red Fawn. I give you my word that no one from this village will hinder your leaving."

Jeremiah nodded. "Many will hear that Chief Great Hawk honors his word." He refrained from adding that just as many would hear of his son's dishonor.

As he watched the chief walk away slouch-shouldered, an unexpected twinge of pity struck Jeremiah. The man knew he'd fathered a blackguard, and perhaps even harbored guilt that he bore some responsibility for his son's ignoble character. A resolve to never bring shame on his own father hardened in Jeremiah's chest.

"Praise the Lord, Jeremiah!"

At Zeb's choked voice Jeremiah turned around, and he found himself engulfed in the older man's embrace. He returned Zeb's fierce hug then pushed away, clearing the tightness from his throat. "The Lord heard our prayers."

"And maybe her prayers, too?" Zeb's head bobbed, and his gaze trained on a point beyond Jeremiah's left shoulder.

Swerving around, Jeremiah saw Red Fawn walking toward them. The smile had left her face, but a look of stark relief swam in her glistening eyes.

"Mother says you must be favored by the Great Spirit. No one else has ever won such a contest against Flying Hawk." Along with the wonder in her voice, Jeremiah thought he detected the hint of a grudging tone.

Zeb grinned at Red Fawn and slapped Jeremiah on

the shoulder. "'Many are the afflictions of the righteous; but the Lord delivereth him out of them all.'" He cocked his head and gave her a wink. "By God's grace, Flying Hawk chose a skill the boy can actually do. He don't know that back home Jeremiah is the tomahawk throwing champion of three counties." He cast a knowing look between Jeremiah and Red Fawn. "Yes'um, the Lord showed who was the better man today."

Jeremiah's neck and ears prickled warmly under Zeb's praise. He hoped Red Fawn didn't take her uncle's words as an endorsement of Jeremiah as a suitor in the place of Flying Hawk. Considering her cool attitude toward Zeb, he couldn't think of a better way to sour her on the notion.

Zeb glanced upward at the gray clouds filling the sky, and his mood sobered. "We'd better get packed and on our way before the weather holds us here. I'm thinkin' it might not be advisable to stay another night while Flying Hawk stews about his loss."

"Perhaps my mother is wrong," Red Fawn said as they watched Zeb saunter toward the longhouse. "Maybe it was your skill and not the Great Spirit that brought your victory today."

Beyond needing to glorify God for saving his life, Jeremiah must not waste an opportunity to testify to Red Fawn of the Lord's love and grace.

He shook his head. "No, I owe my triumph to Providence alone—the will of the Great Spirit. For all my skill, a gust of wind could have blown the blade off course, or a flash of sun could have blinded me at a crucial moment."

The question roiling in his heart forced its way out. "Are you sorry it turned out as it did?"

Her sweet smile made his chest ache. "I am glad you won. Mother says Flying Hawk needed to learn the bitter taste of defeat."

That she hadn't voiced her gladness at Jeremiah not having to forfeit his life didn't matter. Her eyes told him. Emboldened, he took her hand in his.

"Your mother is right...about everything."

~*~

Your mother is right about everything.

As her horse bore her to the crest of yet another hill, Jeremiah's words of three weeks ago echoed in Red Fawn's mind. With all of her heart, she hoped he was right.

Beneath her legs, the mare's sleek gray sides expanded and contracted as the animal huffed a deep breath with the exertion of the climb. Cold weather and miles of hilly terrain had taxed both the travelers and their horses. The trip had proven every bit as difficult as Red Fawn imagined. With the exception of stops at the occasional settlement fort, most nights they'd been obliged to make camp in the forest, constructing pine-bough lean-tos for shelter.

Although Mother never once complained, Red Fawn had watched the miles etch deeper lines in her face and daily sap strength from her feeble frame. So yesterday at sunset when they made camp on the eastern bank of the Wabash River, Zeb's announcement that they were within a day's ride of her father's grave site had sent relief rolling through Red Fawn's chest.

She glanced back at Mother, who lay on the travois Zeb and Jeremiah had constructed four days ago from deer hide and birch saplings. Nine days into their journey Mother had grown too weak to ride astride. They'd had no choice but to wrap her in blankets and secure her to the travois which they attached to the sorrel horse.

All day the sun had hid its face, but Red Fawn didn't need to see the sun to know that midday had long passed. The biting wind gusted, turning the light snowfall into stinging needles. She tugged her blanket tighter around her.

The hide canopy they'd fashioned to shelter her mother's head should keep the dampness from her face, but the jarring the travois doubtless caused her great discomfort. Before she could announce her intention to dismount and check on Mother, Zeb stopped her.

"I believe we have reached the place you are seeking."

The men joined her on the rise. Below them, a stream twisted through a wooded glen.

Zeb leaned forward in the saddle until his beard brushed his horse's pale mane and gazed at the valley. "Down yonder is the spot where Pigeon Creek flows into the Ohio River."

The faint smell of wood smoke tickled Red Fawn's nose as she followed his gaze to the wooded hollow. They must be near the town of Evansville. The birth of that white man's town nine winters ago had pushed her tribe to the banks of the Mississippi River.

Tears sprang to Red Fawn's eyes—not because she remembered the place, but because she could not. Nothing looked familiar. After nine winters, could they still find evidence of Father's grave?

She turned to Jeremiah. "That is Pigeon Creek?"

"It is." Zeb answered her. The older man smiled at her across the back of the sorrel that bore her mother's travois.

She whipped her gaze back to the valley, uneasy at the shadowy memories Zeb's kind expression always evoked.

"After we pay our respects to...your pa's restin' place..." His tone withered. Although she grudgingly understood Zeb's difficulty in thinking of Painted Buck as her father, his hesitancy to refer to him as such still grated.

His voice hurried on, lifting with renewed enthusiasm. "At least tonight, we should have a proper roof over our heads. I am confident that in Evansville, we shall find shelter and sustenance at the home of my good friend Reverend William Medford."

As they made their way down the snowy slope, doubts crowded Red Fawn's heart like the pale gray clouds that filled the sky. Mother would not leave until she'd found Father's grave and nightfall would come soon. To find a gravesite in a dark forest altered by nine winters seemed an impossible task.

At the creek bank Red Fawn dismounted and hurried to her mother's side. When she bent and peered beneath the hide canopy, the serene smile on Mother's face surprised her.

"We are here, Mother. We are at the place where the Pigeon Creek spills into Spelewathiipi." She began untying the strips of hide that secured her mother to the travois.

"I know. For many miles, I have felt it in here." Mother tapped her blanket-swathed chest and sat up with a groan. "You must help me up, Daughter. My legs have become stiff."

As Red Fawn grasped her mother's hands to assist her, Jeremiah hurried to Falling Leaf's other side, supporting her with a steadying arm.

Unsure which direction to go, Red Fawn glanced about the little glade. Mother couldn't walk far, so they mustn't waste time searching in the wrong direction.

"Mother, can you tell if we are near father's grave?"

Mother looked southward past Zeb, who stood tethering the horses at the creek's edge. "We are on the west side of the stream?"

"Yes." Mother's calm demeanor helped to soothe Red Fawn's rising anxiety.

"How far are we from Spelewathiipi?" Speaking in Shawnee, Mother directed her question toward Jeremiah, so Red Fawn translated.

Jeremiah cocked his head southward. "Zeb says we are about a hundred paces north of the Ohio River."

Mother turned and pointed northward at a distant stand of birch trees, their white-barked trunks poking up like skeletal fingers from the forest floor. "The grave house is this way, beside the black rock."

At her mother's mention of the black rock, sad memories draped Red Fawn's heart like the lengthening afternoon shadows. Images of the funeral fires flickering against a large dark rock flashed in her mind. She remembered how, in keeping with the Shawnee custom, fires had burned for four nights atop her father's grave.

Now joined by Zeb, the four started in the direction Mother had indicated with Red Fawn and

Jeremiah supporting Mother on either side. But after a few steps, Mother stopped and shrugged off their help.

"I can walk. It is not far." Straightening her back, she led the way into the birch thicket with strong, purposeful strides that amazed Red Fawn.

At last they came upon a little clearing centered by a dilapidated structure, which Red Fawn recognized as the remnants of her father's grave house—a symbolic spirit dwelling erected over a Shawnee grave. A couple strides away stood the dark boulder she remembered, though it looked smaller than the last time she'd gazed upon it. She remembered the rock towering over her nine-year-old frame, but now its summit came only to her chest.

Many emotions poured like water through Red Fawn as she watched Mother lovingly stroke one of the remaining upright birch logs. To her surprise, she found no sadness among the mix. Instead, happy memories of her father embraced her. Regret that she'd had such a short time to learn from the man she called Father struck again as it had so many times over the past nine winters.

Zeb and Jeremiah stood a respectful distance from the grave site, their heads bowed and hats in hand.

Mother turned slowly as if reluctant to pry her gaze from the little snow-covered mound before her.

"Daughter, I must be alone for a while. Go build a fire and make my tea of hawthorn leaves." Mother looked unaffected by the cold wind that buffeted the edges of the blanket swathing her from head to knee. Something about the distracted look in her eyes sent a finger of fear slithering through Red Fawn, but she nodded in obeisance.

"I will come for you when I have boiled the water

for your tea."

Without another word, Mother turned back to focus on the grave.

Red Fawn walked to Jeremiah and Zeb. Her heart pinched at the thought that her mother didn't wish to share this moment with her. But Mother had waited many winters and had endured many miles of difficult travel for this time with her husband's memory. Red Fawn would respect her wishes, but she would stay within earshot in case Mother needed her.

As they moved away from the gravesite, Zeb and Jeremiah put their hats back on their heads.

"There's a nice stand of pine beside the creek," Zeb said. "I'll go cut some boughs for a lean-to if you two will hunt for wood dry enough to burn."

Watching Zeb slump away, guilt pricked at Red Fawn's conscience. Although she avoided him as much as possible, he continued to show her and her mother nothing but kindness.

"He is a good man, you know," Jeremiah said as if he read her thoughts. "He and your Aunt Ruth will provide you and your mother with a good home."

Red Fawn shuffled through snow and ankle-deep dead leaves toward a fallen birch tree that should provide plenty of dry fire wood. She pondered how to explain to Jeremiah that it wasn't Zeb or his generosity that she resented, but having the white man's way of life forced upon her.

"I do not think Zeb is a bad man." Glad for an excuse not to meet Jeremiah's eyes, Red Fawn bent and snapped off a dry branch the size of her thumb. "My mother and I are Shawnee. It is not right that we live as white women. The white man's way is not better than the Shawnee way, and their houses are not better than our wigwams."

Jeremiah pulled out the little axe he carried in his belt and began hacking off small branches from the dead tree.

After a long moment he said, "I agree. But your mother understood you would both be living with Zeb and Ruth when she decided to leave your tribe."

Red Fawn stopped gathering the kindling wood into a pile. Facing Jeremiah, she pointed northward where, beyond their vision, Mother stood at Father's grave. "And you can see that the journey has almost killed her!" She threw a twig on the pile of wood so hard it bounced, landing in the snow several steps away.

"I believe it took a very strong love for her to insist on making this trip." His soft voice and the tender look in his eyes made her heart pound.

She averted her warming face and pretended to search for more kindling.

"Yes, she loved Father very much—we both did." Red Fawn's voice faded, hoping his ears hadn't detected the hint of resentment that had crept unbidden into her voice. Though she'd tried, Red Fawn had failed to rid her heart of the deepening pain she'd felt since the day Mother announced they'd be traveling to this place. It hurt to think of Mother's willingness to sacrifice their home and Red Fawn's future for a few moments at Father's grave.

"God has blessed you both to have known such a love."

Irritation squiggled up Red Fawn's spine at his use of the white man's word for *Mis-s- Mon-nit-to*, but she held her tongue. Though she would continue to call the Great Spirit by His Shawnee name, she had no desire to quarrel with Jeremiah.

Jeremiah went back to chopping at the tree. For a while, they allowed the sound of the axe falls echoing among the trees to fill the silence.

When Jeremiah finally spoke, he did so slowly, as if carefully considering his words. "But I do not think Falling Leaf made this trip for herself."

Resentment rose like vapor in Red Fawn's chest. How could any white man presume to know her mother's heart—any Shawnee's heart?

Red Fawn whirled on him, no longer caring if her anger broke free. "Then who did she make this journey for? She did not do it for me. You know I never wanted to leave my tribe."

"I think you are exactly why she did it." Though kind, his voice took on a stern tone.

"Then you are *wan-ni-ne*!" Glaring at him, she tapped her temple. "And I don't think even Mother can cure someone crazy in the head."

Instead of the angry response she expected, he threw back his head and laughed.

She liked the sound. His mirth infected her and she couldn't stop the grin tugging at her mouth.

He slipped the axe back into his belt and stepped over the birch log to stand before her. Like two blue flames, his eyes smoldered into hers. He took her hands, sending her heart bolting like a frightened deer.

"My dear Red Fawn." His voice sounded husky as his calloused thumbs caressed the backs of her hands. "I do not know what the future holds for you, but I'm convinced it was God—the Great Spirit—that compelled your mother to take you from your village. And I know you believe as I do that the Great Spirit wants only good for you."

Daylight dimmed, and the wind blew colder and fiercer, snatching at her blanket, but she didn't care. She wanted to stand here forever with her hands enveloped in Jeremiah's warm, strong grasp.

"What I can promise you," he continued, his smile bristling the several days' growth of tawny whiskers that covered his cheeks, "is that you and your mother will find only love in the home of Zeb and Ruth McLain."

Of the many emotions swirling in Red Fawn's chest, guilt emerged first. She opened her mouth, unsure if her constricted throat could make a sound and was somewhat surprised when it did. "I am sorry. I should not have called you wan-ni-ne. I do dishonor to my parents who taught me to always show others respect." Her gaze slid downward.

His soft chuckle rumbled deep in his chest before emerging into the snowy air, and she lifted her face back to his grinning one.

"If how I am feeling now is crazed, I don't think I want to be cured." The husky tone that made her heart quiver returned to his voice.

His head lowered toward hers and confusion reigned in her chest. She felt as rooted to the ground as the trees surrounding her.

A crash sounded, reverberating through the forest and breaking the spell that had enveloped them. They both looked to the north, the direction from which the sound had come.

Fear shot through Red Fawn. Had something happened to Mother? Letting go of Jeremiah's hands, she ran through the snow and underbrush toward her father's gravesite, ignoring the brambles and thickets grabbing at her skirt and blanket.

When the gravesite came into view her hammering heart vaulted to her throat. Her mother lay face down atop her father's grave with a beech log the thickness of two fists across her back.

11

Red Fawn raced past Jeremiah and reached her mother first. He arrived and lifted the small log with ease and pitched it to the side.

Fearing what she might see, Red Fawn struggled to control her erratic breathing as Jeremiah tenderly turned her mother onto her back. Deep down, Red Fawn suspected Mother had planned all along for this to be the place where she stepped from this life into the land beyond the sunset.

Mother emitted a weak groan, and the band of fear constricting Red Fawn's chest eased a bit.

Jeremiah scooped Mother into his arms as if she were a child. "We need to get her away from here. More of these logs could fall."

"No." Though weak, Mother's voice held a strong tone of defiance. Her eyes open now, she rolled her head against the crook of Jeremiah's arm until her gaze locked on Red Fawn's. "Do not take me from this place."

Red Fawn took the blanket from her own back and

laid it on the ground in the shelter of an ancient cedar tree. "We will not take you far, Mother," she said as Jeremiah lowered her mother to the blanket. "But I need to see how badly you are injured."

Jeremiah took off his wool coat, rolled it up, and gently placed it under Mother's head. "I will bring some wood so we can build a fire and get you warm."

Mother grabbed his arm. "No. You stay." Her tongue peeked out to lick her lips. She swallowed and her chest rose as she pulled in a deep breath. "I have only a little time to say what I must say."

Jeremiah obeyed, though worry lines wrinkled his brow.

Anger and grief warred for supremacy in Red Fawn's chest. Despite her weak heart, if Mother wished to stay in this world, she would summon the strength to stay. But she obviously preferred to join Father in the land beyond the sunset rather than stay here with Red Fawn.

Knowing Mother would chide her for any show of grief, Red Fawn allowed the anger to win out. "You cannot leave me, Mother." Blinking back hot tears that threatened to spill down her face, Red Fawn reached beneath the blanket shrouding her mother's body and grasped her hand. "You cannot leave me alone to live in the white man's world. I need you to help me keep the Shawnee ways. And I do not yet possess all your knowledge of healing herbs that will make me a great Shawnee healer."

A smile etched half-moon wrinkles at the sides of Mother's mouth. "For twelve winters I have taught you. You know enough, more than you think you know." Her grip on Red Fawn's hand felt surprisingly strong.

Mother's dark eyes appeared extra bright as they searched Red Fawn's. "You will keep the Shawnee ways, for you are and always will be, Shawnee." She winced as she drew in another deep, trembling breath. "But you belong to the white man's world, too. It is my wish that from this day forward, you would be known by both your white name and your Shawnee name—Ginny Red Fawn McLain. Embrace your white family, my daughter. Open your heart to them and to the good things they, too, can teach you."

At her mother's words, the urge to argue rose up in Red Fawn. Mother had gotten her wish. She had returned to her husband's grave, and her spirit would step into the land beyond the sunset from the same spot his had. If Red Fawn did not acknowledge her mother's request, there'd be nothing to prevent her from returning to her tribe. Nothing except that without her mother's protection, Great Hawk could force Red Fawn to marry Flying Hawk.

Her heart sank as her will surrendered. Even if the threat of marriage to Flying Hawk did not exist, Red Fawn's love for her mother would not allow her to disobey her dying request.

She gave her mother's hand a gentle squeeze. "I promise to do as you ask, Mother."

Mother reached out her other hand and grasped Jeremiah's. She placed his hand on top of Red Fawn's. "Jeremiah Dunbar, in my dreams, I saw one such as you, with hair the color of ripe corn, guarding my daughter. She is strong and brave, but she has no memory of life among your people. I put her in your keeping. Protect her as you did in my dreams."

At the touch of Jeremiah's hand nestled over hers, comforting warmth radiated up Red Fawn's arm.

Once again, she swallowed down the objection that clawed at her throat for escape. She wasn't a child needing protection—especially protection provided by this white man who turned her insides into a swarm of butterflies.

Jeremiah's throat moved with a hard swallow. "I will. And I promise you that Zeb and his wife Ruth will love her and protect her as if she were their own daughter."

Mother's breathing became shallower. The lines around her mouth relaxed, giving her a more peaceful look, but her face had taken on a grayish hue.

A sudden gust of wind moaned through the forest, carrying with it a whiff of cedar and decaying leaves. It whipped a loose strand of silver hair across Mother's forehead.

"Daughter." Mother's voice became faint. "Bury me beside my husband in the Shawnee way with my head to the east and my feet to the west."

"I will, Mother." Red Fawn abandoned any attempt to hold back the tears now streaming down her face.

Mother rolled her head from side to side, and though her eyes shown with loving indulgence, her voice held a gentle chide. "Let Pepoonki, grandfather of the North, dry your tears with his cool breath, my daughter. It is the will of the Great Spirit that I return now to the Creator. You must not show selfish tears to the Great Spirit."

"Jeremiah Dunbar." Mother's voice sounded raspy as she turned her attention to him. "Many days I have listened to you and McLain tell of this Jesus you say is the Son of the Great Spirit." She paused to draw in another deep breath. "In my heart I believe it is true. Is it also true that He is waiting to welcome me to the land beyond the sunset?"

"It is true. Do you accept Jesus Christ as your Savior?" Jeremiah's voice held an odd thickness.

"Yes." Mother's weakening voice made Red Fawn want to shake her and demand that she not go. But she'd rather her mother's last memory of her be one of pride, not shame.

The sun that had not shown all day appeared now at its setting, poking golden fingers into the forest. A shaft of the waning light slanted across Mother's face, making her appear as if she already belonged to a brighter world.

She smiled at Jeremiah. "Pray to the Son of the Great Spirit. Tell Him I am coming, and ask Him to meet me in the land beyond the sunset."

Jeremiah nodded, and in a voice thick with emotion, prayed the prayer Mother requested.

Mother's head rolled toward Red Fawn. "Now Daughter, you must sing a traveling song. And then one of celebration when I step into the sunset and take the hand of the Son of the Great Spirit."

"Yes, Mother. It will be done as it has always been done with our people." Hoping her voice wouldn't betray her deep sadness, Red Fawn began singing, one hand still grasping her mother's, the other enveloped in Jeremiah's large hand and resting on her mother's mid-section. She couldn't deny her gratitude for Jeremiah's presence at this moment which at once, broke her heart and changed her life forever.

~*~

Too many emotions to discern whirled in

Jeremiah's chest as if caught in a cyclone. A will stronger than he knew he possessed kept him from reaching across Falling Leaf's body and gathering Red Fawn into his arms.

Hot tears stung the back of his nose, but his heart sang with the clear, sweet notes of Red Fawn's celebration song. Because he and Zeb had taken the gospel to her Shawnee village, Falling Leaf communed this moment with Christ.

A hand on his shoulder caused him to jerk his attention upward. Zeb stood, somber-faced, his hat in his hands. When the last notes of Red Fawn's celebration song faded in the winter gloaming, Zeb reached out to his niece.

Jeremiah let go of Red Fawn's hand so Zeb could embrace her, an embrace she surprisingly seemed to welcome.

"Your mother was a good, wise, and courageous woman, Red Fawn." Zeb continued to grip Red Fawn's shoulders as she stepped back from his embrace. "I heard her confession of faith, and I join you in your celebration. Our loss is heaven's gain."

Red Fawn lifted clear eyes to Zeb, and Jeremiah marveled at her composure. "For four days we must remain here and perform the traditional burial ceremonies of my...mother's people."

The marked pause in her voice along with her reference to the Shawnee as her "mother's people," suggested to Jeremiah that perhaps Red Fawn had taken to heart her mother's dictate to embrace her white family.

Zeb patted her hand. "Everything will be done exactly as you wish, Red Fawn."

A dark cloud of pain crossed Red Fawn's face then

passing, left behind a look of serenity.

Her chin lifted in a resolute jut. "Respecting my mother's wishes, I shall now be called Ginny Red Fawn McLain."

Joy beamed from Zeb's smiling face. He gave his niece another quick hug. "Everything will be as you would have it, Ginny. Me and Jeremiah will see to it."

And it was. For four days they camped beside Pigeon Creek while Jeremiah and Zeb assisted Red Fawn, now called Ginny, in carrying out her mother's burial ceremony in keeping with Shawnee customs.

That first night, in the pine-bough lean-to Zeb had constructed, Ginny kept watch over her mother's covered remains while Jeremiah and Zeb spent the night in a second lean-to close by.

Jeremiah slept little that night and suspected he wasn't alone in his wakefulness. It tore at his heart to think of Ginny sitting alone in her drafty lean-to, keeping her grim vigil. But he would respect her tradition.

At the break of dawn, he rode into Evansville and borrowed a shovel for the burial from Zeb's friend the Reverend William Medford who was a kind and generous man and in whose home he and Zeb had stayed one night on their trip west.

In addition to the shovel, Jeremiah left the reverend's home laden with more than enough linen sacks full of food to sustain the three of them during Falling Leaf's funeral rites. Reverend Medford also made him promise that he, Zeb, and Ginny would spend a day or two in his home before boarding a steamboat for Charlestown, Indiana.

Each of the four nights following Falling Leaf's burial, in keeping with Shawnee custom, Ginny, Zeb, and Jeremiah shared recollections of Falling Leaf while a fire burned atop her grave.

Though he wished he had known the woman better, Jeremiah was glad to recount the expert care Falling Leaf had given him during his illness and how her medicines had cured him.

Ginny's childhood recollections of her mother touched Jeremiah deeply. Through her words he glimpsed the frightened little white girl, who, under the loving care of her adopted Shawnee mother, had blossomed into the beautiful and remarkable woman before him.

Tonight, for the last time, they gathered near the grave. Once again, a cheery fire crackled atop the newly turned mound of dirt where four days ago, they'd placed Falling Leaf's body in a grave dug in the Shawnee fashion—exactly four-feet deep in an east-west orientation.

Tonight, Ginny alone would speak. Silhouetted against the dark boulder that overlooked her parents' resting place, she stood for a long moment, gazing in silence at the flames. The firelight burnished her braids to gleaming copper, reminding Jeremiah of the description of Celtic maidens he'd read about in books.

She hugged her blanket around her as the gusting wind sent orange sparks flying into the inky sky. Her chin lifted in that familiar strong, determined tilt. Yet her eyes held a vulnerability that stirred his protective instinct.

The life-changing events she'd endured over the past weeks and hours as well as the ones looming ahead, were enough to shake the constitution of the heartiest soul.

Yet here she stood a mere slip of a girl, strong,

brave, and defiant. Facing with courage and grace, the most heart-wounding of life's barbs.

Something twanged deep within Jeremiah. As if an invisible hand had reached into his chest and plucked his heartstrings, sending a sweet note vibrating clear to his soul. He knew without a doubt he would lay down his life for this girl.

As he remembered Falling Leaf's request to protect Ginny, Jeremiah's chest swelled with both determination and trepidation. On this eve of the next to last leg of their trip home, the concern that had plagued him since they left the Shawnee village gripped him hard.

How would the people of Underwood accept Ginny? Many had lost family members during the massacre at Pigeon Roost, and Jeremiah knew a number of residents still harbored strong feelings against the Shawnee. The thought of Ginny struggling to assimilate into life in Underwood had concerned him enough when he thought Falling Leaf would be there to provide her companionship, support, and wisdom. It pained him to imagine her as the lone target of hurtful comments and hateful looks.

Without question, Zeb and Ruth McLain would do their best to protect her from any unkindness, but Jeremiah had trouble envisioning Ginny confiding in her aunt and uncle. And, with Jeremiah living in Jackson County some forty miles away from Underwood, he'd have limited ability to keep watch over her.

At least she'd agreed to be called Ginny instead of Red Fawn, which eased his growing anxiety to some degree. He prayed she'd also choose to adopt the dress and hair styles of her white neighbors. That, too, should go a long way in gaining her a measure of acceptance and in helping to diffuse even the most ardent Shawnee haters.

Ginny turned to face Jeremiah and Zeb, who stood a few paces from the gravesite.

"Zeb. Jeremiah. By respecting my mother's wishes, you have honored her spirit. I thank you for that."

Her voice took on a harder, almost bitter tone.

"You know it is not my wish to live among the whites. But I promised my mother I would try, and I will not dishonor her spirit by breaking that promise."

Her chin jutted and her back stiffened poker-straight. At her stubborn demeanor the concerns smoldering in Jeremiah's chest flamed anew.

"But I would not honor my mother by turning my back on all that she and my father taught me." Her gaze narrowed to a near glare as it swung between Zeb and Jeremiah.

"I will live in the white man's world, but I will not live as a white woman. I will live as what I am and always will be—a Shawnee woman. A Shawnee healer."

12

Ginny's heart quickened as she started down the steep metal steps to the steamboat *Jefferson's* main deck. After six days aboard the cramped boat, she longed to walk on land again. Last night at supper, Zeb said they should make the landing at Charlestown, Indiana, by mid-morning today. Underwood, he'd told her, lay within an easy day's ride of Charlestown.

Inching down the stairs, she grasped the cold iron railing with one hand while lifting the hem of her black skirt from her moccasin-clad feet with the other. She would not want to trip and tumble like a raccoon from a tree and land in a heap amidst a room full of fancy white people eating breakfast.

The white man's love of height still baffled her. After leaving Pigeon Creek, they'd stayed two days in the large log home of the man, Medford, and his family. Though she appreciated all the kindnesses the Medfords showed her, she'd found many of their customs odd. One of which, was the notion of sleeping in lofts built high off the ground. And as if that wasn't high enough, their beds were made so they slept at least knee-high above the floor.

Ginny had been obliged to share the loft with the family's two daughters, who were near her age. The girls had graciously offered to let her share their bed, but the thought of sleeping so far off the floor had unnerved her. She'd wanted to say that she did not care to roost in the trees like a bird. Instead she'd thanked them and insisted on sleeping on a pallet of quilts on the floor, to which they exhibited both surprise and disbelief. She suspected the girls surmised she hadn't wanted to crowd them in their bed.

When they boarded the steamboat, she learned that the women slept in little rooms they called cabins located above the main deck while the men slept in cabins on the level below. Perhaps only white *women* preferred to sleep high up.

Bewildering!

Since then, she'd observed many other odd customs of the whites. Their last morning at Pigeon Creek, Ginny had bathed in the cold stream before dawn while the men still slept. Yet Medford's wife had insisted that before they embark on the steamboat, Ginny take a warm bath with lye soap in what looked like a short dug-out canoe. So while the men went into Evansville to sell the horses for money to pay for their ride on the steamboat, the Medford women had subjected Ginny and her clothes to a thorough washing.

Stepping onto the main deck, Ginny expelled a relieved breath. All her life, she had climbed up and down steep hills, maneuvering over and around many natural obstacles like rocks and logs. But these man-made steps required a skill her leg muscles had not yet learned.

Now safely down, the pleasant scent of cooking food teased her nostrils and made her mouth water. Black men in black coats and pants and snowy white shirts carried steaming containers of food. They maneuvered between many round tables where the boat passengers sat eating breakfast. This, she understood. Guests should be served food.

As she'd done many times since boarding, Ginny gazed in wonder at her shiny surroundings. Everything sparkled like a river gleaming in the sunlight.

Again, she marveled at the vast amount of glass, which seemed to be everywhere. Above her, a line of huge brass candleholders draped with glass beads hung from the ceiling and ran the length of the deck. She felt uneasy sitting or standing directly beneath them and tried to always stay a safe distance away in case one might fall.

White cloth covered the dark wood tables that dotted the area. Eating vessels made of glass and painted with colorful birds and flowers circled the table tops. Zeb called them plates. Glass drinking vessels—clear, shiny, and delicate as a thin film of ice accompanied the plates.

Everyone sat around the tables on chairs as if afraid to sit on the floor. That, especially, made no sense as a red, gold, and blue blanket as thick as moss, covered the floor.

She searched for Zeb's and Jeremiah's faces among the many people sitting around tables but couldn't find them. Perhaps they had not yet emerged from their cabins.

The chattering sound of many voices talking at

once stilled suddenly like a tree full of birds when she approached. Many pairs of eyes turned toward her, and a surge of warmth flooded her face. Although the Medfords' daughters had expressed interest in her clothes and the way she wore her hair, as a whole, the family had treated her with respect.

She sensed no respect in the curious stares of her fellow steamboat passengers. The rude looks caused her skin to prickle and made her want to hide in shame, yet in her heart, she knew she had nothing to be ashamed of.

By now, she'd come to expect the stares, gasps, whispers, and giggles whenever she walked into this big room called the main deck, but they still bothered her.

With each day's travel up the Spelewathiipi, Ginny's misgivings about living in the white man's world grew. But at the same time, her determination to cling to her Shawnee customs also increased.

Her skin crawled as if covered with insects beneath the unfriendly looks directed toward her. Her gaze darted about the room, and she prayed the Great Spirit would make Zeb and Jeremiah appear.

"Excuse me!"

A sharp jab at Ginny's shoulder blade accompanied the harsh female voice behind her, jarring her from her spot at the bottom of the stairway.

A woman dressed in an incredibly soft material the color of a mourning dove glared at Ginny as she stepped from the stairway and brushed past her. She carried what looked to be a stick covered in a shiny gray material—obviously the weapon she'd used to inflict the sharp pain to Ginny's back.

Ginny's courage withered. She turned to race back

up the stairs to her cabin when she felt a strong, comforting arm wrap around hers.

"There you are." Jeremiah's bright voice and friendly smile made Ginny want to embrace him. But she'd endured enough stares. She'd rather not bring more on herself, or upon Jeremiah.

"I—I could not find you." Ginny hated the tremble in her voice, but Jeremiah didn't seem to notice.

"We chose a table near a window so we could watch the scenery pass by." As he guided her around and between the tables, she caught a whiff of a clean, woodsy scent about him. It reminded her of the forest. "I hope you're hungry, because Zeb and I have ordered flapjacks and bacon all around."

Ginny had no idea what flapjacks were, but the way her empty stomach groaned, she didn't care. So far, she'd found most of the white man's food, though strange, generally palatable and some even tasty.

"Good morning, my dear." Zeb rose from his chair, his actions sending a hint of the same scent she'd smelled on Jeremiah to her nose. Perhaps the shaving soap Medford gave the men in Evansville contained the smell.

"Good morning...Uncle Zeb." The word *uncle* caught in her throat, but Ginny had decided she should begin addressing him by that title. It seemed to please him as his smile widened.

Jeremiah pulled out a chair, and Ginny carefully lowered herself to the seat, once again wishing she could sit on the floor and not have to worry about falling off of some silly perch.

Zeb shook his head as Jeremiah pushed Ginny's chair up to the table. His eyes looked extra shiny as he reached over and gave her hand a squeeze. "What a blessing you will be to your Aunt Ruth. I just wish I could have let her know you're coming, but you'll be a wonderful surprise for her."

Ginny managed a tepid smile, unsure how she felt about meeting her aunt.

A man laden with plates of sweet smelling food stepped to the table, saving her from any further comment.

To her happy surprise, the food looked and smelled very familiar. Though larger than she'd ever seen—nearly covering the plates—these flapjacks appeared to be nothing more than large corn ash cakes she'd eaten all her life. They came drenched in melting butter, the oil made from cow's milk that the whites seemed to adore.

The man also placed on the table a plate heaped with strips of fried meat and two little glass containers filled with a thick amber liquid. Ginny had tasted bacon at the Medfords' and liked it well enough. From the look and smell, she recognized the amber liquid as a familiar sweet she'd enjoyed since childhood—maple syrup!

"Let us say grace." Zeb bowed his head, and Ginny and Jeremiah did the same as Zeb prayed, asking the Great Spirit he called God, to bless the food.

This custom of the whites, Ginny approved. In fact, after Jeremiah visited their wigwam and said a prayer of thanks for the food they'd served him, she and Mother adopted the practice. Mother had remarked that they should always thank the Great Spirit for everything.

"Amen." When Zeb finished his prayer, Jeremiah uttered the word with which the whites always ended their prayers, but Ginny had no idea of its meaning.

One day I must ask Jeremiah.

The thought jarred her. She had no doubt that Zeb and his wife both knew the word's meaning. But her mind—*and heart?*—instinctively turned to Jeremiah.

She wished again, as she had done many times since Mother's death, that Jeremiah lived in Underwood instead of Deux Fleuves, a journey of two days from Underwood, he'd said.

The men began eating—stabbing their flapjacks with their two-pronged forks and slicing off chunks with their knives.

The use of the white man's metal eating utensils confused Ginny, and the metal felt uncomfortable in her mouth. Most times, she ate with her fingers as she'd done all her life. She certainly saw no need of sharp metal tools to eat ash cakes.

She drizzled maple syrup on her flapjack and then tore off a piece and popped it into her mouth. For a moment, she luxuriated in the familiar taste and grainy texture of the corn cake. For the first time since leaving her village, she felt at home.

"Look, the red-haired injun woman is eatin' her flapjack with her fingers." The child's voice came from somewhere behind Ginny, and she turned around.

As she swallowed down the bite in her mouth, she found herself gazing into the scowling face of the woman who'd poked her back with the stick. The woman sat at a table about three paces away with a tall, dark-haired man and a boy who could not have seen more than six winters.

"Don't stare, Jack!" The woman grabbed the boy's arm and yanked him around in the chair. "They're savages. They live like animals."

The man—likely the woman's husband—snorted.

"You ask me, they ought to make the dirty Injuns eat out on the promenade deck with the slaves. They ain't fit to eat amongst decent people."

The hateful words cut deep and tears sprung into Ginny's eyes. She didn't blame the curious child, but the parents should know better. Did the people she'd soon live among share the attitude of these hateful people? The thought sent a chill through her body.

She glanced at Zeb. Sorrow clouded his eyes, and his gaze drifted away as if ashamed to meet hers. He shook his head and then reached over and patted her hand. But while her uncle's sympathetic gesture touched her heart, Jeremiah's reaction frightened her.

Stiffening, he shoved his chair from the table so violently the plates rattled, water sloshed out of the glass containers, and the legs of his chair screeched as they scraped against the deck floor.

Beneath his neatly combed pale hair, his face turned bright red. His handsome features twisted with anger making him almost unrecognizable.

He shot to his feet, and Ginny grasped his arm. His muscles felt hard and tense beneath her fingers, reminding her of an animal ready to spring at its prey.

Fear, like a leather strap, cinched her chest tight as a vision of shattered glass and mayhem flashed before her eyes.

"Please, Jeremiah, do nothing. I do not wish you to cause trouble."

He yanked his arm free from her grip and blue flames of fury leapt in his eyes.

"No, Ginny, I won't allow anyone to say such things about you!" He trained his murderous look on the ones who'd spoken the insults. "And they already caused the trouble. I'm just going to finish it."

13

"Easy, son." Zeb's even voice reminded Ginny of the tone her father had often used to calm her own anger.

Jeremiah stood with his fists clenched at his side but, thankfully, Zeb's admonishment had kept him at their table.

Jeremiah shot a barbed glance at the offending couple. "Ginny's your blood, Zeb. Surely, you can't listen to those people call her a savage and let it pass?"

A wizened smile lifted the corner of Zeb's mouth. "I doubt anything you or I could say, or even a beating from you, would change their way of thinking."

He shook his head. "Remember Proverbs 19:11. 'The discretion of a man deferreth his anger; and it is his glory to pass over a transgression.'"

Jeremiah's scowling face reflected the war raging in his heart. Ginny hurried to take advantage of his indecision.

Lifting pleading eyes to his, she curled her fingers around his now unclenched hand. "The man may deserve a bloody nose, Jeremiah, but his son does not deserve to see it."

The tension drained from Jeremiah's face. He let his hand slip from hers, and he sat back down with a thud, allowing her to release her held breath.

His eyes appeared a deeper blue as they smoldered into hers. They held a tenderness that stole away Ginny's breath as if she'd run a long distance.

"Let us finish our breakfast in the Lord's peace." Zeb's voice broke the invisible connection lashing Ginny's spirit to Jeremiah's. Though gentle, her uncle's tone held an unmistakable command.

Ginny and Jeremiah obeyed, and no one said much throughout the remainder of the meal.

Emotions raged inside Ginny like a storm, robbing her of her appetite. Glancing at Jeremiah's brooding profile as he picked unenthused at his corn cake, she wondered if the same storm rolled through his chest.

For the second time, he'd put himself in danger for her. At the thought, joy bloomed in her heart like the first flowers of spring.

Guilt wilted them.

Such a thought should not make her happy. Undoubtedly, she could expect to endure many more such insults among the whites. If Jeremiah felt obliged to fight every man who tossed an insult her way, he'd be in constant danger of injury or death.

Fear for him popped up its head like a snake from its hole and slithered down her spine. She dropped the piece of flapjack in her fingers back onto the plate. It now held no more appeal than a piece of leather.

"I must get my belongings bundled before we reach Charlestown." Maybe if she left the main deck, Jeremiah would feel less inclined to fight someone.

She pushed away from the table, and Jeremiah stood to help her up. Though she didn't need the help, she enjoyed the feel of his strong hand wrapped around hers.

"And Jeremiah and I should do the same, my dear." Zeb stood and smiled.

Jeremiah didn't smile. Neither did he frown. But his eyes never left her, gazing into her face as if he'd found something unexpected and wonderful.

Her heart throbbed with a deep ache. She cared for this man far too much. Keeping her vow to hold tight to her Shawnee culture in the white man's world would be difficult enough without giving her heart to a white man.

Somehow, she managed to wrench both her gaze and her fingers from Jeremiah's and wend her way between the dining tables to the stairway that led to the upper deck. She tried to ignore the staring eyes and hushed whispers as she passed. At least the couple who'd made the rude comments and their young son had left their table.

A few minutes later, she stood on the outside deck near the back of the boat listening to the *shug, shug, shug*, of the big red paddlewheel as it pushed the steamboat up the river.

An icy breeze nipped at her cheeks and blew the gray smoked belching from the tall black pipe at the front of the boat back to tickle her nose. Somewhere below on the main deck, the sound of a musical instrument wafted up. It sounded like the stringed instrument she'd seen played on the boat, which Jeremiah had called a banjo. Its lively tune did nothing to cheer her sagging spirit.

She hugged her blanket around her and watched

the barren trees along the snowy river bank slip past.

Fast. Too fast.

The hateful comment by the man at breakfast still echoed in her ears. A dark fear filled her chest until she could hardly breathe. How could she endure life in a place where everyone hated her?

She pulled in a deep breath of icy air to squelch the panic rising inside her. Closing her eyes tightly against her hot tears, she thought of her village on the White River and swallowed down the sob.

"Mother, why did you make me come here? These are not our people. These are not *my* people."

Nothing answered but the caw of a hawk. The big black bird sent a shower of snow into the air as it flew from its perch in a skeletal oak along the river's northern bank to make lazy circles against the gray sky. Weak sunlight filtered through a thin veil of clouds and glinted on the bird's dark wing.

The sight made Ginny think of Flying Hawk, the man who'd tried to win her affection. Would it have been better for her to have stayed in the village and become his wife? Mother had not thought so. Ginny's heart agreed, recoiling from the thought of being tied forever to the chief's ill-tempered and often drunken son.

Your mother is right about everything.

Jeremiah's words from before they left her village whispered comfort to Ginny's troubled heart.

Jeremiah.

Had she left her village to get away from a man she didn't love or to be near one she did?

"You shouldn't be out here in the cold."

At the sound of Jeremiah's voice, Ginny jerked and whirled around, feeling as though her thoughts had caused him to appear.

"I am used to the cold." She turned back to the rail, hoping her voice didn't sound as shaky to him as it did to her.

"Your aunt would not be happy with me and Zeb if we allowed you to catch a lung fever." His voice, too, sounded odd.

"I will not get sick. And if I did, I have my mother's medicine bag full of herbs to cure me." She glanced down at the calico sack by her feet that held all her possessions, including Mother's bundle of precious healing herbs. Ginny couldn't help smiling at the white man's odd belief that the cold could make someone sick. Did they think the bad spirits that caused sickness became more active during the moons of Pepoonwi? The thought joined a flock of questions her mind had gathered concerning the bewildering ways of the whites.

Stepping nearer, Jeremiah angled his large frame so his body sheltered her from the cold wind. He chuckled, that pleasant happy rumble that seemed to rise from the depths of his broad chest. With his movement, a gusting breeze carried his woodsy scent to her nose.

"Having once been your patient, I can attest to your healing abilities." His voice softened.

"If you had fought that man, I might have had to use my herbs to heal you again." She hoped her light tone would ease the tension building between them. It didn't.

"I'm sorry you had to hear the hateful things they said."

"Are there many who feel as those people do?" The question flitting around in her mind flew from her mouth before she could stop it.

For a long moment, her words floated on the chill air unanswered.

"A good number, I reckon." When he finally spoke, his voice held a quality she couldn't quite identify.

"Then do you plan to fight them all?"

"I have no right to fight any of them." His voice sagged.

At the unmistakable tone of guilt in his voice, confusion filled Ginny. Did his Christian beliefs make him ashamed to fight for even an honorable cause? If so, she wanted no part of his Bible book.

She twisted around so her back rested against the rail. With her head close enough to lean against his broad chest, she fought the urge to do so. She must keep talking.

"Why? Because of what it says in your Bible book?"

"No."

His gaze skittered away to the passing riverbank, and she watched the muscles move in his clenched jaw. He turned his gaze back to hers, meeting her look squarely. "Because I once felt the same way they do."

~*~

Ginny's stunned expression smote Jeremiah like a sharp slap across the face. His heart reverberated with the shock of having actually voiced the confession and then seized in fear as he waited to see disdain replace the surprise in her eyes. But he'd rather she hear the truth from him than from an offhand remark made by one of Zeb's neighbors.

"But you do not feel that way now?" Instead of disgust, a flash of pain crossed her face and gouged at his heart.

"Surely you know I do not." He reached out and grasped her hand, an instinctive reaction as if he could physically prevent her affections from fleeing him. Realizing what he'd done, he fully expected her to pull away. To his amazement, she did not. Instead, she allowed her hand to remain nestled in his and cocked her head at him, her face full of curiosity.

"And why do you not?"

The wind had tugged loose a copper strand of her hair from her braids and set it dancing across her forehead. The urge to reach out and touch it became almost overpowering. Instead, he rubbed his thumb across the back of her hand. It felt like silk to his rough skin.

"Because I have learned better." The simple statement didn't come close to explaining the changes God had wrought in his heart over the past two months. Or expressing the shame that still seared his soul over the mean, close-minded opinions he'd held before this trip. "I—I wouldn't blame you if you thought ill of me."

Confusion knitted her brow. "Ill? You believe I should think you are sick?"

He grinned in spite of himself and shook his head. He must remember that English wasn't her dominant language. "No, I would not blame you for being upset with me for thinking as I did about the Shawnee."

"And what did you think? That Shawnee are bad people?" She slipped her hand from his sending his heart spiraling to his feet.

"Yes, I suppose I did." He turned to the rail,

unable to meet her gaze, and focused on the trail of white froth the boat's churning paddles left in their wake. Though he had no hope that an explanation would redeem her regard for him, he nevertheless felt compelled to offer one.

"I was twelve when the...incident at Pigeon Roost happened. For nearly a month—one moon—a few Shawnee warriors kept my family and our neighbors holed up in our fort at Deux Fleuves." He shrugged. "We supposed they were loyal to Tecumseh. We never knew for sure."

A glance at her somber expression heartened him to continue.

"The food soon gave out, and the Indians dammed up the creek to deprive us of water. I watched people starve to death. Each night I went to sleep with my belly empty and my mind full of painted Shawnee warriors screaming and waving scalping knives."

"I am sorry some of my people did that to you, Jeremiah." A tiny V etched between her eyes, and she pressed her hand on his arm.

Despite her look of regret and the sincere ring of her voice, it vexed him that he hadn't once heard her ask about the fate of her birth parents and her brother.

"And what about John, Carolyn, and little Joe McLain? Are you sorry for what the Shawnee did to them?" The moment it left his mouth, he wished he could call back the blurted question. He had no idea if she'd witnessed any of the atrocities carried out on her family members all those years ago. If so, she'd clearly buried the memories in some deep, dark chasm of her mind.

She didn't answer, but he thought he saw her wince an instant before she turned her attention to a keelboat passing a few feet off their port side. The two men working the poles of the passing boat stopped singing a ribald song and waved in their direction. Ginny waved back, but her arm lowered when the words "red-haired squaw" along with several indecent proposals couched in laughter wafted back on the frigid air.

For the second time that morning, Jeremiah wanted to pummel a man senseless. But the keelboat had slipped far into their wake, and the men had once again taken up the bawdy song.

Jeremiah touched her shoulder. "I'm sorry those men were disrespectful to you. If I could have reached them, I'd have—"

"You would have fought them. I know." When she turned to face him, a smile played over her lips. Her eyes glistened with moisture, but whether from the gusting wind or gusting emotions within, he couldn't tell.

She scanned the forested bank where gray plumes of chimney smoke curled above the trees. They were nearing another town.

When she turned back to him, her smile had been replaced by a look so intense that it felt almost like a glare. "There are bad Shawnee and bad white men. Bad Shawnee killed my white family, but bad white men killed my Shawnee father, Painted Buck."

She bent and picked up her calico bag from the deck and clutched it to her middle as if to throw up a barrier between them. "I am sorry for what bad Shawnee do, as you are sorry for what bad white men do." She shrugged. "My father once told me 'Even the best trees have some rotten fruit.'"

"Your father was a wise man."

She sniffed and ran a hand under her nose, and Jeremiah moved to better block the wind from reaching her. They should be getting below, but he sensed they needed to finish this conversation.

"Why do you think I was taken from my white family?" Her unflinching gaze pierced him like the biting wind.

Jeremiah's mind raced in search of an answer to her unanswerable question. In the end, he fell back upon the only thing that made sense of life's mysteries. "God's will, I suppose. What you call ka-tet."

She drew her blanket closer around her and turned to study the snow-dusted forest. "Shawnee children are not named until their second winter."

Surprised by the irrelevant comment, Jeremiah said nothing.

She continued to peruse the passing shoreline. "My people believe that if parents are not worthy of their child, the Creator may take it back before two winters pass. So before they name their baby, they wait to see if they are worthy to keep it."

Indignation sparked in the pit of Jeremiah's belly at her inference. How could she impugn her own blood—people of whom she professed to have no memory? "Are you saying your birth parents were killed because God somehow deemed them unworthy to be parents?"

Her dispassionate glance made him sad and, at the same time, riled his sensibilities. "I believe the Creator made a mistake and gave me first to the wrong people."

Jeremiah tried to douse his flaring anger with cool reason. Her conclusion might very well make sense to her in light of her Shawnee beliefs. Yet to malign in such a way the people who gave her life, smacked of callous disrespect.

He gripped her shoulder, and she turned innocent, questioning eyes to him.

"John and Carolyn McLain were good people, and God doesn't make mistakes." He couldn't stop the anger that sliced through his words like the December wind, but the thought of her repeating such hurtful things to Zeb and Ruth McLain felt unbearable.

She glanced at his hand still clamped on her shoulder and fear flicked in her eyes, sending a wave of remorse swirling through him. He took his hand from her.

Arguing with Ginny would not help his efforts in opening her heart to the scriptures or easing her into her new life. Soon they would land in Charlestown. From there, a rented horse and wagon should get them to Underwood by nightfall. Unless he could convince Ginny to at least make an effort to assimilate into the community, he feared her experience at breakfast would prove a bitter foretaste of worse things to come.

He took off his hat, shoved his fingers through his hair, and then blew out a long, steadying breath. He prayed for patience as the chill wind prickled his scalp and cooled his steamy humors.

"Look, Ginny, I know you don't want to be here, but by the will of God, you are here." He reached out to grasp her hand, but she jerked away causing a painful prick near his heart. Wincing, he ploughed on. "Getting used to a new life—new ways—will be hard enough. I just think things might go smoother if you keep your beliefs to yourself."

Her face reddened, and she skewered him with a glare. "You traveled many miles to take your beliefs to my people. I am a proud Shawnee woman. Now that I am among the whites, I will not allow you or your people to shame me into hiding my beliefs." Her chin tipped up in that now familiar sign of stubbornness.

Jeremiah struggled to think of a credible counter that might nudge her from her mulish attitude, which he feared would invite trouble. As he pondered without success, the boat's whistle sounded two deafening blasts announcing their approach to Charlestown landing.

14

Ginny grasped Jeremiah's shoulders as he lifted her down from the wagon's bed. His large hands, wrapped firmly but gently around her waist, lent a measure of reassurance to her wobbly legs. She hadn't liked the idea of climbing into the high-built contraption when Zeb said he'd found an acquaintance willing to transport them to Charlestown in his wagon. Zeb had assured her of the wagon's safety and insisted that making the two-and-a-half-mile trek on foot would expend too much time and energy.

Glad to be on firm ground again, she glanced over to where Zeb stood talking with the wagon driver. Though he never said so, she sensed Zeb's eagerness to reach his home again. She knew how he felt. They had left her village in the waning of Kini kiishthwa, the Long Moon, and now the waning of *Washilatha kiishtha*—the Eccentric Moon neared. The trip had taken almost a month in the white man's way of measuring time.

Looking around at the brick and wooden

structures of Charlestown, she blinked hot tears from her eyes. She was a long way from her home.

Home.

Soon the word would describe something strange and unwelcoming and very different from her snug little wigwam on the banks of Missouri's White River, which she would doubtless never see again. A longing in the pit of her belly gnawed like a beaver working its way through a birch log. She missed Home...and Mother.

Mother, why did you leave me?

Did Mother speak often of her to Father as they walked together in the land of the sunset?

She blinked the tears from her eyes, glad for the gusting wind that dried them on her cheeks. Even with Zeb and Jeremiah close by, she felt alone in an alien world.

Jeremiah's face held none of her dread. Instead, a look of eager anticipation shone on his features as he scanned Charlestown's tall buildings and the wide dirt road between them. Occasionally, a passerby would wave and call his name. He'd reciprocate, adding a tip of his hat if the person happened to be female.

A pretty young woman about Ginny's age cast a smile over her shoulder at Jeremiah as she clung to an older woman's arm while they crossed the road. When Jeremiah waved and smiled in return, the girl's cheeks bloomed pink as wild roses beneath the odd head-covering the white women called a bonnet.

Something uncomfortable knotted in Ginny's middle as she wondered if Jeremiah had gestured out of politeness or if he knew the women.

Either way, Ginny's spirit sagged as if draped with the heavy folds of a wet blanket. These were Jeremiah's people. Whether he knew them personally or not, he knew their customs. Their ways were his ways.

Jeremiah was where he belonged.

Like a drumbeat, another thought answered. *And you are not.*

She glanced down at her black skirt decorated Shawnee style with bright ribbons the color of the sunset running down each side from waist to hem. The tops of her brown doeskin moccasins stuck out from beneath her skirt. She didn't need the curious stares of passersby to remind her she was as out of place as a fish trying to live on land or a bird trying to live beneath the river.

"Heyaa!" the wagon driver hollered. The wagon jerked and rolled away, leaving two dark lines in the snow-covered road.

Zeb ambled up, his smiling face mimicking Jeremiah's. He cocked his head toward the retreating wagon. "Mr. Findley said he's headed to Vienna and will be happy to take us on into Underwood. But first he needs to stop at the blacksmith and get a shoe replaced on his haw-side horse."

Jeremiah grinned. "Good. That'll give us time to get a warm meal." His gaze turned to a brick building a few paces away, and he rubbed his middle. "Those breakfast flapjacks have pretty much worn off."

Ginny's gaze followed his to the flat piece of wood swinging between two poles in front of the building. Though she couldn't read the white man's words, the image of the white man's eating and drinking utensils on the piece of wood made the message clear.

As the three crossed the road, Jeremiah linked his arm with Ginny's, and she wished her heart didn't sing at his touch. They had scarcely spoken since their tense exchange of words on the steamboat's deck. And though in body, he remained near, she sensed his spirit had drawn away from hers and turned as stiff and cold as the icy breath of Pepoonwi, father of the winter.

Zeb nodded and gave Ginny a wink. "The food at Harper's Inn don't hold a candle to your Aunt Ruth's, Ginny-girl, but it'll be warm, and there'll be plenty of it."

Inside the inn, a rush of warmth and the tantalizing aroma of a meat stew greeted them, making Ginny's mouth water. She glanced around in wonder at the large room—as large as the main deck of the steamboat—and with a ceiling so high a man could stand on another's shoulders and the top of his head would still not touch it.

At least here, no fancy glass decorations hung from the huge wood beams overhead. A cheery fire crackling in an enormous fireplace built into one wall lit the dim space. The bottom steps of a stairway jutted out from behind the fireplace. They probably led to a sleeping area since the whites loved to sleep so far above ground. The thought sent a shiver through her.

Several people sat at square wooden tables eating. Unlike on the boat, few stopped to stare at Ginny, and their looks held no hostility, just friendly curiosity. It heartened her that the room didn't become still, and no one pointed or whispered. Indeed, the place continued to buzz with a pleasant mix of unintelligible conversations.

Jeremiah led her to a table near enough to the fire to be warm, but far enough away to not be uncomfortably hot.

A big man wearing a stained white cloth tied around his middle bustled over to their table. He smiled and nodded when Zeb asked for three bowls of stew with bread and some coffee for him and Jeremiah.

"My niece will have sassafras tea if you have some." Zeb glanced at Ginny, and one of the big man's eyebrows shot up. But he grinned and said "Yes, sir," then scurried off.

When the food came and Zeb had said a prayer over it, Ginny ate quietly while the two men discussed the day's plans.

"Of course, you must stay with us tonight, Jeremiah," Zeb said around a bite of bread. "I know you're eager to get back to Deux Fleuves, but we'll be fortunate to make it to Underwood before nightfall. You wouldn't reach Salem and the next inn before midnight."

Ginny paused in lifting her stew-laden wooden spoon to her lips and glanced at Jeremiah. A little rabbit of panic jumped in her chest, and she hoped he'd accept Zeb's offer. She didn't feel ready to interact alone with her aunt and uncle.

Jeremiah nodded and scooped up another spoonful of stew. "I'd be much obliged, Zeb. I've been gone over three months, so I reckon another couple days won't matter." He flashed a smile at Ginny, the first he'd given her since their argument, setting her heart beating like the wings of a captured bird. "Besides," he said, "the sky looks like it might snow. Wouldn't want to be caught benighted in a blizzard."

Stifling a relieved sigh, Ginny remembered the food on her spoon and popped it into her mouth. At least here the eating utensils were made of smooth, soft wood instead of cold, hard metal. Thick with root vegetables and savory venison, the stew reminded her of the kinds of foods she and her mother had cooked.

The taste warmed her heart as well as her stomach.

Zeb nodded. "Reckon we'd better hurry up and eat so we don't miss our ride."

For the next several minutes, they all focused on finishing their food. Ginny even ate the yeasty wheat bread. Aside from needing to fill her belly so she'd stay warm for the wagon ride to Underwood, she figured she might as well get used to the white man's food.

When they finished eating and Zeb paid the man who wore the cloth around his belly, they headed for the livery stable.

Jeremiah's prediction about the weather proved accurate. By the time they reached the livery, a fine wet snow had begun falling.

Inside the dim, dusty building, the combined smells of horses and their manure, leather, and dried grasses assaulted Ginny's nose. Horses neighed from individual wooden pens. A man stopped raking the soiled straw from one of the empty pens and leaned the rake against it.

"What can I do for you fellers... and ma'am?" Glancing at Ginny, he lifted his floppy black hat displaying a flash of a bald head before covering it again with the hat. His jaw bulged with something he chewed. The brown stain meandering from the corner of his mouth to his chin suggested a wad of tobacco.

"We're lookin' for a feller by the name of Abner Findley," Zeb said. "S'posed to be havin' a horse shoed here."

The man's gaze flitted back to Ginny and lingered for an uncomfortable moment.

Jeremiah stepped in front of Ginny, blocking the man's view. "Mr. Findley offered us a ride to Underwood in his wagon. That is, when his horse gets a new shoe." His tone took on a sharp edge, and Ginny hoped he didn't think it necessary to fight the man.

The man reached for the rake. "The smithy's behind the livery." He cocked his head toward a narrow doorway at the far end of the building from where the ringing sound of metal striking metal emanated.

"Thank you, kindly." Zeb gave the man a nod and then strode toward the opening with Ginny and Jeremiah following several steps behind.

"Hey, missy."

At the livery man's words, Ginny and Jeremiah halted and turned back to him as Zeb disappeared through the door.

"You ain't any relation to Bluelegs, are ya?" Still chomping his chew, the man dragged off his hat and scratched at his head with filthy fingers, ruffling a few wispy gray hairs.

"No." Ginny and Jeremiah answered in near unison.

The man spat a brown stream into the dirty straw. "Thought mayhap that half-breed smithy had a sister runnin' around we didn't know about."

Ginny sensed Jeremiah tense beside her. His eyes flashed, and he skewered the man with his blue glare.

"The lady's name is Ginny Red Fawn McLain." His words came out hard and flat as if pushed through a locked jaw. "And her only living relatives are her uncle Zeb," he jabbed a thumb at the open doorway through which Zeb had disappeared, "and Zeb's wife, Ruth. And I'll ask you kindly not to spit in her presence."

"I meant no disrespect." The livery man went back to raking. "But I reckon she wouldn't be kin to

Bluelegs. Not with that hair."

Fearing the man's next words or actions might further inflame Jeremiah, Ginny tugged him toward the opening and out of harm's way.

Welcome warmth greeted her as she passed through the low, narrow portal. The roof sloped down covering three sides of the area behind the building, with the back left open. All manner of iron objects littered the ground around a brick fire pit.

In front of the fire pit, a young man stood pumping air into the furnace with some sort of pleated bladder. Sparks flew, and the coals glowed brighter red.

Although his actions interested her, Ginny found the man himself even more intriguing. His brown calico shirt hung to his knees. The shirt's sleeves were rolled up above his elbows revealing massive copper-colored forearms. Though he wore white man's breeches, they were tucked into calf-high fringed, deerskin moccasins. A beaded leather band wrapped around his blue-black hair cut in the short, white man's fashion.

The design of the colorful beading on his headband as well as on his moccasins marked him as a member of the *Lenni Lenape* tribe.

Zeb and Jeremiah stood several steps away, talking to the man named Findley who'd brought them from the landing into Charlestown this morning. But Ginny couldn't help staring at the blacksmith who picked up a horseshoe with a kind of iron grabbing tool and shoved it into the midst of the glowing coals. As she watched him, the livery man's words came back to her. This must be the man called Bluelegs.

"Are you Lenni Lenape?" he said in a quiet voice,

his gaze never leaving his work.

"Shawnee." That he'd noticed her without looking directly at her, impressed Ginny. "I am pleased to meet one of the Grandfather people."

She'd learned since childhood to consider all other tribes of the Algonquin nation distant kin. But the Lenni Lenape, or Delaware tribe as the white man called them, were especially respected and revered by the Shawnee. Their languages were similar enough to be almost interchangeable.

"*Kee-wes-si-an-na*?" Bluelegs glanced in Jeremiah's direction as he pulled the white-hot horseshoe from the belly of the fiery furnace with the grabbing tool. His softly enunciated question in Shawnee made her face heat with warmth that had nothing to do with the furnace. Of course, Bluelegs would assume Jeremiah was her husband.

"No." The tinge of sadness in her voice surprised her.

Focusing back on his work, Bluelegs picked up an iron mallet and gave the horseshoe several fierce blows, sending orange sparks flying.

He gave a quick nod toward Zeb. "*Coo-tha*?"

She shook her head at his second wrong assumption, explaining in Shawnee that Zeb was her uncle, not her father. Though unsure why Bluelegs preferred to converse with her in Shawnee rather than English, she guessed he figured Zeb and Jeremiah didn't know Shawnee. The glint in his dark eyes also suggested he thought it sport to speak in a language only the two of them understood.

Using the grabbing tool, Bluelegs plunged the hot horseshoe into a bucket of water, causing a loud hissing sound and sending up a cloud of steam.

"I am called Bluelegs Cavanaugh." He reached out a massive hand.

"I am Ginny Red Fawn McLain." She gripped his hand which felt even more calloused than Jeremiah's, and gave it the customary quick Algonquin shake. She explained that they were on their way to the home of her aunt and uncle in Underwood.

"You live with them?" While his question struck her as too personal for a stranger to ask, his smile, full of friendly curiosity, put her at ease.

"I will." Mother had always warned her to reveal no more to strangers than necessary for politeness.

"You are called Red Fawn for the color of your hair?" He continued to speak in Shawnee as he lifted the horseshoe from the bucket of water and held up the dripping piece of metal, studying his work.

"Yes. I was given the name when I was adopted into my Shawnee family as a child." Mischief struck and she added with a grin. "And your legs are blue?"

He grinned in return, making pleasant crinkles at the corner of his dark eyes. "No, but there is a story about how I was named. Maybe there will be a time when I can tell it to you." For the first time, he openly appraised her with a studying gaze. "*Ulethi oui'thai-ah*," he said softly.

At his compliment on her lovely hair Ginny's face, again, grew warm.

Thankfully, Jeremiah strode to her side, saving her from any further comment. His glance bounced between Ginny and Bluelegs, and his pale brows rode low over his narrowed eyes.

"Mr. Findley wonders how much longer it will be before you have his horse shod." A hint of anger honed a sharp edge on Jeremiah's impatient tone.

Bluelegs flashed a bright smile and offered Jeremiah his hand. "I'll have him ready to go in two shakes, Mister—?"

"Jeremiah Dunbar." Jeremiah paused for a moment as if reluctant to accept Bluelegs's outstretched hand. When he did, the handshake appeared even briefer than the custom Algonquin greeting.

Though meeting a fellow Algonquin felt somehow reassuring, Ginny hoped Jeremiah never found it necessary to fight Bluelegs. Her heart trembled at the thought, unsure Jeremiah could win such a contest.

~*~

Jeremiah wanted to punch his fist through... something. Anything. A wild, unreasoned fury brewed deep in his chest. Bumping along the rutted road to Underwood in the back of Abner Findley's wagon, he couldn't remember when he'd felt so wretched and tried to make sense of his surly mood.

In truth, he knew the cause. She sighed softly, shifting her head against his shoulder in her sleep.

He glanced up at the sky, streaked with purple and vermillion in the deepening winter gloaming. It reminded him of a bruise—a bruise he would like to put on the nose of Bluelegs Cavanaugh. Yet the blacksmith back in Charlestown had given him no reason to do so.

At least, no honorable reason.

The blanket slipped off Ginny's shoulder with the wagon's jostling. He reached over and tucked it beneath her chin again.

Jeremiah could no longer deny it. Watching Ginny

laughing and carrying on a conversation in Shawnee with the young blacksmith had soured Jeremiah's humors. He should be glad Ginny had found someone with whom she could speak Shawnee.

But he wasn't.

And there lay his shame. The words of James 3:14 convicted Jeremiah's heart. *But if ye have bitter envying and strife in your hearts, glory not, and lie not against the truth.*

The ugly feeling festering in Jeremiah's heart had a name and he knew it.

Jealousy.

Jealousy that made him want to smash his fist into the face of a man who'd done him no wrong and could potentially assist in making Ginny's transition into her new life, easier.

If he truly cared for Ginny. *And he did.* Jeremiah knew he should want the best for her. As the apostle Paul said in his first letter to the Corinthians, "Charity suffereth long, and is kind; charity envieth not; charity vaunteth not itself, is not puffed up. Doth not behave itself unseemly, seeketh not her own, is not easily provoked, thinketh no evil."

But try as he might, Jeremiah could dredge up scant charity for the blacksmith.

Still, he knew nothing of the man. Surely, it would be prudent of him to keep a watchful eye on Cavanaugh in case the blacksmith attempted any romantic overtures toward Ginny. Not for the first time, Jeremiah considered making Underwood his permanent residence.

Dear Lord, help me to protect Ginny, and to do it with a pure heart.

The instant he'd sent the prayer heavenward, the

wagon stopped.

"Jeremiah. Ginny. We are home." At Zeb's excited voice, Ginny stirred. Sitting up with a jerk, she blinked and rubbed the sleep from her eyes.

"I—I did not intend to sleep." Her eyes wide, she drew away, and Jeremiah fought the urge to pull her warmly back against him. Instead, he stood in the wagon bed covered with straw that still smelled of the smoked hams Abner Findley had sold to the steamboat.

"It's been a long day." He reached down and grasped her hands to help her up. "But tonight, you will sleep in a proper bed."

Jeremiah climbed down from the wagon and then turned to help Ginny. Lifting her from her perch on the wagon's wheel to the ground, he wished he could hold her in his arms like this forever.

But the next moment, they were expressing their thanks to Abner Findley and waving their good-byes as he drove away into the gathering darkness.

When the rumble of the wagon faded, they turned toward Zeb's two-story cabin. It stood quiet and dark. Too quiet. Too dark.

"Zeb, there is no smoke coming from the chimney." Jeremiah wished he'd tried harder to keep the alarm from his voice.

Although disappointment registered on Zeb's face, his shoulders lifted in an unconcerned shrug. "Ruth must be stayin' with one of the neighbors. Tomorrow, we'll ask around and find where she is, but right now we need to get Ginny inside and get a good fire going."

The latchstring hanging outside the door confirmed Zeb's assumption. If Ruth was home and had gone to bed, the latchstring would be pulled in and the door barred from the inside.

The cabin's dark interior felt almost as cold as the outdoors, and Jeremiah yearned to get a fire going. Zeb shoved a broom straw into the faintly glowing coals on the hearth's floor, catching it afire, and lit a taper. The candlelight cast a warm glow around them, but did little to dispel the darkness that clung to the corners of the room.

Jeremiah started to head back outside to fetch wood from the rick he'd noticed on the porch when a soft moan sounded from a shadowed corner of the cabin, and he turned around.

Zeb plopped the candleholder back on the table and ran to the bed in the corner. Ginny followed with the taper in hand.

"Ruth! Oh Ruth, we didn't think you were here." Zeb sank to his knees beside the bed, his voice thick with emotion.

Ruth answered with another moan, and Zeb looked up at Jeremiah and Ginny, his face a stricken mask in the flickering candlelight.

"She's burning up with fever."

15

Three days later, Ginny jerked awake at the sound of voices.

"Zeb. Zeb."

"I'm here, my love. I'm here."

A wave of shame rolled through Ginny. A good medicine woman never fell asleep while caring for a sick person.

The startling realization that Ruth McLain had finally awaken in apparent possession of her senses, swept away Ginny's embarrassment. Since their arrival at the cabin, Ruth had lain in the grip of fever, her spirit undecided whether to stay in this life or step into the next.

Ginny rose from her bed of quilts on the wood floor and blinked at the shaft of morning sunlight streaming through the cabin's front window. She took two steps toward the bed in the corner of the cabin then stopped, not wishing to intrude on the intimate moment between the couple.

My aunt and uncle.

The thought still felt as uncomfortable against her mind as another person's moccasins might feel on her feet.

Zeb sat on the edge of the bed holding his wife's hand while tears streamed down his cheeks and onto his black and gray beard. "Praise be to God. Praise God. Praise God." He kept repeating the words between kisses to his wife's hand.

"Zeb, are you here? Are you really here?" Ruth's voice sounded raspy as she looked up at her husband, her brown eyes growing large as buckeye nuts. "Tell me you are here, and I am not mad."

Zeb grinned through his tears. "You are not mad, my love, but you have been very sick."

Ruth closed her eyes and rolled her head on her pillow. Her hair, which Ginny had braided to keep away from her face, bounced on her shoulders like two short black and gray ropes. "I was sure I was mad...or had died."

She gripped Zeb's hand with both of hers. When she opened her eyes again, they widened as she searched her husband's face. "Zeb, I do think I glimpsed heaven. I saw Carolyn, but her hair was not light. It was red like Ginny's was. You remember how Ginny's hair—" A fit of coughing cut off her words and shook her slight body like a stiff wind buffeting a sapling. When the coughing eased, she lay back gasping. The sight pinched Ginny's heart, reminding her of her mother's illness.

Zeb glanced over at Ginny, his wide grin splitting his face. "It is our Ginny you saw, my love. We have our Ginny back home with us."

Ruth's head rolled on the pillow and followed Zeb's gaze.

"Dear Lord, can it be true? Is it possible God has returned our little Ginny to us?" Despite her questions, the tears streaking her pale cheeks as she appraised Ginny acknowledged her growing belief in her husband's statement.

"Come here, child." Zeb reached his hand out to Ginny, and she stepped reluctantly to her aunt's bedside and took Zeb's free hand.

Though she willed her countenance to remain calm, Ginny squirmed inside like a trapped animal. She would live here because she had to. But she did not wish to be part of this family and would not be forced to be someone she wasn't.

"Ginny has been tending you." Zeb beamed up at her. "It is by God's grace and Ginny's good medicine that you are still here with us."

Ruth's face scrunched up and her tongue peeked out to lick her lips. "I remember something tasting bad."

Ginny grinned in spite of herself. "I boiled the root of the butterfly weed and made a tea." She touched her aunt's forehead and gave a satisfied nod at the feel of cool skin beneath her fingers. "It was the butterfly weed that took away your fever. You must drink more to heal your lungs."

Ruth's wonder-filled gaze suggested her mind skipped over Ginny's words, chasing other thoughts. "You have been with the Indians all these years?"

Pride stiffened Ginny's back and lifted her chin. "I am Shawnee. Like my mother, I am a Shawnee healer."

The cabin door opened and Jeremiah came in with a rush of cold air, his arms full of pieces of wood. With one look at Ruth, he dropped the pile of wood onto the hearth with a clatter.

"Ruth." He crossed the cabin in three strides, his smile broadening with each step. "Praise God!"

Zeb and Jeremiah began recounting to Ruth how they'd found Ginny at her village on the White River.

"It was God's own hand that led us to her." Moisture glistened in Zeb's eyes.

Ginny pulled her hand from his grasp. "I need to make more medicine," she mumbled, brushing past Jeremiah as she crossed to the hearth. A dull ache gnawed at the center of her chest. She wanted to close her ears as the men talked of her village, her mother, and her mother's death on the banks of Pigeon Creek.

Zeb, Ruth, and Jeremiah might consider taking Ginny away from her village a good thing, but Ginny didn't share their joy. She missed her village and the members of her tribe. Even old Spotted Bird and Flying Hawk. But mostly, she missed Mother and the close bond they'd shared. She missed speaking Shawnee instead of English and daily learning from Mother's wisdom and knowledge of healing.

She picked up the empty water bucket from the stone hearth. Filling the bucket would give her a reason to leave the cabin and not have to listen to the others talk about her and the home she missed.

Outside, the sun sparkled on the new fallen snow. Ginny drew in a deep breath of the cool, refreshing air. She looked up into the maple trees that surrounded the cabin and could almost imagine she was back in her village.

But this was not her village. The shock she'd seen in the eyes of the woman she must call *Nik-kea* made plain what Ginny already knew. She did not belong here.

She made her way through the shallow blanket of

snow to the little stream that snaked behind the cabin. As she plunged the bucket into the water that glinted in the sunlight as it gurgled over smooth brown stones, a woman's stern face flashed before her eyes.

Ginny McLain, don't you fall in that creek. You'll catch your death!

Ginny jerked the bucket from the water and stood up, her heart pounding. The vision of a yellow-haired woman evaporated in the sparkling water of the moving stream. Since their arrival here three days ago, she'd experienced a rash of such troubling visions.

Memories?

She couldn't be sure. But it was the vision of the woman she'd just seen—the one with Ginny's face, but yellow hair—that troubled Ginny most. Was it to this woman the Creator had first sent her?

I won't, Ma.

Ginny shivered. Had she once called the strange white woman with yellow hair by the odd white man's word for mother that sounded like a bleating goat? Or was she just remembering the word Jeremiah had used when speaking of his own mother?

At the sound of snow crunching behind her, Ginny turned around. She sensed Jeremiah's presence before she saw his broad-shouldered shadow stretch across the snow beside her.

"I'm leaving for Deux Fleuves." He reached out and took the dripping bucket from her hands. "Now that your aunt is out of danger, I reckoned I'd best be getting home. Zeb offered to loan me one of his horses for the trip." The corner of his mouth jerked in a tight, fleeting smile as he cocked his head in the direction of the structure beyond the cabin. She'd learned it housed two horses and a cow. "I wanted to say good-bye."

Quivering heat like a dancing flame rose in Ginny's chest. She fought the urge to beg him to stay. Jeremiah's presence had offered a kind of shield between her and Zeb. And Ruth waking from her fever only minutes earlier hadn't given Ginny enough time to discern what attitude her aunt might take toward her.

But she had no right to delay Jeremiah from reuniting with his family, whom he hadn't seen for many moons. If not for Ruth McLain's illness, he'd have left three days ago.

For the first time, she wondered if he had a sweetheart waiting in his village of Deux Fleuves. The thought deepened the shadow of sadness creeping across her heart.

Afraid to trust her voice, she nodded, and they walked together to the front of the cabin in silence.

"I'll be back in a few days to return Zeb's horse and help him plan the bigger church he wants to begin building here in Underwood this spring." He grinned. "Your Aunt Ruth put her foot down. No more circuit riding or long trips for your Uncle Zeb."

At his promise to soon return, joy rose from Ginny's chest on gleeful wings. She stifled a grin and shook her head. "Why do the whites think *Wos-so Mon-nit-to* will hear them better when they are inside a building?"

Jeremiah chuckled. "That's a good question."

He set the bucket on the flat brown rock in front of the cabin door and took her hands into his, making her heart flutter like the wings of a fledgling bird.

The smile left his face and his blue eyes turned somber. "Ginny, I know the white man's ways seem strange to you. But remember, the Shawnee ways seem strange to most whites, too."

Ginny tried to ignore the prickling sensation stiffening her spine. She'd rather not revisit the argument they'd had on the steamboat. She'd made it clear that she wouldn't be forced to live as a white woman, and she didn't want their parting marred by a quarrel.

He looked down at their clasped hands. "Your aunt and uncle love you very much. They will honor your ways, but you must be willing to honor theirs as well."

She swallowed down the anger rising in her throat and filling her mouth with a bitter taste. With her hands nestled in Jeremiah's warm grasp, Ginny was prepared to promise him anything.

"I will try," she managed to murmur as the rough skin of his thumbs rasped across the backs of her hands, sending pleasant tingles up her arms.

"I'm glad." His tilted smile that had become dear to her since his arrival in her village during the waning days of the Wilted Moon, caressed her face and heart.

She gripped his fingers a little tighter and said, "*Paselo,* Jeremiah Dunbar."

"Does that mean good-bye?"

"It means take care."

"Then Paselo, Ginny Red Fawn McLain." His voice softened to a near whisper and his blue gaze held hers. "I will pray that God will keep you in His care."

The moment he slipped his fingers from hers she missed his touch. She watched him walk through the snow to the barn knowing she would be whispering Jeremiah's name in her own prayers to Wos-so Mon-nit-to and waiting impatiently for his return.

So four days later, her heart jumped with

anticipation when a knock sounded at the cabin's front door. She'd just applied hot ashes wrapped in buckskin to her aunt's chest.

Compassion filled Ginny at the pain lines that etched Ruth McLain's face with each breath she took. A true affection for the woman had sprouted and grown in Ginny while she'd treated her aunt's ills. She'd even begun to enjoy hearing the stories Ruth told of how she'd taught Ginny to count and read when she was small, though she had no memory of such lessons.

"You'd best call out a 'Who's there?' Ginny." Ruth paused to draw in several wheezy breaths. "Zeb's still out milkin', and I don't have the wind to holler."

"Who's there?" Ginny called toward the door while still keeping a watchful eye on Ruth. The beads of sweat forming on her aunt's forehead and upper lip told her the poultice of hot ashes was doing its job.

"Ben and Esther Collins. Is that you, Ruth? Don't sound like you."

At the unfamiliar voice, Ginny's heart sagged, and she faltered in her trek to the door. The smile blooming on her lips in anticipation of seeing Jeremiah wilted.

She glanced at her aunt who nodded and clutched the hide poultice to her chest.

Ginny opened the door to reveal a man and woman of about forty winters. With one look at Ginny, their eyes flew wide open and then quickly narrowed. A scowl drew down the man's features. Beneath his wide-brimmed black hat, his bushy dark brows rode low over his squinted eyes. The woman gasped and stepped behind her husband. She peered at Ginny from the depths of her brown wool bonnet, fear shining from her gray eyes.

"Who are you, and what have you done to Ruth?"

The man shoved his wife further behind him and leaned forward, jutting his scraggly bearded chin toward Ginny.

Ginny stood her ground and met his menacing green-slitted glare. "I am Ginny Red Fawn McLain, niece of Zeb and Ruth McLain."

Ben Collins blinked, and his face that had grown red turned nearly as white as the snow on the ground behind him.

"Ben. Esther. Come in and shut the door. That wind is cold." A spate of coughing followed Ruth's words, sending Ginny to her bedside.

The couple shuffled in and shut the door behind them. Keeping a wary eye on Ginny, they crossed the cabin to stand beside Ruth's bed.

Ruth struggled to push up to a sitting position. Though she would have preferred her aunt keep the poultice on longer, Ginny set it aside and helped Ruth to sit up and placed pillows behind her back to support her.

"This is John and Carolyn's girl, Ginny, we lost twelve years ago." Ruth smiled at Ginny and then pressed a rag to her mouth to stifle another cough. "Zeb found her out in Missouri on his trip to take the gospel to the Shawnee," she added when sufficient breath returned.

"Raised by injuns?" The man's scowl deepened as he raked a critical glare over Ginny's black skirt with its colorful ribbons, her brown calico blouse, and her braided hair.

"Your lungs are still sick, Nik-kea. You should not talk so much." Ginny glanced from her aunt to the couple and returned the man's cool glare. She hoped the rude visitors would take the hint and cut their stay short.

"We heard you'd left the Ketcham place and come back home." Ben Collins directed his full attention to Ruth while his wife continued to peer from behind her husband at Ginny. "We hadn't heard Zeb was back and thought we oughta see to ya."

"I thank you for your concern." Ruth offered the couple a weak smile. "It got cramped at the Ketcham's when Edith took in her widowed cousin." She paused to cough. "Besides, I missed working my rug loom." Her smile widened. "And Zeb had promised to come home before Christmas."

"If I knew you were ailin', I'd have come sooner." The woman named Esther, who reminded Ginny of a timid mouse, stepped from behind her husband and then glanced at Ginny and stepped back.

"I appreciate that Esther, but Ginny has been taking very good care of me. She was taught the healin' arts by her adoptive mother."

"Do you think that's wise? I mean really..." Esther Collins's critical glance reminded Ginny of the rude looks she'd experienced aboard the steamboat.

"She healed my lung fever in three days, and now she's treating my pleurisy." Ruth's back straightened, and a wave of gratitude washed over Ginny at her aunt's defense of her healing abilities.

"But she's a heathen!" The man named Collins spoke as if Ginny were not in the room.

A storm cloud crossed Ruth's face, but she said nothing. Instead, after a moment's pause, she turned and smiled at Ginny. "Ginny, dear, would you please fetch your Uncle Zeb? I'm sure he will want to know we have company."

Ginny lingered, reluctant to leave. Too much

talking wasn't good for her aunt's sick lungs, but she sensed Ruth wished to speak privately with the couple.

She retrieved the short blanket she used as a wrap from her sleeping spot beside the hearth. She appreciated that Zeb and Ruth McLain had not insisted she sleep in a bed suspended above the floor. In truth, they'd made no demands that she replace any of her customs for theirs.

Ginny headed toward the door at the back of the cabin, making her way through the room where Ruth kept her large weaving loom. When she reached the back door, the angry voice of Ben Collins caused her to pause. Though the breach of privacy pricked her conscience, Ginny felt compelled to listen in the event she needed to defend her aunt.

"It was bad enough that Zeb left his congregation here in Underwood to go on a fool's errand, preaching to blood-thirsty heathen, but to bring one back..." Collins snorted.

"She is our little Ginny—Zeb's blood." Ruth's tone sounded the sternest Ginny had heard her use.

"So she says." Another snort from Ben Collins.

"She does favor Carolyn a good deal as I recollect," mousy Esther said.

"Be quiet, Esther!" The man's harsh voice made Ginny sorry for his wife.

"Whoever she is, she was raised by the same animals that killed your kin and ours twelve years ago, Ruth. So you and Zeb had better see to it that little heathen turns from her injun ways, or I can guarantee you there'll be trouble."

16

Jeremiah's heart bucked at the distant sight of Ginny's russet red braids dangling at the sides of her bent head. Urging his mount up the snow-covered path toward the McLain's barn with Zeb's horse in tow, he spied her hunched figure near the building.

For a full fortnight, he'd had to rely upon the memory of her sweet visage to salve the aching wound their parting had inflicted on his heart. A three-day blizzard and his mother's entreaties that he stay home for a while after his long absence had kept him in Deux Fleuves far longer than he'd intended.

As he approached the barn, Ginny stood and lifted a hand in greeting. The noonday sun glinted off the knife blade in her hand. Scarlet splotches colored the snow at her feet, suggesting she was skinning some sort of small animal.

Many nights over the past two weeks, concern over how Ginny was adapting to life here in Underwood with Zeb and Ruth had robbed Jeremiah of slumber. That she still dressed as a Shawnee woman caused the familiar worry to slink out once again to gnaw in earnest at his chest.

"It is good to see you again, Jeremiah Dunbar." She sent him a quick smile before bending again to her work.

Jeremiah's heart quickened. Had he imagined the joy he'd glimpsed on her face? "It is good to see you, too, Ginny." The understatement sounded stupid to Jeremiah's own ears. He dismounted and led the horses toward the barn feeling as awkward as a youth of sixteen years. "I would have returned sooner, but the blizzard had us snowed in. I pray your Aunt Ruth's health continues to improve."

Jeremiah added the last with a fair amount of caution. He'd left too soon to get an indication of how the two women might get on. Ginny's quick smile brought him a measure of relief.

"Every day she grows stronger." Ginny swiped the skinning knife across the snow, leaving red slashes on the pristine whiteness. "The days Pepoonki blew his fierce breath across the land, my nik-kea taught me how to work the big loom that makes rugs."

Frustration inched its way up Jeremiah's back. He fought the urge to tell Ginny that the earth is the footstool of the one and only God, who, with the Son at His right hand, dictates all weather that sweeps across the globe. But there would be time later for such discussions. Now, he simply wanted to enjoy Ginny's company and drink in her beauty. The apples of her cheeks and her full lips flushed deep pink in the chill air. The sunlight burnished her hair to spun copper and set the snow around her to sparkle like a million glass crystals that wreathed her in a near angelic aura. She took his breath away.

He watched her finish peeling back the hide of the second rabbit with deft skill to match that of the most accomplished trapper. "Your Aunt Ruth is a wonderful woman. I'm glad to hear she is enjoying better health," he said, desiring to keep her engaged in conversation.

"Jeremiah!" With a wide grin stretching his bearded cheeks, Zeb emerged from the cabin's back door and slogged toward them as quickly as the two-feet of snow cover allowed.

After tethering the horses to a sapling beside the barn, Jeremiah hurried to meet Zeb, offering his hand in greeting.

"I came as soon as the weather broke and I heard most of the roads were passable."

"We had no need of an extra horse, snowed in like we were." Zeb glanced at the roan gelding. "Thank you for the good care you took of him."

As they walked toward the barn, Zeb turned his grin toward the two plump, skinned rabbits Ginny had retrieved from the snow. "My, those are a couple of nice fat ones, Ginny girl. You did yourself proud." He cocked his head toward the house. "Your Aunt Ruth's got the pot boilin', and she's cleanin' root vegetables for that first-rate rabbit stew of yours."

Though she made no comment, it did Jeremiah's heart good to see the pleased look on Ginny's face. From every outward sign, she appeared content.

"Tell Ruth to set another place at the table," Zeb called after Ginny who'd headed for the cabin with the rabbits in hand.

"I will, *Shee-tha*." Smiling, Ginny sent the words over her shoulder to Zeb, but her gaze sought out Jeremiah's face.

Though her smile made Jeremiah's insides quiver

like gelatinous meat broth, her use of the Shawnee word for uncle bothered him more than he would have thought.

When she'd disappeared into the cabin, Jeremiah turned to Zeb. It troubled Jeremiah that Zeb seemed unbothered by his niece's insistence on clinging to her Shawnee ways, including the language.

"How is she...adjusting?" Though eager to learn of Ginny's progress, Jeremiah didn't want to sound critical.

A cloud passed over Zeb's face. "She hasn't tried. At least not that you'd notice." It was the first indication that Zeb, too, found her resistance to assimilate into her new life worrisome.

"Has she shown any interest in learning more of the scriptures, or about Christ?" Jeremiah knew the answer before Zeb shook his head.

Zeb rammed his hands into his coat pockets and let loose a sigh that lifted his shoulders then dropped them down again. "In her own way, she joins us in prayer before meals and never interrupts when I read aloud from the scriptures. But she refuses to attend worship services at church, even the Christmas service last week. And though Ruth has offered several times to teach her to read from the Bible, Ginny won't have any of it."

Disappointment pressed heavily on Jeremiah's heart. Despite Ginny's vow to cling to her Shawnee ways, he'd hoped that, with daily exposure to the scriptures, she, like Falling Leaf, would come to accept Christ as her Savior.

Zeb heaved another sigh. "I've never known a more patient woman than Ruth. But when Ginny goes on about the grandfathers of the four winds and burns tobacco in the fireplace to draw the Great Spirit's attention to her prayers...well, even Ruth's patience is showin' signs of frayin' around the edges."

"And the neighbors, how are they taking to her?"

The scowl deepening the furrows on Zeb's forehead sent a stab of fear through Jeremiah. "Some pretend she's not here while others treat her like a curiosity. Best I can tell, only Ben Collins has spoke against her."

"Ben Collins?" The name sounded vaguely familiar, but Jeremiah couldn't place him.

"Ben lost his first wife and three kids at Pigeon Roost. He'd gone to borrow a mule from a neighbor. When he got back..." Zeb hung his head and gave it a sad shake. "The baby hadn't even made it into the world yet," he continued. "They found it torn from its mother's body, scalped, and laid on her mutilated belly." Zeb's voice thickened and his eyes glistened with the telling of the horrific tale. "Reckon I can't blame Ben for how he feels about the Shawnee, but I won't allow him to visit his spite on our Ginny."

A wave of anger doused any sympathy the story had sparked in Jeremiah. "Has the man threatened her? If he has, he'll get an unpleasant visit from me before the sun sets today."

"No, no. Nothing like that." Zeb held up his hands as if to restrain Jeremiah. "He just said she needs to dress and act like a white woman."

A measure of anger seeped away from Jeremiah's tense muscles. He didn't want to cause trouble between Zeb and his neighbors, but Jeremiah still wondered if it might be prudent to pay Collins a visit. At least he could make the man aware that if he caused any harm to Ginny or her kin, he'd have to answer to someone capable of administering a righteous smiting.

An hour later, as they all took their seats around the little oak table across from the fireplace, Ginny and her well-being continued to dominate Jeremiah's thoughts. He'd struggled to focus his attention on Zeb's conversation while the women prepared the rabbit stew. Ginny's every move, every smile, held him captive. During their time apart, he'd almost hoped his feelings for her might have dissipated. But if anything, they'd grown stronger.

His heart thumped harder at her nearness as she bent and placed a bowl of steaming stew before him. Glancing upward, he murmured his thanks. With great difficulty, he managed to wrench his gaze from her cheeks sprinkled with golden freckles. *Like bits of grated cinnamon floating atop thick cream.*

Jeremiah struggled to steer his mind from Ginny's charms as Zeb offered a prayer of thanks for the meal and Jeremiah's safe trip from Deux Fleuves. Remembering Zeb's earlier comment that in her own way Ginny would join Zeb and Ruth in prayer, he couldn't help himself from sneaking a peek.

She sat with her face tipped upward, her eyes wide open, and her hands lifted toward the heavens. The same prayerful attitude he had witnessed many times among the Shawnee including Ginny and Falling Leaf suddenly grated against a nerve. Her lips moved in a soundless prayer...*to whom?* The One true God Jeremiah worshipped or one of the several imagined deities to whom the Shawnee paid homage?

A deep ache filled Jeremiah's chest. She hadn't promised to change her ways, and he'd been a fool to think she would. Jeremiah had pledged his life to preaching Christ's salvation to the lost. He would need a Christian wife beside him. How could he minister to others and be unequally yoked to an unbeliever?

The answer to that question screamed through his mind with a tortuous echo. Until such a time as Ginny Red Fawn McLain embraced Christ as her Savior, he could not entertain the notion of linking his heart—or his life—with hers. Though every emotion within him resisted the thought, he knew he must somehow constrain his errant heart and try to view Ginny as nothing more than a dear friend. As much as he'd once regretted the distance between their homes, he now saw the forty miles as a blessing. If the love and Christian influence of Zeb and Ruth McLain couldn't entice Ginny into Christ's fold, what chance did Jeremiah have in doing so?

Yes, it would be better for both he and Ginny if he prayed for her salvation from afar and resolved to stay clear of Underwood for the foreseeable future.

"I promise you; it tastes even better than it looks." Zeb's teasing tone jerked Jeremiah's gaze up from his untouched bowl of stew.

With a sheepish grin at having been caught musing, Jeremiah shoveled a generous spoonful of stew into his mouth. The succulent pieces of rabbit married perfectly with the soft chunks of potatoes, carrots, and onion. Cornmeal thickened the stew, adding a graininess he found pleasing to the tongue. A blend of herbs and spices—sage and pepper being two he could name—seasoned the dish to perfection.

"See, I told you Ginny's rabbit stew is somethin' special," Zeb said as Jeremiah filled his mouth with a second spoonful.

"It's very good, Ginny." Jeremiah managed to mumble around the bite of stew. She responded to his muted praise with a shy smile.

When he turned his attention from Ginny to Ruth, inquiring after the older woman's health, he glimpsed a look of disappointment flit across Ginny's face. He steeled his heart against it. Whatever affection Ginny might hold for him, he couldn't allow it to grow, just as he must quash his growing affection for her.

Zeb reached into the basket of bread Ginny had placed in the middle of the table. Jeremiah had noticed with interest that the basket held both leavened wheat bread and Shawnee style flat corn cakes.

"I wanted to speak with you about a project God has put on my heart, Jeremiah." Zeb paused in slathering a slice of wheat bread with butter. "Underwood is growin'. At Christmas service, the little meetin' house looked to be fixin' to bust at the seams." He waved the piece of bread in front of his face. "I ain't complainin', mind you. I praise God for every soul who comes to worship our Lord. But I truly believe the time has come to build a larger sanctuary. I'd like to begin the work in the spring."

Jeremiah nodded. His pa's congregation at Deux Fleuves had faced the same situation a couple years past, which they'd solved by expanding the church to three times its original size.

"Since you and your pa did such a fine job planning the addition to the church in Deux Fleuves, I was hopin' you might lend us a hand here."

"I would be glad to." Jeremiah shot Zeb a quick smile. "I'm not sure how much help I can be though, since I'll be riding the circuit by then."

"That's what I wanted to talk to you about." Zeb's serious expression pricked Jeremiah's curiosity. Was Zeb considering riding circuit? But that made no sense.

That would leave him no time to shepherd his flock here in Underwood, let alone time to build onto the church.

Zeb leveled his gaze on Jeremiah's face. "I'd like you to come and help me with the church here instead of riding circuit. There's a little empty cabin behind the church you could use."

Jeremiah dropped his spoon into his bowl with a clink. Warning bells clanged in his head, drowning out Zeb's words.

"I—I don't know." Surely, there was a credible reason to decline the offer, if only Jeremiah could think of one.

But he couldn't. In truth, he hadn't relished the notion of riding circuit and had planned to do so only until he secured a congregation of his own.

Ruth reached over and pressed her hand on Jeremiah's forearm. "Please consider it, Jeremiah. The men of the congregation will be busy tilling their fields come spring and won't be able to offer much help with the building." She cast a fond smile at her husband. "Zeb has his head set on building onto the church. I fear if left alone, he may cause himself an injury."

A battle raged in Jeremiah's chest. Ginny's hopeful gaze warned him of the danger to his heart if he agreed to move to Underwood while Ruth's plea-filled eyes begged him to consider the physical danger to Zeb if he declined.

17

Ginny reached up and plucked several of the fragrant white blossoms from the dogwood tree beside the Renaker cabin. She couldn't resist the opportunity to add to her store of medicinal herbs.

Spring had brought with it an abundance of wild vegetation. With the coming of the Sap Moon, she had begun foraging in earnest for the plants *Melo'kami*, the grandfather of the East who sits where the sun rises, now scattered over the greening earth.

Sadness filled her as she tucked the flowers with their four red-tipped petals into her basket. Soon it would be time for the Spring Bread Dance. For the first time in her remembrance, she would not be helping the women of her village grind the corn or make the bread for the festival. This year, she would not talk and laugh with her mother as they prepared for the sacred celebration that ushered in the season of planting. No more would she feign indignation when Mother asked which young man she planned to choose as a partner for the dances.

Ginny swiped at a rogue tear that escaped the corner of her eye. Despite her deep heartache at the loss of her parent, the thought of Mother walking happily with Father in the land of the sunset gave her comfort. Mother wouldn't be pleased if Ginny dishonored her by giving in to selfish grief.

But the memory of Mother's teasing brought another visage to mind which also pressed painfully against Ginny's bruised heart.

Jeremiah.

When Jeremiah had come to live in Underwood, the moon was new; now it waned to half—two weeks in the way the white man marked the passing of days. During that time, he'd visited her uncle's home but once.

Zeb had attributed Jeremiah's scarceness to his busyness refurbishing the cabin behind the church. But remembering Jeremiah's distant attitude toward her, Ginny wondered if she was the reason he stayed away.

She'd heard Zeb and Jeremiah talking. Jeremiah would be preaching alongside Zeb at the church. Perhaps, like Sadie Renaker, Jeremiah worried that an association with Ginny would invite ill will among the people of Underwood.

Glancing back at the Renaker cabin, she glimpsed Sadie peering through the glass window. The sight spurred Ginny on. She didn't wish to cause trouble with her neighbors.

With perhaps the exception of Ben Collins, Ginny had seen no sign that Zeb and Ruth's neighbors were angry with them for providing a home for Ginny. Instead, the attitude of most people toward the McLains seemed more of pity, viewing Zeb's and Ruth's actions as one of shameful duty.

Even when they learned Ginny had cured Ruth of the lung fever, the neighbors continued to eye Ginny with both curiosity and suspicion. So it came as quite a surprise when three days ago, Sallie Renaker appeared at Zeb and Ruth's home asking Ginny for medicine to cure her baby's colic and loose bowels.

The woman's request kindled an unexpected spark of enthusiasm in Ginny. She was a healer, and a healer had no purpose if the sick spurned the healer's medicine. If Sallie Renaker was willing to seek her help, perhaps eventually, others would as well. And maybe through her healing abilities, Ginny could gain acceptance among these people.

It had hurt when Sallie requested Ginny enter her home through the cabin's back door and to tell no one of her visit. But Ginny understood the young mother's concern. She also doubted Sallie would have allowed Ginny to come if the cabin hadn't been nestled in a secluded clearing at the edge of a small forest, away from the view of neighbors.

The past two mornings, Zeb had brought Ginny to the Renaker's cabin in his wagon before heading to the church. But not fond of riding on the high, jostling wagon, Ginny had insisted on walking this morning, having now learned the way.

Using a method she'd seen Mother use effectively many times, she treated the infant boy alternately with teas of boiled cedar leaves and prairie willow root. This morning the sight of a happily cooing baby, apparently devoid of the stomach pains, had rewarded her efforts.

Sallie, a girl about Ginny's age, had warmed to Ginny, giving her a hug and tucking a jar of honey in her basket.

Ginny's spirits lightened as she slipped among the

trees and headed back home through the wooded glen. The forest would hide her from curious eyes while providing her access to many of the healing herbs available only in wooded areas in the springtime.

The shade enveloped her in a delicious coolness. The sweet scents of pine, cedar, and blossoming trees blended with the pungent, earthy smells of mud, decaying leaves, and mosses. Beneath her feet, the dead leaves that covered the soft, marshy ground rustled as Ginny made her way through the woods. She stopped often to gather a variety of bark, new leaves, mosses and the pale-colored growths Ruth called mushrooms, which Ginny liked to use in cooking.

The sound of hammering brought her head up from where she knelt to pluck a large mushroom from beside a decaying stump. Curious, she placed the honeycomb-like mushroom in the basket and followed the sound to the edge of the woods.

Peering through the trees, she saw a cabin in a clearing. In front and to one side of the cabin stood another structure, a larger one with crossed sticks fixed atop it.

Zeb's church. The cabin must be the one Jeremiah now occupied.

Ginny's heart quickened, filling with a desire to see Jeremiah again. Without giving her head time to talk her heart out of it, she emerged from the woods and strode toward the buildings. She would invite him for supper. More than likely, Zeb would be working at the church as well and would add his own invitation.

As she made her way alongside the cabin toward the back of the church, she noticed the hammering sound had stopped.

"Ginny."

Ginny whirled to see Jeremiah step from behind the cabin.

"Are you looking for your uncle?" His voice sounded strangely stiff, almost as if he were talking to a stranger. His tone inflicted a stab of sadness to her chest. "I'm afraid he's not here just now—"

"No, I was looking for you." Ginny hoped her voice sounded steadier to his ears than it did to hers. "My nik-kea would be pleased if you sat with us at supper." It was but a partial untruth. Ruth had said that very thing to Zeb many times. Just not today.

Though the sun still shone, a cloud seemed to pass across his face. "I'd planned to work until dark." He turned his gaze toward the church as if looking for a reason to focus on something other than her face.

"My shee-tha says you work too much." The words jumped from her mouth like a rabbit flushed from a thicket, and she regretted them the moment she spoke. Zeb hadn't given her his permission to repeat his thoughts. Her embarrassment gave way to joy at Jeremiah's laughter.

"Zeb is probably right." Some of the stiffness left his voice, and she felt a flash of the warm friendship they'd once shared. His bright smile and the sparkle in his blue eyes gave her courage.

She stepped toward him. "Then you will come?"

"Yes, but you should not have come here alone just to ask me to supper." His pale brows slipped together and his voice turned serious. "You know there are some in Underwood who do not look kindly upon you because you are Shawnee. Until they get to know you better, you'd be safer to walk about Underwood with Zeb or Ruth."

It pricked Ginny's heart that he didn't include himself as a protector. "I had another purpose to be out this morning." She told him of her invitation to treat the Renaker baby.

"And how is the child?" He sounded both surprised and worried.

"He is well, as I knew he would be." She couldn't keep a note of pride from creeping into her voice. "My mother taught me well."

"Yes, she did." At his gentle tone, tears sprang to her eyes. Memories of the times she, Jeremiah, and Mother had shared flooded her mind. Ginny blinked away the wetness.

She needed to speak of something else. "This is your home?" She turned her gaze to the little building of hewn logs, scant larger than most wigwams back in her village.

"It is." Turning toward the cabin he smiled, and his voice lifted like a bird taking wing.

This was the Jeremiah she knew. The one her heart had fastened itself to.

"Come. You must see the inside." He grasped her hand and led her around to the front door.

Instead of facing the road as the church did, the cabin's front looked past the back of the church. Ruth told her it had served as her aunt and uncle's first home after their marriage.

Inside, the sparseness of the space surprised Ginny. No table or chairs cluttered the room. The only furniture consisted of a lone bench against one wall and a low bed against another. Smoldering coals glowed red in the fireplace. Jeremiah pitched two short pieces of wood on top of them sending orange sparks up the chimney. Bright little tongues of flame quickly rose to lick about the wood.

"Last week's rain found some places on the roof that needed mending," he said, "but I think I've fixed them all." Now his voice turned tight again, almost nervous. "I suppose the next rain will prove the quality of my work."

Ginny's gaze swept the place. While she approved of the absence of chairs and other usual white man clutter, the addition of rugs and baskets would bring warmth and color to the drab space. "When you come for supper, I will give you some rugs for your floor. Nik-kea and I made many while the snow was deep."

He emitted a deep, rich chuckle. "You are a Proverbs thirty-one woman for sure, Ginny Red Fawn McLain." Wonder filled his voice, and his gaze caressed her face with a touch as gentle as a butterfly's wing.

His use of her Shawnee name along with her white name strengthened Ginny's longing to recapture the close relationship they'd once enjoyed. She remembered the time she bargained with Silver Fox for the horses and how Jeremiah had likened her to a wise and industrious woman in his Bible book. She'd told him she didn't want to hear about anything in the book but then later regretted her angry words. Now she had a chance to make up for them. If she let him tell her more about this woman of whom she reminded him, maybe she and Jeremiah could grow close again.

"Who is this woman you speak of?" She put down her basket and settled herself on the floor beside it to show her readiness to listen.

He walked to the bed and picked up the same black book she'd seen him carry and read from in her village and on their journey here. From this book, he'd read over her mother's body words he said were those of the man called Jesus, the Son of the Great Spirit.

All winter, Ginny had listened to Zeb and Ruth read from their own Bible book the words of the man called Jesus and those who followed him. As a custom, her uncle and aunt set aside time each evening to read aloud from the book. Ginny suspected they used these occasions to teach her more about Jesus. And so they had.

Though she took care not to show it, the words had soaked into Ginny's heart. More than once, the story of Jesus' death had caused her eyes to fill with tears of sadness, while the story of his resurrection had brought tears of joy. She'd written on her memory many of Jesus' words, like "Come unto Me, all ye that labor and are heavy laden, and I will give you rest."

Still, she resisted praying to Jesus, or asking Him to be with her always as Mother had done before she died. Mother's desire to step into the land of the sunset with the Son of the Great Spirit at her side seemed understandable. Unlike Ginny, she wouldn't face the struggle to remain Shawnee in the white man's world. If Ginny accepted Jesus and became a Christian, she'd doubtless be expected to give up her Shawnee ways and live like a white woman.

She could no longer speak of the fathers of the four winds. Or call the Great Spirit Wo-so Mon-nit-to, but must call Him by His white name, God. No longer could she wear the clothes of a Shawnee woman, or braid her hair. She could not burn tobacco to get the attention of the Creator when she prayed. No. Mother said she must be both white and Shawnee, and Ginny could not see how she could be Christian without giving up the part of her that was Shawnee.

Enthusiasm filled Jeremiah's face as he settled himself on the hearthstones. Ginny sat patiently with her hands folded in her lap while he searched the book, the turning pages whispering against his thumb.

"Ah, here it is." He glanced up as if to assure himself of Ginny' attentiveness, and she stifled a giggle at his earnest look. Something about the way his pale hair fell across his broad forehead and the shadow the firelight cast along his strong jaw caused her heart to thump harder.

"'Who can find a virtuous woman? For her price is far above rubies.'" He stopped reading to explain that a ruby was a very prized red stone. He went on to read about a woman whose works, wisdom, and compassion brought her the praise of her husband, her children, and all who knew her.

"'Favour is deceitful, and beauty is vain: but a woman that feareth the Lord, she shall be praised,'" he read. "'Give her of the fruit of her hands and let her own works praise her in the gates.'"

A pained expression crossed his face as he closed the book and set it down beside him on the hearthstones.

"You say I am like the woman in the story" Ginny said, feeling the need to say something. "But the woman in the story has a husband. I do not."

Jeremiah rose slowly and walked over to where she sat against the cabin wall. He reached down and grasped her hands, his strong arms lifting her up. At the intense expression on his face, her insides quivered.

"You could be that woman, Ginny Red Fawn McLain." His husky voice, hardly above a whisper, set her heart prancing. "And the man who will call you 'wife' will be blessed."

The way his gaze melted into hers snatched Ginny's breath from her lungs. She fought to breathe as he touched his fingertips to her forehead and brushed aside a stray lock of hair.

When he lowered his face to hers and pressed a tender kiss on her lips, her heart felt as if it stopped beating. Had she alone or the cabin begun to spin? She didn't care. She cared only about the joy flooding her heart as she stood in Jeremiah's strong, yet tender embrace.

Too soon, he gently released her shoulders and stepped back. His face turned the color of vermillion paint and he looked as stunned as if she'd struck him.

"I'm sorry. That shouldn't have happened." His expression vacillated between bewilderment and anger.

Confused, Ginny stood in a dizzying fog, fighting for both breath and balance. Had she done something wrong? She knew nothing of the white man's ways of courting. Ginny felt no sorrow for the kiss, and hearing Jeremiah express sorrow for it jabbed at her heart like spear.

Heat flooded her face. Perhaps the kiss convinced him she wasn't like the woman in the Bible book after all. Should she have refused his kiss? The woman in the story seemed to always do the good and right thing. Was the kiss some sort of test? Anger sparked in her chest at the thought. She wouldn't make the same mistake again. In the future, she'd prove to him that she had the same strength of will as the woman in the story.

With an unsteady hand, she snatched up her basket. "I will tell my nik-kea you will come to supper," she managed with a breathless warble as she shot out of the cabin.

"Ginny..." His voice behind her sounded almost strangled, but Ginny didn't look back.

Moving at a near trot, she entered the forest, doubting Jeremiah would follow her there. At least she hoped he would not.

Thankfully, as she stepped among the trees, she heard behind her the distant sound of Zeb's voice calling to Jeremiah. Long before suppertime, when she must face Jeremiah again, Ginny would have gained control of her galloping heart and flaming face. A part of her hoped he'd change his mind and decide not to come for supper after all, but she'd never known him to go back on a promise.

With her head and heart still reeling, she hurried through the woods in a daze and emerged at a spot she thought was near her aunt and uncle's cabin. But seeing nothing familiar, her heart sank in dismay. Before her lay a rut-pocked road—the one she assumed ran through Underwood. Across the road and a few paces north stood what looked like a barn with both front doors yawning wide.

A sign hung above the door and just below the pitched roof. As she made her way across the road and toward the structure, Ginny wished for once that she'd let Ruth teach her to read the white man's words.

The place reminded her of the livery stable in Charleston, which made her think of Bluelegs Cavanaugh. Zeb had mentioned that the young Delaware blacksmith recently opened a shop in Underwood.

Nearing the building, she peered into the shaded interior and sure enough, the glow of a furnace glared back like a large, red-gold eye. The *clang, clang* of metal striking metal emanated from the depths of the barn's dark throat.

Relief washed over Ginny. At least she'd met Bluelegs before in Charlestown and had shared a friendly conversation with him. She had no doubt he could point her in the direction of her uncle's home.

The smell of molten metal filled her nostrils as she stepped into the building. Bluelegs stood near the furnace hammering a red-hot horseshoe, which he held against a flat piece of iron using a long-handled gripping tool.

Shirtless, he reminded her of the men of her village. Most wore shirts only in the coldest part of the winter. In the light of the furnace, sweat glistened on his coppery arms and torso.

He looked up, and Ginny had to stifle a giggle when his dark eyes flew open wide.

"Red Fawn, it is nice to see you again."

The look of surprise vanished from his face, impressing her by how quickly he gained control of his features.

"What brings you to my shop?" He went back to hammering on the horseshoe, making little sparks fly.

Remembering her promise to Sallie Renaker, she told him she'd lost her way in the woods while gathering plants for medicines. "Do you know in which direction is the home of Zeb McLain?"

Using the tongs, he dropped the hot horseshoe into a waiting bucket of water, sending up a loud hiss amid a cloud of steam. "Your home is only a short walk to the south, my little lost fawn." He cocked his head in that direction and his lips formed a grin. "I will take you there if you like."

"No. I do not wish to take you from your work,

and I would rather walk alone." While her aunt and uncle refrained from any idle talk, she'd noticed that many of the whites enjoyed gossiping about their neighbors, a crime punishable by death among the Shawnee. She would not like her name to be linked romantically with Bluelegs, especially if Jeremiah were to hear it.

"So my little fawn, are the medicines for your own use, or are you a healer?" He planted his balled fists on his narrow hips as he faced her.

"I am a Shawnee healer, as was my mother." Ginny's chin lifted. Though she didn't like him calling her his "little fawn," she sensed he meant no disrespect.

"Does your mother live here in Underwood, too?"

"My mother walked into the land of the sunset at the rising of the Eccentric Moon." She told him of their journey from the banks of Missouri's White River to the place where the Pigeon Creek flows into the Spelewathiipi. "I think my mother decided long before we left Missouri that she would be buried beside my father."

"I am sorry for your loss, but happy the Great Spirit granted your mother's wish." Unlike the whites, including her aunt and uncle and even Jeremiah, Bluelegs' voice, though kind, held none of the over-sympathetic tones that stirred sadness in Ginny.

"I miss her most now as the time of the Bread Dance nears." Ginny managed a wobbly smile. "I miss the celebration of the Bread Dance, too."

"And which was your favorite dance?" Taking a wide stance he folded his massive arms across his chest and fixed her with an attentive gaze as if waiting for an answer of great importance.

"The Pumpkin Dance was my favorite."

"Ah, the last dance before prayers." He nodded his approval, his dark eyes twinkling. "I have no turkey wing, but I see no reason we cannot share a dance to celebrate spring as our people have always done."

To her surprise, he walked to her and took her hands in his. Though not a general occurrence, she recalled several occasions when members of the Grandfather People were invited to her village for such festivals as the Spring Bread Dance.

Facing her, he released her hands and took two steps backward.

"*Ya ne hoo wa, ya he hoo wa no.*" He began chanting in a rhythmic fashion, swaying side to side as he shifted his weight from one foot to another.

Mirroring his movements, Ginny slipped into the rhythm of the dance with glee. She echoed his song, allowing the memory of drumbeats from celebrations gone by to guide her feet as she stomped out the dance steps.

Swaying side to side and stepping forward and back, they sang in Shawnee of their thanks to the Great Spirit for the coming of spring and their prayers for a bountiful and peaceful growing season.

At last, he stepped so close to her that the toes of their moccasins almost touched. He stopped chanting and grasped her hands in his then stomped twice, signaling the end of the dance.

"*Ouisah meni-e-de-luh,*" he said with a grin, his dark gaze melting into hers.

Ginny echoed the Shawnee words for "Good dance." Still clinging to his hands, she giggled. She would never have imagined that here in this village of white men, she'd have the opportunity to share a Shawnee dance with someone. The past few moments had wiped a measure of homesickness from her heart.

At a sound near the doorway of the blacksmith shop, she turned her still smiling face in that direction. What she saw snatched the smile away, along with much of the breath from her lungs. She had just enough air left to gasp out one word.

"Jeremiah."

18

A week later, as he stood in his cabin attempting to scrape the whisker stubble from his clenched jaw, the memory of Ginny holding hands with the blacksmith still slashed at Jeremiah's heart. He'd redoubled his resolve to stay clear of her, but the hurtful image refused to fade.

To his shame, Jeremiah had stomped away from the smithy half-hoping Ginny would come after him. She hadn't. Neither did she mention the incident later that evening during supper at Zeb and Ruth's home. In truth, Jeremiah had given her scant chance, declining dessert and excusing himself from the table early. Although he couldn't imagine a more perfect pairing than Ginny and Bluelegs, Jeremiah wasn't ready to hear from her lips that the young blacksmith had won her heart.

Her lips.

The punishing slashes against his heart resumed with the memory of her lips—soft and sweet as flower petals—touching his, caressing...

Bad enough that he'd given in to Zeb and Ruth's cajoling and moved here to Underwood after vowing to stay away from Ginny. That he'd allowed himself to compound the folly by foolishly kissing her strained comprehension. In truth, he should be thankful to Bluelegs for effectively removing the possibility of developing a romantic relationship with Ginny. But of the many emotions tangling in his chest, thankfulness wasn't among them.

"Jeremiah."

At the sound of her voice, Jeremiah's hand holding the shaving razor jerked, sending a stinging pain along the side of his chin.

He turned from the mirror and winced, both from the pain of his cut chin and the pain Ginny's visage inflicted on his bruised heart.

She stood framed in the cabin's open doorway. Her smile wavered, and her gaze avoided his face. Was she, too, remembering the kiss they shared in this room?

"I have brought you the rugs and baskets I promised for your cabin." With a rolled-up rag rug tucked under one arm and a basket dangling from the other, she stepped in uninvited, and Jeremiah fought the urge to suggest she take them to Bluelegs.

"Thank you." How could he live with these things, look at them daily, and not be tortured by thoughts of the one who made them? Remembering the soap on his face, he grabbed the scrap of linen from the washstand and, with awkward motions, swiped it across his face.

She placed the basket by the hearth and then spread the rug beside his bed. Made of varying hues of blue cloth sprinkled with a smattering of yellow-gold calico, the rug reminded him of a summer sky.

"They are very nice, but..." He needed to think of a response that convinced her he didn't need her offerings while not sounding ungracious.

As he puzzled how he might word a polite rejection, Ruth McLain sashayed in laden with more rugs.

"Doesn't our Ginny do wonderful work, Jeremiah?" Ruth shot him a quick smile and set the rugs on the floor. "I never saw anyone take so quickly to rug making."

"It is very kind...of both of you." Surrendering to the inevitable, Jeremiah managed a weak smile. They'd left him no choice. He must keep the gifts.

Ruth's eyes welled as she gazed fondly about the little cabin. "It seems impossible I've not set foot in this house since moving into our larger one these five years past."

Having learned that Ruth and Zeb spent their first years of marriage here, Jeremiah wondered at the memories that must be playing through her mind.

Ruth lifted her apron hem and dabbed at her wet eyes. "I'm happy to see it become a home again." She bounced a smile between Jeremiah and Ginny as Ginny scattered the rugs about the floor. "Well, I must go now and have Zeb show me the progress you two have made on the church since I was last here." She hurried out of the cabin before Jeremiah could think of a reason to call her back. At the thought of being left alone with Ginny, panic seized him, and he started to follow Ruth out the door.

"You have cut your face."

Ginny's soft voice drew his attention from Ruth's retreating figure. He touched the place on his chin that still stung and brought away fingers smeared with blood.

"It is nothing." Of course, as a healer, Ginny felt obliged to doctor his injury. The thought of her lingering here and touching his face, battered his heart. He dabbed at his wound with the linen cloth. "It will stop bleeding soon."

To his dismay, she ignored his dismissive comment and opened the ever-present medicine pouch attached to the deer hide belt she wore around her middle. After a moment of searching, she drew out a piece of what looked like fir bark, popped it into her mouth, and chewed it. She then spit the wad of brown goo into her fingers and began slathering it on his chin.

Jeremiah winced, not from the slight burn of the fir resin, but from Ginny's tender touch. Her fingertips blazed a trail of fiery tingles along his jaw, dancing over his skin like heat lightning.

Unable to bear it any longer, he reached up and covered her hand with his, holding it close and warm against his face. He must be mad. Had he lost his wits altogether? He didn't care. Nor did he care that Bluelegs might well call him out or simply pummel him senseless. Nothing mattered but Ginny's upturned face, so close to his he could almost count the golden freckles sprinkled like honey drops over her delicate nose and across her soft cheeks. He marveled at how the light turned her lashes to wispy curls of spun gold. Her pink, full lips were slightly parted, inviting... He lowered his face.

To Jeremiah's shame, she yanked her hand from beneath his and sprang back, her face turning the color of a ripe strawberry.

"I—I'm sor—"

"Big Brother! Did you not hear me knocking?"

Before Jeremiah could finish forming an apology to Ginny, his brother Joel strode in with their sister Lydia following close at his heels.

Jeremiah stood stunned, from both the shock of Ginny's reaction to him and the appearance of his siblings. A blast of heat shot up his neck and filled his face. How much had they witnessed? A greater concern quickly swept that thought away. "Is something amiss at home?"

"You did forget!" Lydia huffed out an impatient breath. Still unmarried at one and twenty, she'd earned the pet name Little Mother in the family. She justified the moniker by turning to their eighteen-year-old brother. "See, Joel. I told you he would forget."

"Forget what?" Now completely confounded, Jeremiah glanced toward the fireplace to assure himself that Ginny hadn't fled the cabin—something a part of him was glad about while another part wished she had.

"Don't worry, brother," Joel piped up. A couple spindly legged strides brought his post-thin frame next to Jeremiah's. He gave Jeremiah's shoulder a thump. "We won't tell Ma you forgot her birthday is Wednesday next."

Jeremiah groaned. Though Mother annually complained about the fuss, Father always insisted the family gather to celebrate her birthday.

"You seem to have forgotten your manners as well, Jeremiah." With pert movements that always reminded Jeremiah of a bird, Lydia maneuvered her petite form around Joel and headed for Ginny.

"I apologize for my brother's bad manners." Lydia stuck her hand out toward Ginny. "I'm Lydia Dunbar, Jeremiah's sister."

Jeremiah managed to stifle a groan. From the time they were small, Lydia had seemed to find it her life's mission to correct him.

Lydia glanced at Joel. "And this is our brother, Joel."

Joel bobbed his head in Ginny's direction. "And you must be Zeb and Ruth McLain's niece, Ginny. I've heard so much about you from Jeremiah."

"Yes, I am Ginny Red Fawn McLain." Smiling, Ginny accepted Lydia's hand and gave it a quick shake. "I would like to hear what your brother has said of me." She quirked a grin toward Jeremiah and he held his breath. He never could predict what might pop out of his sister's mouth.

"He said you were beautiful, and I can see he was not in the least exaggerating."

Another wave of heat flooded Jeremiah's face. Joel snorted in a failed attempt to stifle laughter. Later, Jeremiah would make him pay for his burst of mirth.

"So I'm assuming Pa sent you two to fetch me for Mother's birthday celebration." Jeremiah needed to turn the conversation in another direction.

Lydia spun toward him, making her brown calico skirt twirl like a whirligig maple seed. "Actually, it was my idea. Of course, Pa would not let me come alone, so he made Joel come with me."

Joel nodded and shrugged his shoulders in mute agreement.

"In fact," Lydia turned back to Ginny, "we would like to invite you to come, too."

Ginny's face mirrored Jeremiah's surprise. Moments earlier, he had accepted this unexpected development as God's way of removing him from the temptation of Ginny's presence. Lydia's impulsive invitation dashed that assumption.

When he found his voice, Jeremiah said "I'm not sure Zeb and Ruth would—"

"Last Sabbath, Ma was talking to Annie Martin, one of our neighbors." Lydia prattled on to Ginny, ignoring Jeremiah. "Ma mentioned to Annie that you'd returned to Underwood, and Annie said she would like very much to meet you. Annie was taken by the Shawnee the same year you..." In an apparent flash of self-awareness, Lydia, to Jeremiah's great relief, stopped talking. After a moment his sister shook her head, reminding him of a small dog shaking off water.

"In any event," Lydia continued brightly, "my family and I would like to invite you to come visit us at Deux Fleuves, Ginny."

The tightness in Jeremiah's chest eased a bit. He couldn't imagine Ginny accepting such an invitation. With her still so new to Underwood and with Bluelegs here now.

"I would like to visit your village, Lydia Dunbar, and meet this Annie Martin." Ginny's quiet reply touched off a war in Jeremiah's chest.

God, I trust You, but what are You doing?

Beaming, Lydia clasped her hands together and gave a little bounce. "Oh, we shall have a grand time, shall we not, Jeremiah?"

Jeremiah forced a weak smile. Spending a near fortnight in close proximity to the woman he loved, yet could not have, seemed more like the definition of torture than Lydia's "grand time."

~*~

"I'm starving! I do hope Mother has some scraps

of supper left on the hearth." Lydia Dunbar's voice sounded like the squawks of a bird in Ginny's ears as they bumped along on the wagon seat behind Jeremiah and Joel.

Though possessed of a kind heart and friendly manner, Lydia, Ginny observed, seemed to talk for the sheer joy of hearing her own voice. In the two days since they'd left Underwood, she'd scarcely stopped talking except to sleep. Last night at the inn in Salem where the two had shared a room, Lydia had talked into the night as she lay in bed, requiring Ginny to answer only with an occasional murmur from her pallet on the floor until sleep overtook them both. She also noticed that much of Lydia's talking consisted of complaints.

"I dare say you must be hungry too, Ginny, and cold." Lydia shivered as she shifted on the seat, nestling further into the quilt in which she'd wrapped herself against the early evening chill. "Even with your blanket, I don't know how you bear this cold air without a bonnet. Your ears must be frozen."

Ginny opened her mouth to say that she could endure the cold a lot easier than the punishment the jostling wagon seat inflicted on her bottom, but Joel spoke up before she could.

"I'm sure you've kept her ears warm with all your hot air, Lydia." He glanced over his shoulder, his tone as flat as an ashcake.

"Pay no attention to Joel, Ginny. He's horrid." Lydia's face pruned up in a petulant pucker.

Ginny suppressed a giggle. The sister and brother had entertained her much of the way with their good-natured teasing. But it bothered Ginny that throughout their journey, Jeremiah remained unusually quiet—

even for him. More than once, she'd sensed, as now, that he wasn't especially happy to have her here. The thought pinched her heart, and she fled the sadness it caused by focusing back on Lydia's incessant chatter.

"Now what was I talking about before Joel rudely interrupted?" Lydia tapped her pursed lips for a moment. "Oh yes, food. Wait until you taste our sister Elizabeth's biscuits, Ginny." Lydia stuck her hand out of the quilt and gave a little wave. "I must admit, even at sixteen, our little sister has the lightest hand with biscuits I've ever seen. I wouldn't be a bit surprised if some young man didn't snatch her up for a wife very soon."

"Oh, I do hope so," Joel said. "I'd love to see you have to dance in the hog trough, Lydia."

Lydia reached out and gave the back of her brother's shoulder a punch, making him cry out in pain amid his laughter. "It is too bad brothers don't have to dance in the trough, because our sweet baby brother, Isaac, will likely find a bride long before you do," she shot back. "And he's only fifteen!"

A barely audible chuckle rumbled from Jeremiah, earning him a punch to the arm from Joel.

Intrigued, Ginny turned to Lydia. "Is this dance a wedding custom?" She'd witnessed many Shawnee marriage dances but had never seen anyone dance in a trough.

Lydia stiffened. "Oh, it's a silly tradition that if a younger sister marries first, the older sister has to dance in a hog trough at the wedding celebration." She snorted. Since our sister Dorcus married last summer, it's actually Jeremiah's turn to choose a bride. Unless..." Lydia's tone turned sly. The grin she slid in Ginny's direction made Ginny squirm. "He has already chosen."

"Look, there's home!" Jeremiah's voice broke in as they crested a hill, thankfully cutting short the uncomfortable turn the conversation had taken. He pulled back on the reins, jerking the wagon to a sudden stop just before the road took a steep slope downward.

Ginny peered around Jeremiah and followed his gaze. Nestled between the surrounding wooded hills lay a little valley. In its center sat a fort with weathered gray pickets poking up at the purple sky streaked with the gold and vermillion glow of the setting sun. Scattered around the fort were several cabins of various sizes and shapes. The sight reminded Ginny of a grouse hen gathering her chicks to her as they settled down for the night, their golden eyes winking up at her.

"Thanks be to God!" Lydia's words *whooshed* out on a single breath of air. "The tapers are still burning, so we won't have to wake everyone up."

Knots tightened in Ginny's middle as they neared a tall cabin. Despite Lydia's repeated assurances that her parents were eager to meet Ginny, she still couldn't help wondering what sort of welcome awaited her behind the cabin's log door.

Jeremiah helped Ginny down from the wagon while Joel helped Lydia down from the other side.

In Jeremiah's warm embrace, Ginny's heart danced. For an instant, she glimpsed in his eyes the same tenderness she'd seen when he kissed her and again when she treated his cut chin. But as if remembering himself, he quickly let her go, turned, and stepped up to the cabin's door.

The Dunbar's cabin reminded Ginny of her uncle and aunt's home in Underwood. Judging by the two windows above the front door and below the roof, this cabin, too, had an upstairs.

While Jeremiah pounded on the door and called out for someone inside to open it, Ginny wondered if she would be sleeping upstairs tonight. That concern fled when the door finally flew open, revealing an older woman with a drawn face and red eyes.

"Praise God, you are home!" With a muffled sob, the woman collapsed into Jeremiah's embrace.

19

"Ma, what is the matter?" Stepping into the cabin, Jeremiah gently drew his mother aside to allow Ginny, Lydia, and Joel to enter.

"It's Isaac." The woman's eyes welled with tears. He was drivin' the cows into the barn for the night and got rattlesnake bit not half an hour ago."

"Is he much sick from the poison?" Ignoring Lydia's gasp and Joel's and Jeremiah's groans, Ginny strode across the cabin to where the boy lay on a bed, moaning and writhing in pain. Sweat plastered his light brown hair to his forehead. A girl about his same age, evidently the sister called Elizabeth, stood near her stricken brother, holding at the ready a bucket that reeked of foul, bloody vomit.

"Bad as I've ever seen, I reckon." A big man with pale hair and beard rose from a chair beside the boy's bed to face Ginny. This was, without a doubt, Jeremiah's father, Obadiah Dunbar. Besides their same coloring, the two men shared similar large frames and bright blue eyes. Obadiah's drawn face and fear-filled eyes matched his wife's anxious expression. "I sucked out as much poison as I could, but the leg keeps swellin' and the bleedin' and vomitin' won't stop."

Nearing the bed, Ginny could see the man's words were true. Isaac's pant leg was cut away at the knee, exposing the affected limb, mottled with purple and swollen to twice its normal size. A bloody cloth swathed the boy's ankle. This would be the point of the bite.

"Did you put any medicine on it?" Ginny took care to keep her voice calm as she studied the extent of Isaac's injury while his family members clustered near the bed. The sooner she determined how much poison the snake had given the boy and what treatment he'd had, the better she could determine what best to do for him.

"A poultice of salt and gunpowder to draw out the poison, but it don't seem to be doin' much good." Obadiah ran an unsteady hand across his broad brow.

Ginny stifled a snort. Despite her poor opinion of the white man's treatment, she must show respect.

"I have seen bites by timid snakes that have little poison, and bites by angry snakes that have much poison. Your son was bitten by a very angry snake. It will take stronger medicine to cure him."

"You are Zeb's niece, Ginny." Obadiah's words were not a question. He stuck out his large hand and she gave it a quick shake. "I'm Obadiah and this is my wife, Bess." He glanced at the woman Jeremiah had called "Ma."

"I am Ginny Red Fawn McLain. Like my mother, I am a Shawnee healer.

"Then we welcome you and any help you can give our boy." Obadiah's tight smile faded as he turned back to his injured son.

Without another word, Ginny stepped closer to the boy's bed. She unwound the bloody cloth from Isaac's ankle and dabbed away the blood to reveal two tiny pin pricks oozing blood. The miniscule wounds suggested a young offending serpent which hadn't yet learned to control the amount of poison its bite released. A more mature snake would have left larger marks and might have given a warning bite, releasing no poison at all.

Isaac thrashed his head from side to side, his face contorted in agony. "My leg's on fire. Do somethin' to stop the burnin,'" he said through clenched teeth.

New concern for Jeremiah's brother sparked in Ginny's chest. Schooling her face to not show her worry, she dug in her medicine pouch for the ever-present snakeroot. She handed the dried roots and leaves to the boy's mother. "Boil these until the water is brown with the juice. Make a poultice of the leaves and then boil the juice with some milk for Isaac to drink." She forced her lips into what she hoped was an encouraging smile. "I have never seen this remedy fail."

"Thank you, Ginny." Her blue eyes swimming with tears, Bess Dunbar hurried to carry out Ginny's instructions assisted by a purposeful Lydia.

Isaac retched and added to the foul contents of the bucket his sister held for him, and Ginny sent a silent petition to the Creator that the boy would be able to keep enough medicine down to cure him.

Supper forgotten, Ginny and the Dunbar family spent the evening attending to the sick boy. Throughout the night, she refreshed the poultice while continuing to dose Isaac with the medicine. As she'd feared, nothing stayed on his stomach for long. But due to his ravenous thirst, he eagerly drank the milk and snakeroot brew. When the first rays of dawn stained the cabin's puncheon floors with streaks of pink, Isaac finally slept.

"Ginny."

At the sound of her whispered name and warm touch on her shoulder, Ginny roused from sleep. Straightening in her chair beside Isaac's bed, she looked up at Jeremiah's gentle smile.

"I'm sorry to wake you, but I was afraid you might fall out of your chair." He grinned and handed her a steaming cup. "I brewed some sassafras tea."

"Thank you." Shame that she'd once again fallen asleep during the care of a patient filled her. She took the cup in her hands, and its welcome warmth suffused her even before she sipped its honey-sweetened contents.

"How is he?" Jeremiah's gaze turned to his brother's sleeping countenance.

"The worst is past. Your brother will recover, but slowly, I think."

"Praise God." A look of relief eased the tense lines from Jeremiah's face. He turned again to Ginny. "It's to your healing ability that we owe Isaac's life."

Ginny fidgeted beneath his grateful gaze. In truth, she hadn't been half as sure of Isaac's outcome as she'd portrayed. She focused on bits of sassafras bark swirling atop the steaming tea. "I should not have allowed sleep to overtake me. Mother would never have done so."

Jeremiah's expression turned bemused as he pulled a chair up to sit beside her. He glanced around the cabin at his sleeping family members scattered about the wood floor on quilt pallets. "You outlasted the rest of us. I woke only a few minutes ago myself." His sweet smile and tender blue gaze spread warmth through her that no cup of tea could generate. "I think your mother would be very proud of you."

Ginny blinked back the hot tears that sprang into her eyes. A truth she could no longer deny throbbed with every beat of her heart. She loved this man beyond all reason. The realization snatched away her breath and with it, her ability to reply.

Thankfully, Jeremiah's parents chose this moment to rise and hurry to their son's bedside.

"How is my boy?" Bess Dunbar bent over her sleeping son. The forced cheerfulness in her whispered voice couldn't mask the apprehension shining in her red-rimmed eyes. Worry and lack of sleep etched deep lines in her plump face and smudged dark shadows beneath her eyes.

Ginny stood, eager to comfort this woman whose stoic strength reminded her of her own mother. "The danger is past. The leg is not as swollen today. The fever is gone, and the bleeding and vomiting has stopped."

"Praise God." Bess sank to the chair Ginny had vacated and heaved a ragged sigh.

Obadiah scrubbed his hand across his own haggard face. He stepped up behind his wife and gripped her shoulders. "Let us pray." Bowing his head, he launched into a prayer of thanks to the Great Spirit he called "God" for sparing his son's life.

Despite the unease she always felt during the white man's prayers, Ginny bowed her head with Jeremiah and his parents instead of stubbornly keeping her face lifted. For once, the need to feel part of this family's prayer of thanksgiving superseded her discomfort in petitioning the Great Spirit with her head bowed instead of facing heavenward.

"Amen and amen." A female voice at the cabin's open door echoed Obadiah's conclusion to his prayer.

Ginny looked up to find a smiling young woman with a reed basket on her arm.

"Annie, come in." Bess rose to meet the visitor. "A snake bite put our Isaac in peril, but God sent us Ginny to save him."

Obadiah explained what had happened and made introductions between Annie and Ginny.

The woman stepped into the cabin. A half-head shorter than Ginny, she walked toward her. Dark brown curls peeked from beneath Annie's faded blue bonnet to frame her pleasant face. A smile replaced her look of concern at Bess's words, and she reached out her free hand to Ginny. "Ah, Ginny Red Fawn McLain. *Bezon*! I've been wanting to meet you."

Annie's use of the Shawnee greeting both surprised and pleased Ginny. She gave the woman's hand a quick shake. "Bezon. I have desired to meet you, too, Annie Martin."

Annie's attention turned to Isaac, now rousing from sleep, and Ginny described her treatment of the boy's injury. "The snakeroot is working well, but I think adding a poultice of black ash buds would hasten the healing."

"There is a large black ash tree by the fort. It's only a short walk from here. I will show you when I've emptied my basket." Annie handed her basket laden with dandelion greens and two small covered earthen jars to Bess. "Brock and the boys found a bee tree the other day. Thought you might like some of the honey and a mess of dandelions I picked on my way here."

Bess smiled the first relaxed smile Ginny had seen on the woman's face since they arrived last evening. "Thank you, Annie, what a welcome treat. I was gettin' low on my store of honey, and with Isaac sick, I hadn't got a chance to hunt for greens." She emptied the basket's contents and handed it back to Annie. "You two run along and fetch what you need for the poultice." She tilted a fond smile down at her stricken son and brushed his sandy-colored hair from his forehead. "We'll see to Isaac."

Ginny followed Annie outside and down a worn dirt path. The scent of spring blossoms fragranced the crisp morning air. The rising sun bathed the dew-drenched landscape in a golden glow, giving Ginny her first clear look at Deux Fleuves settlement. A few yards ahead rose the fort's gray weathered stockade. Blossoming spring wildflowers, white wood sorrel, blue violets, and yellow dandelions studded the greening grasses along the path.

"Jeremiah tells us your mother was also a Shawnee healer." Annie smiled over her shoulder to Ginny as they made their way single file down the narrow dirt path. Undoubtedly, Annie had learned of Falling Leaf's recent death from Jeremiah and his family. Yet neither her voice nor her smile held any of the maudlin sympathy whites tended to gush on those who'd recently lost loved ones. "You honor her with your work."

"*Neahw.*" Without thinking, Ginny uttered the Shawnee word for thanks. "You speak as a Shawnee. Jeremiah tells me you were with my people for a time. How long?"

"Here it is." Appearing to ignore Ginny's question,

Annie stepped from the path and waded through the dewy, ankle-deep grass toward a large ash tree near the weathered wooden walls surrounding Fort Deux Fleuves. "I was with them for a month from the middle of the Raspberry Moon until the beginning of the Blackberry Moon." Her voice remained conversational with no hint of any negative emotion.

"Were you treated badly? Is that why you left them?" Ginny regretted the question the moment it left her tongue. Proper manners prohibited asking such a question of a stranger, but curiosity overpowered her sense of propriety. To cover her lapse of etiquette, she reached up to a low-hanging branch and stripped off a handful of velvety, purple-black buds and dropped them into Annie's basket.

"No, I was treated very well." Annie reached up to pluck buds from the supple branch Ginny had pulled lower. "I still think often of my Shawnee sister, Yellow Bird, and our grandmother, Winter Moon Bird, and pray for them."

"You were adopted into the bird clan, then?"

"No. I left the evening before my adoption ceremony was to take place."

"Why?" Feeling the need to further quench her burning curiosity, Ginny blurted the improper question.

"I was carrying my eldest son in my belly." Her voice turned wistful as her hand went to her now flat midsection. "He needed to be born on the land his father had left to him."

Ginny nodded despite the many questions gathering in her mind. The tribe that had planned to adopt Annie would not have allowed her to leave. Annie must have escaped. Respect for the bravery of the woman beside her sparked in Ginny's chest. Though her curiosity itched, the good manners her parents had taught her wouldn't allow her to scratch it by asking Annie about her escape. Turning her attention to the fort, she changed the subject. "Jeremiah tells me it was in this place that his family went for safety from Tecumseh's warriors."

"*Oui*. Everyone in Deux Fleuves settlement did." Annie's voice, that held the accent of French voyageurs who'd traded with Ginny's tribe, turned somber and a look of remembered pain flashed in her brown eyes.

Ginny could only imagine the terror Annie, as well as Jeremiah and his family, must have experienced during such a siege.

The vision of a painted-faced warrior flashed in Ginny's mind. A hot barb of remembered fear slashed at her mid-section. The frightening childhood memory hadn't visited her in many moons. Ignoring the sweat breaking out at the hairline of her forehead, she mentally shook off the image and willed her voice to calmness. "I'm sorry my people brought such trouble to you. My father often said that Tecumseh was a great warrior, but that his passion for his own people had turned his heart to stone against all others."

Annie dropped a handful of buds into the basket and turned a kind smile toward Ginny. "Ugly things happen in times of war, Ginny. The Bible tells us to not be overcome by evil, but to overcome evil with good. We can let the bad things that happen to us make us bitter or, through forgiveness, we can use them to make us kinder toward others."

Ginny sensed that Annie's comments were in regard to Ginny's past experiences as much as to her own. New hope budded in her chest like the velvety sprouts on the tree's branches. If, like Annie and the Dunbars, most whites believed and follow the words in their Bible book, perhaps, in time, they would accept Ginny despite her Shawnee ways. With a few exceptions like Ben Collins, Ginny had experienced more curiosity than outright hostility from her white neighbors. Perhaps she could even allow her heart to believe in the possibility of her and Jeremiah having a future together.

That hope grew and blossomed over the next couple days. The medicine Ginny made from the black ash buds seemed to help speed Isaac's recovery. As the boy's symptoms subsided, the general mood inside the Dunbar cabin lifted. Lydia suggested that their mother's birthday dinner go on as planned and Isaac agreed. Now able to sit up and even manage a few tentative steps with the help of his father or brothers, he seemed much improved. A persistent numbness around the point of the snakebite remained his singular complaint.

The day of the birthday dinner Ginny worked beside Lydia and Elizabeth, preparing a meal of roast young turkey, cornbread, and a mixture of dandelion and chickweed boiled with chunks of boar's fat. Jeremiah and Joel had gone out hunting while their parents traveled a few miles north to fetch the oldest sister, Dorcas, and her husband.

As usual, Lydia kept up a constant chatter as the three women worked at the hearth. "I can hardly wait to see Dorcas." She turned the spit that suspended the turkey over the fire and then spooned drippings from the pan beneath it onto the roasting meat. "It seems like an age since she and Rudd came for a visit."

"It's only been a month, Lydia." Elizabeth gingerly

lifted the lid from the iron pot banked with hot coals to check the baking cornbread. "And their cabin is but four miles away in Brownstown. You talk as if they live as far away as Madison or even Louisville." Her flat tone suggested strained patience with her talkative sister.

"Well, it seems longer." Lydia's tone turned defensive. "And now that she is—" Lydia glanced across the cabin to where Isaac lay sleeping on his bed and lowered her voice to a whisper. "In the family way. Mama needs to keep a closer watch on her."

Ginny stirred the pot of bubbling greens, not wanting to intrude on what seemed a private family conversation between the sisters. But Lydia's odd expression and secretive demeanor set her curiosity itching. "What is it you mean by 'in the family way?'"

"Dorcas is with child," Elizabeth said, ignoring her older sister's shushes and concerned glances at their sleeping brother. "As Isaac is aware," she added with a giggle. "Don't be such a prude, Lydia."

"And you would do well to behave a bit more prudently, sister." Pressing her fists against her waist, Lydia leveled an aggravated glare at Elizabeth.

Sounds of a wagon and horse team outside interrupted the sisters' quarrel. At once, Lydia and Elizabeth shrieked and ran for the open cabin door.

"What, what has happened?" Isaac sat up in bed and rubbed sleep from his eyes.

"I think your parents have arrived with your sister and her husband." Ginny smiled and walked to Isaac's bedside. "Do you feel strong enough to stand?"

"Yes, I think so." Isaac swung his legs over the side of the bed and tentatively pressed his injured foot on the woven rug. "It's still some numb, but it don't hurt much, just a little tender."

Ginny helped to steady him as he stood and took a couple halting steps. She couldn't help feeling pride at the rapid healing her medicines had brought about. The sudden thought struck that Mother would be proud when she told her of it. A flash of embarrassment followed the thought. How odd to forget that Mother could no longer praise her accomplishments. At the realization, a painful pang of sadness struck her chest, and she blinked away tears. How she longed to see Mother's gentle face smiling her approval.

She swallowed down a lump of sorrow as the Dunbar family, with the exception of Jeremiah and Joel, flowed through the cabin door.

"My poor baby brother!" A woman that looked like a younger version of Bess Dunbar ran to Isaac and threw her arms around him. Dorcas, Ginny presumed, cupped her brother's face in her hands. "Ma and Pa told me about you gettin' snake-bit. I was that worried!" Dorcas's blue eyes glistened with tears.

Isaac's face reddened, and he wriggled out of his sister's grasp. "Aw don't fuss, Sis. Ginny here says I'll live."

For the first time, Dorcas turned her attention to Ginny. Her eyes welling with appreciation, she grasped Ginny's hands. "Thank you. Thank you for saving my baby brother. I don't care what Rudd says, we owe you—"

"Dorcas, get away from that savage! Do you want to mark our babe?"

20

"Rudd, you may be my son-in-law, but this is my home, and Ginny is my guest. I will thank you not to speak about her in that way." Anger flickered like blue flames in Obadiah Dunbar's eyes as he chastised the angry man with the scraggly dark beard and slouch hat. Obadiah's measured tone reminded Ginny of Jeremiah's when he'd stood to fight for her honor on the steamboat.

A smiling Jeremiah ducked into the cabin followed by Joel, making Ginny feel as if her thoughts had caused him to materialize. "Dorcas. Rudd. Joel and I hallooed from the edge of the woods, but you must not have heard us. Glad to see you! Rudd, that Kentucky long rifle you lent me is a dead-sure shot." His smile faded as he took in the somber expressions around the room.

Obadiah cleared his throat, and Bess busied herself at the hearth. "We were just fixin' to make the introductions, son." His pointed glance at Rudd broached no contradiction before his gaze slid to

Ginny. "Dorcas, Rudd, I'd like you to meet Ginny Red Fawn McLain, Zeb and Ruth McLain's niece. Ginny, this is our eldest daughter, Dorcas, and her husband, Rudd Callahan."

For a long moment, silence filled the cabin until Ginny could hear the hissing sound when the juices from the roasting turkey hit the hot hearth. Rudd glared at her, and her heart quaked at the hatred smoldering in his dark eyes. Only the presence of Jeremiah and his father gave her the courage not to flee the cabin.

"I'm so glad to meet you, Ginny." Dorcas, who'd jumped away from Ginny at her husband's earlier barked order, stepped forward again to take Ginny's hand while avoiding her husband's glare.

"I am happy to meet you, too, Dorcas." Ginny gave Dorcas's hand a quick shake, hoping her action wouldn't further anger Rudd.

Jeremiah put an arm around Rudd's shoulder and turned him toward the cabin's open door. "Come out and see the three fat squirrels I shot with your rifle."

Rudd hesitated, and Ginny held her breath. When he finally acquiesced and allowed Jeremiah to guide him outside, everyone else in the cabin seemed to breathe a sigh of relief. Obadiah and Joel helped support Isaac and the three followed Rudd and Jeremiah outdoors, leaving the women to finish the meal preparation.

While Bess, Lydia, and Elizabeth gathered at the hearth to oversee the cooking, Dorcas lingered near the table with Ginny. She placed her hand on Ginny's forearm. A mixture of embarrassment and remorse played across her pleasant, round face. "I'm sorry for what my man said to you, Ginny." The anguish in her blue eyes welling with tears touched Ginny's heart, and she longed to alleviate the woman's concern.

Ginny covered Dorcas's hand with her own. "Do not be troubled by your husband's words. This is not the first time I have heard such things since I left my village in Missouri."

As if unwilling to let the conversation go, Dorcas gripped Ginny's arm tighter and her expression turned imploring. "I want you to know that Rudd is not a bad man. He..." She glanced at the open door as if gathering her thoughts before turning back to Ginny. "He had a terrible experience with the Shawnee as a child. His father was killed during the siege of Fort Deux Fleuves back in 1812, just after the attack at Pigeon Roost." Cringing, Dorcas stopped talking and glanced down as if she'd said more than she would have liked.

Ginny shook her head, ready to assure Dorcas that her mention of Pigeon Roost did not upset her. But to confess that she had no memory of the attack or her murdered family might be misunderstood by the Dunbar family and perhaps even considered callous, so she simply smiled and patted Dorcas's hand. "I understand. It was a bad time."

Without another word, Ginny and Dorcas joined the other women in finishing the meal preparation and getting the dinner on the table. When they called the men in for the meal, the light-hearted mood and air of celebration appeared restored. Rudd's demeanor, however, remained sullen, and Ginny noticed that he chose a seat at the table as far away from her as possible and out of direct eyesight.

Obadiah offered a prayer of thanks for the food, everyone present, and especially Isaac's healing, and then the Dunbar family members began chatting among themselves. For the most part, Ginny remained quiet, speaking only in response to direct questions.

"This sure is a feast," Rudd said. "'Member when we was boys, back durin' the siege, Jeremiah? Them Shawnee savages starvin' us out? Why we dreamt about food like this every day."

Jeremiah didn't respond.

Undeterred, Rudd continued to talk, his grim tone turning bitter. "Starvin' wasn't the worst, though. Losin' Pa to a Shawnee arrow was the worst." He leaned forward and for the first time, sent a challenging glare down the table at Ginny. "The Injuns killed your pa, ma, and baby brother too, didn't they, Ginny?" The emphasis he put on her name made it sound like an insult. "But I don't reckon you remember your family much, do ya?"

"Rudd, please." Dorcas's soft plea sounded close to tears.

Ginny had no answer to Rudd's question—the same one Uncle Zeb and Aunt Ruth had asked, albeit far more gently. Indeed, Ginny had asked herself the question many times since Zeb and Jeremiah first arrived in her village. At night, in the dark stillness as she lay abed unable to sleep, the question had haunted her. Sometimes she thought she could remember faces; a woman with yellow hair; a man much like Uncle Zeb, but different; the sound of a baby squalling; and a doll made of corn husks. All these things flashed in her mind and then flitted away like winged insects. The instant she felt she might grasp them, the images vanished.

When the silence became uncomfortable, Jeremiah cleared his throat and spoke of his and Joel's morning of squirrel hunting, saving Ginny from any answer.

~*~

Three days later, back in Underwood, the question continued to plague Ginny. Did she remember her white family? Did fleeting bits and pieces of visions constitute remembering?

In the several months since she'd come to Underwood, not once had she considered visiting the graves of the parents and brother she only knew through the stories of Uncle Zeb and Aunt Ruth. But now she felt compelled to remember. Jeremiah's words from months ago came back to her like a challenge. *I can remember much from the age of six and even younger.*

Though confused as to why she'd come, Ginny stood in the spot she'd avoided since arriving in Underwood. Here in this quiet clearing shaded from the late morning sun by the surrounding pine grove with only the sounds of a soft breeze playing though the trees, the musical gurgling of the nearby creek, and the cheerful chirping of birds, it seemed impossible to envision the horror that had happened here.

The tear that escaped her eye to wet her cheek surprised her as she gazed at three wooden crosses among a small group of other such markers. These were her people. They were as much her people, maybe more her people, than Falling Leaf and Painted Buck had been. Who were these dead white people who had given her life, whose blood coursed through her veins? A sudden ache to know throbbed deep in her chest and, with it, a feeling of grief and loss.

A faint rustling sound behind her told her she was no longer alone, but with tears drying on her cheeks she wasn't yet ready to turn around.

"They *were* good people." Jeremiah's quiet voice felt like a gentle caress, causing new tears to spring into her eyes. "Your parents did love you, even if you can't remember them."

"Chickens." The three weathered wooden crosses faded before Ginny's gaze. She was a child again, out feeding the chickens on a warm September afternoon. "Ma had sent me out to feed the chickens corn and gather the eggs before Pa brought the cow in from the meadow. Sadie. The cow's name was Sadie." Why these memories hadn't visited Ginny until this moment, she couldn't begin to guess, nor did she care. All that mattered at this moment was that she gave them voice. It didn't matter to whom she said the words. It just mattered that she said them. But that it was Jeremiah hearing the words, gave her comfort and courage. For years, she'd shied from the memories, had pushed them into the shadowy dream-life from whence they came. But even the times when her courage overcame her fears, and she'd tried to grasp the strange images that flitted through her mind like flashes of light, she couldn't hold onto them any more than she could catch a beam of morning sunlight.

"You don't need to tell me this if—"

"Yes, I do." She turned to him, no longer caring if he saw the tears streaming down her face. "For many moons, I could not remember these things. For most of my life, I did not want to remember them. They frightened me, so I would shoo them away like I might stomp on the ground to shoo away a snake. Then later, when I wanted to remember, I couldn't."

Jeremiah stepped closer and took her hands in his. The tender expression on his face threatened to dissolve her courage. How easy, how comforting it would be to simply melt into his embrace and weep, and let the invading memories slink back into the recesses of her mind like a dank fog. She resisted the temptation. Now that she finally had a firm grip on the frightful memories from her childhood, she needed to know what had happened to her. More importantly, she needed to face what had happened to Ma, Pa, and baby Joe.

She slipped her hands from Jeremiah's and turned again to gaze at the small cross with three marks of what the whites called letters: JOE. "I don't remember him much, baby Joe." Despite new tears chasing the old ones down her face, Ginny smiled and pressed her hand against the ache deep in her chest. "That troubles my heart much."

"You were only six and he was...here for such a short time." From behind, Jeremiah's strong hands gently cupped her shoulders, lending her courage.

"I remember he was crying." A little giggle escaped Ginny's throat, surprising her. "Joe was always crying. That is what I remember about him. That, and his blue eyes. He had eyes as blue as an October sky..." She sniffed back the wetness dripping down her nose. "I remember he was crying and Ma was cooking supper. She asked me to feed the chickens and gather the eggs. I was playing with my doll made of corn husks and didn't want to leave her, but I did want to get away from Joe's crying."

Jeremiah's silence encouraged her to continue.

"I remember carrying the bucket of shelled corn out of the cabin. The bucket was heavy and the rope stung my hands, but I was strong." Now the memories seemed to come in a flood, like a rain-swollen river.

She turned and looked at the pine grove, but instead of the trees, she saw a sturdy log cabin. "The shadow of the tallest pine tree had crawled almost up to the cabin's roof. Pa was always home from the meadow with Sadie before the shadow reached the roof. I paid attention to those things. But that day, he did not come home." She turned back to look at the cross with the markings JOHN. A clear vision of a sturdy man with a big chest, his hair and beard the color of a red fox, only a little browner than her own hair. And blue eyes, the same bright blue eyes Joe had. "If Pa had come home in time, maybe..." A wad of new tears threatened to close off her throat.

Jeremiah gave her shoulders a gentle squeeze. "They found him in the meadow. Zeb said they found him tomahawked near the cow. Ginny, I'm sorry. I shouldn't have told you that. I should have let Zeb tell you." His voice turned remorseful then unsure. "It's your family's concern, not mine. I just didn't want you to think ill of your pa."

"Yes, Zeb *should* have told me, either him or Ruth. But they didn't tell me, and it is something I needed to know." She turned back to face him and managed to give him a wobbly smile. "I thank you for that, Jeremiah."

"And your ma? Do you remember your ma?" His voice tiptoed out carefully as if testing the air.

"I remember yellow hair, even yellower than yours." Ginny's smile came easily this time, as did the memory. I remember her laugh. It sounded like music. And I remember her reading to me from the Bible book." Ginny's voice reflected her surprise. So she *had* known of the Bible and its stories before Zeb and Jeremiah came to her village along Missouri's White

River.

The sudden memory of a piercing scream shot through Ginny's brain, making her jerk. Terror gripped her chest like an icy fist, sending a shudder through her body. She fought for breath and composure.

Seeming to sense her distress, Jeremiah took her hands in his. "What is it, Ginny? What do you remember?"

"A scream." Now shaking, she allowed Jeremiah to wrap his arms around her and hold her close to him. When her body finally stilled, she pressed the side of her face against the rough material of his hunting shirt and gasped. "I remember hearing Ma scream. Then she was quiet. Joe stopped his crying too." The enormity of what she was remembering struck Ginny like a pile of large rocks tumbling down upon her, and she wept. Pressing her face hard against Jeremiah's chest, she sobbed until she lost the strength to sob anymore.

Another memory muscled its way into her mind, drying her tears. She pushed away from Jeremiah and looked up into his face, but instead of his handsome, caring features she saw the frightful, painted image of a Shawnee warrior. "I saw a man—a Shawnee warrior. His face was painted in war stripes of vermillion and black ash, and he wore copper rings in his nose and ears. His head was shaved but for his scalplock."

"Your Shawnee father, Painted Buck?" Jeremiah's voice lowered to a whisper.

Another shudder slithered through Ginny's frame. "No. No!" She couldn't help the disgust in her voice as she shook her head and repeated the word. For Jeremiah to think that the horrid man who had bound her hands, carried her into the forest, and later beat her with willow switches all those years ago was the same man who'd lovingly raised and protected her, felt abhorrent. "This man was bad. He told me his name was Missilemotaw." For twelve winters she hadn't thought of the name. Its appearance in her mind sent another squiggle of fear through her, sapping her strength.

She gripped Jeremiah's forearms for support. "He tied my hands so tightly they bled and then he put me on a horse." The awful memory stole her breath and she fought for air to speak. Was this why she disliked riding horses? "When I cried and begged him to take me home, he beat me with willow branches."

"Was the man a member of your tribe? Did he give you to your Shawnee parents?" Though more curious than accusatory, Jeremiah's questioning sounded enough like Rudd's of three days ago that Ginny bristled.

"The man who took me did not *give* me to my parents." She no longer tried to keep the anger from her rising voice. "Father came upon me and the man who took me." At the mention of her long-dead parent, new tears sprang to Ginny's eyes. "When Father saw the man beating me," she glanced down at the faint scar on her wrist she'd carried since the incident, "he bought me with the hide of a buck deer."

"And you are just remembering all this now?" The doubt in Jeremiah's tone stung but in truth, Mother's story of how Ginny became her daughter and the memories now flooding back, mingled until Ginny couldn't separate the two.

Frustration at her inability to deal with the deluge of troubling memories manifested as anger toward Jeremiah's skepticism. She let go of his arms and stepped back away from him. "You do not believe me.

Like Rudd, you think I have known these things all my life but did not care what had happened to my white family."

She glanced at the three wooden crosses illuminated by the afternoon sunlight shafting through the surrounding pine trees. Then she turned and glared at Jeremiah. The flash of anger chasing away her pain felt good.

Jeremiah sighed and looked at the wooden markers. "You said you didn't remember your family or what happened to them before today, so I believe you. But my sister Elizabeth was younger than you that same autumn during the siege of Fort Deux Fleuves, and she remembers every bit of it."

The accusation struck Ginny like a blow across the face. "You preach the forgiveness of the man called Jesus in your Bible book, but in truth, you are no different from Rudd and all the other whites here and in Deux Fleuves. There is no forgiveness in you. You keep alive the memory of what my people did to you. You protect it and nurture it like a precious ember, and when it suits you, you fan it into a blaze again." She yanked her medicine bag from her belt and waved it before his stunned face. "You welcome my medicine that heals snake bites, fevers, and all other sicknesses your white medicine is not strong enough to cure. But still you look upon me as a savage, not to be trusted. Every one of the people whose ills I treated today begged me not to tell their neighbors I had seen them." She waved her arm at the crosses. "I am sorry that the lives of these people were taken early, but I am glad I was raised as a Shawnee. I would rather be a proud and honest Shawnee than be like the Christian whites who profess love and forgiveness with their mouths while their hearts are full of vengeance!"

~*~

Ginny's words slashed across Jeremiah's heart. He'd prayed that she'd be able to look past his brother-in-law's prejudices against the Shawnee and not hold Rudd's prejudices against Jeremiah or his family, but obviously she did. At the same time, her words convicted him. Was he a hypocrite as she had charged? Later he'd turn to the scriptures and deal with the contents of his own heart about the matter, but now he must make amends with the woman who owned a large part of his heart or risk losing any hope of winning her to Christ.

"Ginny. I do believe you. I'm sorry I compared Elizabeth's memories of that time to yours. Everyone's ability to remember is different, I suppose." Was he pulling himself out of the hole he'd dug with his earlier comment, or digging an even deeper hole? All he could do was forge ahead. "As for the hypocrisy of the whites who've treated you badly, we are all sinners. No one is perfect, not one." He held his hands out toward her and prayed she'd be willing to at least listen to his apology. "My family and I have apologized for Rudd. We can't help his actions or how he feels, but the rest of us don't share his feelings."

He stepped toward her, but with his every step forward she took one back, so he stopped. "Surely, you know I don't think of you as a savage. You are dear to me." His throat tightened, and he hoped he wouldn't embarrass himself with a show of emotion. He took another step.

"Dunbar! What is that dirty little heathen doing

here?"

Jeremiah turned.

Ben Collins stomped toward them, his hands fisted at his sides and his face purple with rage.

21

"This is hallowed ground, Dunbar! I won't abide that Shawnee whelp near the graves of my dead kin!" Collins nearly spat the words as he strode toward Ginny.

Jeremiah stepped between her and the irate man, stopping Collins's advance. He didn't know what Collins intended, but the man would have to go through him to get to Ginny. He held his hand out, palm forward. "Don't take another step, Collins. Ginny's kin is buried here, too. She has as much right to be here as you do."

Collins gave a snort and spat on the carpet of pine needles at his feet. "These ain't her kin, not anymore! She might have sprung from John and Carolyn McLain, but them red devils got hold of her and turned her pure Injun. More likely, she's come to dance on their graves and the graves of my dead wife and young'uns them Shawnee devils slaughtered back in '12!"

"That's unchristian, Ben. And ridiculous." Jeremiah strove to keep his voice calm. Hopefully, by appealing to the man's Christian charity and using his given name, Jeremiah could defuse the situation without coming to blows.

Collins gave another derisive snort. "Do not speak to me of Christian ways, Dunbar, when this little heathen"—he glared and shook his fist past Jeremiah's shoulder—"is runnin' around practicin' her evil witchery on the good Christian folk here in Underwood." His lips twisted in an ugly sneer, and he stabbed the air in front of Jeremiah with his meaty finger. "And you, a supposed man-of-the-cloth, are out here in the woods cavorting with the likes of the heathen!"

Rage seethed inside Jeremiah's chest. It took every bit of his willpower not to pummel the hateful man. But Ginny didn't need to see that, and Jeremiah didn't wish to be the cause of trouble within Zeb's congregation. So instead, he fixed the man with a steely glare, all the while keeping his ears keen for any sound of movement from Ginny. Above all, he needed to keep his body as a barrier between her and Ben Collins. "Be very careful, my friend. I am a man of peace, but I will not allow you to impugn Ginny's character or mine."

Despite being delivered in a soft voice, the ominous tone of Jeremiah's measured warning appeared to have the desired effect on Collins. The man visibly shrank back, and for the first time since his appearance, Jeremiah felt comfortable enough to glance back at Ginny. Expecting to find her cowering behind the closest pine tree for safety, he was at once amused and proud to see her standing in the open and eyeing her antagonist with no sign of fear on her stoic features. Jeremiah glanced back at Collins to assure himself that the man hadn't moved and then put a protective arm around Ginny's shoulders. For an instant he feared she might shrug it off, but thankfully, she didn't.

By exerting gentle pressure on her shoulders Jeremiah silently urged her to walk with him while careful to give Collins a wide berth. As they passed the man, Jeremiah offered him a cordial nod. "We will leave you in peace to pay your respects to your kin, and we bid you a good day."

Collins glared at him, his florid face still contorted in murderous anger, and Jeremiah feared that he may yet need to fight the man, but Collins made no move. Instead, he shifted his glare to Ginny and shook his forefinger at her. "I'm warnin' you, you little heathen. Stay clear of this place! And if you know what's good for you, you'll stop practicing that Injun witch-doctorin' around here, or you'll be sorry. And so will Zeb and Ruth!"

Taking the advice of Shakespeare, Jeremiah decided that discretion was the better part of valor. He allowed Collins's warning to go by without a reply and hurried Ginny along, praying she would remain mute as well.

Safely out of sight and earshot of Collins, Jeremiah stopped and turned to Ginny. "I'm sorry he said those hateful things to you. Like I said, you have as much right to visit the graveyard here as Ben does, but you shouldn't have come alone. From now on, have Zeb, Ruth, or me come with you."

Instead of looking shaken from their run-in with Collins, Ginny's demeanor exuded annoyance. Her aggravated scowl as well as the green fire flashing in her eyes both surprised Jeremiah and warned of her willingness to rejoin their earlier verbal skirmish.

~*~

Ginny's growing need to remember her white family had brought her to their resting place. She had hoped that in solitude, with only the spirits of her blood kin near, she might remember the events that had been plucked from her life here. So while Jeremiah's unexpected arrival had lent her a measure of comfort when the memories began to flow over her, his presence had, at the same time, shattered the solitude she cherished. No Shawnee would have intruded on another's grieving time. Such intrusions in the name of caring marked but another irksome example of the differences between the Shawnee and the white man's cultures.

"I will not be coming back, and if I did, I would not need, or welcome, any company." Jeremiah meant well, but he, as well as Zeb and Ruth, needed to learn to respect her traditions.

Since the age of ten winters, Ginny had taken for granted the freedom of roaming the woods alone. But since leaving her village in Missouri, finding time alone had become both difficult and rare, making her feel like a child that required constant watching. Every time she prepared to leave the house to gather medicinal herbs or to treat an ailing neighbor, her aunt and uncle would question where she was going and how long she planned to be gone. Though she knew their questions sprang out of concern for her, living in such a way had become stifling. Most likely, Uncle Zeb had sent Jeremiah to discover her whereabouts this morning and bring her home.

One of Jeremiah's light brows raised and then lowered to pinch together with the other brow. He cocked his head toward the pine grove. "You heard Collins's warning. He may be all bluster, but I don't know the man well or what he is capable of doing."

"I am not afraid of Ben Collins or anyone here."

"Then that makes him all the more dangerous."

Ginny had no interest in arguing any longer, so she voiced the question she'd been about to ask Jeremiah when Ben Collins appeared. "Why did you come to this place?"

"Your Uncle Zeb was concerned—"

"I thought as much." Ginny sighed. Having her suspicions confirmed did nothing to lessen her irritation. "Zeb and Ruth remember me as a child, so they think of me as a child. I am not a child, and I will not be treated as such."

A smile curved on Jeremiah's well-shaped lips. "Of that, I have no argument."

Beneath his tender gaze, Ginny's heart thudded and warmth leapt to her face. For a moment, she thought he might kiss her like he'd done in Zeb's old cabin the day Lydia and Joel arrived. To her shame, she leaned in, hoping it would happen. But his next words felt like a cold wind, pushing her back.

"But your uncle and aunt *are* right that it is not entirely safe for you to go about as you like." He glanced in the direction of the graveyard behind them, his frown deepening. "I hate to agree with Ben, but your presence here has stirred up some sore feelings. Until folks get more used to you being here, it might be best not to go gallivanting all over Underwood by yourself practicing your Shawnee medicine."

A new flash of anger leapt in Ginny's chest, and

she narrowed her gaze at him. "You know I did not wish to return here. I am only here because of my promise to my mother before she joined my father in the land of the sunset. But at her burial, I also promised her I would continue to be a Shawnee healer." She glanced back in the direction of the burial place they'd just left. "The blood of the people buried here may run through my veins, but they are of my dream-life. I am Shawnee, Jeremiah. I will always be Shawnee and not you, Ben Collins, or anyone else can keep me from being who I am—Ginny Red Fawn McLain, a Shawnee medicine woman."

Jeremiah scowled. "You ask me why I came here. And yes, I was looking for you, but not because Zeb sent me. He did not. But he did tell me that Ben Collins had come to him complaining about you practicing your medicine." Jeremiah heaved a sigh and glanced down as if gathering his thoughts. When he looked up, his gaze had turned soft again. "The people around here just need to accept you, to see you as one of them, and that takes time. I think perhaps if you would dress and wear your hair more like the other women in Underwood—"

"You want me to be more white." The realization hurt, and Ginny fought back the tears welling in her eyes. Was Jeremiah ashamed to be seen with her dressed as a Shawnee? When his family had shown Ginny kindness and acceptance, she'd nurtured hope that her friendship with Jeremiah could grow into something far deeper. Even Rudd Callahan's dislike of her had scarcely dampened those hopes. Until this moment, she never thought her Shawnee ways bothered Jeremiah. She stiffened her spine to bring herself as tall as possible and raised her chin. "My skin may be white, but I am Shawnee, and I am proud to be Shawnee. I will not dress like the whites. I will not wear my hair up and hide it under a bonnet like the whites." Hoping to stave off the tears that threatened to overflow and shame her, she fixed him with the hardest glare she could manage. "And I will not worship your white God in your log buildings. I will worship the Creator of the Shawnee in the fields and forests as I have done all my life!"

Now the tears Ginny could no longer hold back, poured. To hide them, she ran and hoped that Jeremiah would not follow.

He called her name twice, but she continued to run. When she finally stopped and turned around, Jeremiah was not in sight.

Slowing to a walk, she found herself on the rutted wagon road that led home. The thought vexed her. When had she begun to think of her aunt and uncle's cabin as home? With her eyes stinging and her cheeks still wet from tears, the notion of Aunt Ruth questioning her held no appeal. Instead, she turned and walked in the opposite direction toward Bluelegs Cavanaugh's blacksmith shop. It would allow her time to regain her composure, and Bluelegs would not ask why her eyes looked as though she'd been crying.

Even from a distance, the ring of his hammer on iron sounded comforting. With Bluelegs, Ginny could be unapologetically Shawnee, if only for a short time. As she neared the building's yawning doors, she craned her neck to peer inside. If there were men loitering about, she would not stop, but would simply walk on. It took a moment for her eyes to become accustomed to the dim light inside the building, but from what she could see, only the young blacksmith occupied the space.

As usual, Bluelegs stood bare-chested before his anvil, hammering a piece of red-hot iron. He stopped his work and looked up as if he sensed he was no longer alone. A wide smile stretched his handsome face. "Welcome, my little fawn. It seems that my prayers to Melo' kami this morning asking for a good day, were heard." His welcoming words and friendly expression encouraged Ginny to venture inside. He leaned forward in an exaggerated display of looking beyond her. "I see no horse you have brought to have shod, so are you lost again my little fawn, or is it simply my charming company you seek?" Gripping the hot iron with his tongs he doused it in a bucket of water, sending up a cloud of steam.

Normally, Ginny would have found such a brazen comment by a young man impolite, but Bluelegs' lighthearted tone and teasing wink showed her he meant nothing improper by it.

"No, I am not lost." Ginny couldn't help giggling, remembering her last time here and how she'd needed to ask the way home.

"Then it *is* for the joy of my company you have come." He cocked his head, and his grin widened. The thought struck that if she'd met Bluelegs a year ago in her village before she knew Jeremiah, she could have easily lost her heart to him. Could she still, if she tried? A part of her wanted to, but deep in her heart she knew it was too late. Whether or not she wanted it to be, her heart was already taken.

"No. Yes." She felt silly, even more so when Bluelegs gave a hearty laugh.

He reached his hand out to her. "Perhaps you have come back for another dance."

"I have come to talk, I suppose." Embarrassed at her awkwardness, she looked down at her hands clasped in front of her.

"Then sit." Bluelegs motioned at an upturned barrel near the forge. "As it happens, I am ready for a rest, and I would not mind a talk." He rolled another barrel closer and sat across from her. "So what is on your mind, my little fawn?"

Ginny sat for a moment studying her linked fingers in her lap, unsure how to put into words the conflict swirling in her chest. Finally, she looked up, not at Bluelegs, but beyond him at the orange flames flickering in the belly of the forge. "How do you do it? How do you live in the white world as a Lenape man?"

For once, Bluelegs grew sober. His lips tipped in a small smile and, after a glance at the dirt floor, he looked at Ginny. "Did I ever tell you how I got the name Bluelegs?"

Ginny shook her head. Obviously, he considered her question improper and didn't care to answer it.

"My white name is Adam, but my father, a trader, always wore blue wool pants, so the members of my mother's Lenape tribe called him Bluelegs. When I came along, my mother began calling me Little Bluelegs." He laughed. "I didn't stay little, and when my father died..." A momentary look of pain crossed his dark eyes. His smile returned. "I became Bluelegs."

Ginny shifted her focus to his face. "I am sorry. My parents are dead, too. All of them."

"By all, you mean both your white and your Shawnee parents?"

"Yes." Ginny glanced out the open doors. "Today I visited the graves of my white parents and brother. It was the first time I remembered any of my life with them."

"And now you do not know if you are white or Shawnee."

At his quiet statement, defiance flared inside Ginny and her voice bristled. "I am Shawnee. I will always be Shawnee."

He nodded. "Yes, but like me, the blood of the white man flows through your veins, so you must also find a way to fit into the white man's world."

He leaned forward with his hands on his upper thighs and gave her an understanding smile. "Every year more whites come, taking the red man's hunting grounds and pushing him farther west." He shrugged. "Just yesterday, I talked with hunters from a Lenape tribe near the town of Madison. They tell me that a band of Ohio Shawnee are now traveling down the Ohio River on flatboats on their way to lands west of the Mississippi River. They said they have heard that Shawnee and Lenape in the southern part of Indiana, including many from a Shawnee village on Silver Creek near the town of New Albany, plan to join the group going west when the boats stop at Louisville for provisions."

Ginny nodded. "We heard in my village on Missouri's White River that the powerful whites in Washington want to move us farther west."

Bluelegs reached out his hand and covered hers. "In that, my little fawn, we are more fortunate than our Indian brothers and sisters. The white blood in our veins protects us from any such laws." His intimate gesture surprised Ginny, but it evoked no other emotion in her.

"You came here for advice, so I will give you the advice my father gave me when I was a boy and seeking the same answers you are seeking now. He told me to learn from both the white and Indian worlds, to take from each and to become my own man." He grinned. "Or in your case, your own woman."

Ginny managed a feeble smile. She would not hurt his feelings by telling him that is exactly what she'd been doing, and still many of her white neighbors would not accept her. Sadly, things were not the same for her as with Bluelegs. Neither he nor his tribe had taken part in the attack on Pigeon Roost.

"Hey smithy, my horse threw a shoe. Reckon you could take time from your courtin' to make a new one?" A burly man Ginny didn't recognize sauntered into the blacksmith shop.

At the man's voice Ginny and Bluelegs sprang from their perches. Bluelegs gave a good-natured laugh. "Sure thing. Bring in your horse, and I will get right to work on it."

Smiling, Ginny offered her hand to Bluelegs. He took it and they exchanged a quick shake. "Thank you, Bluelegs. I will remember what you have told me."

On her walk home, she mulled over what Bluelegs had said. Oddly, Jeremiah's advice that she dress more like her female neighbors kept intruding on her thoughts. As Bluelegs suggested, perhaps she should consider adopting some customs from the white man's world. If she kept her Shawnee beliefs what harm would a calico bonnet do, and it might just make her appear less threatening to Ben Collins and others here in Underwood.

By the time she neared the cabin she now called home, she'd decided to ask Aunt Ruth to make her a bonnet and perhaps even a calico dress to wear whenever she walked around Underwood. Imagining the look of joy her request would bring to Aunt Ruth's face, she smiled.

Her smile wilted as she approached the cabin. On the cabin's doorstep lay a fawn with its throat cut, its bright red blood spilling over the stone step and pooling in the dirt at Ginny's feet.

22

"Oh Ginny! Praise God you are all right." Aunt Ruth's voice caught as she ran from the roadway to gather Ginny in her arms. "I found this, this awful thing, and I've been looking everywhere for you. I was so worried." Her words dissolved into tears as she held Ginny to her.

"I am well, Aunt Ruth." Ginny patted her aunt's back, less bothered by the spectacle of the dead deer than how the sight had upset her aunt. Still in her aunt's embrace, she turned to the grisly scene. "Who could have done this?"

"I don't know for sure, but I have a pretty good idea." Uncle Zeb strode across the road toward them, his face set in grim lines. "Ben Collins came by the buildin' site today, blusterin' nonsense about Ginny bein' a witch doctor and insistin' that she stop practicin' her Shawnee spells." He glanced at Ginny. "I told him you're doin' no such thing, but he wouldn't hear it."

He turned his scowl back to the dead animal. "In

my mind, there is no question about who did this or the message he's tryin' to send. What Ben did to this fawn, he could do to our Ginny." Uncle Zeb's eyes narrowed as he frowned at the slaughtered deer. His voice lowered like the rumble of a distant storm. "This is Ben Collins's handiwork, make no mistake. And I'm gonna tell him plain that he'd best stay clear of our Ginny!"

In light of all that had transpired at the Pigeon Roost grave site, Ginny shared Uncle Zeb's suspicions about Ben Collins. But with Aunt Ruth already upset and Uncle Zeb so angry, she decided that this moment might not be the best time to tell them of her and Jeremiah's encounter with the man.

Zeb turned, presumably to carry out his threat, but Ruth caught him by the arm. "Zeb, don't you go off half-cocked, now. We can't know for sure that it was Ben who did this. Remember what the scriptures say: 'A soft answer turneth away wrath, but grievous words stir up anger.' Don't make this worse than it is. Ben's a decent man at heart and a Christian. If he did do this hateful thing, he's probably got it out of his system now. It might be best if I spoke about it to Esther first—"

"No!" The word exploded from Uncle Zeb like a clap of thunder, and Aunt Ruth jerked against Ginny. "I may be a preacher, but I'm also the man of my house, and I'll not hide behind my wife's skirts and let her deal with those who'd do us harm!"

At Ruth's startled reaction, he took in and expelled a deep breath. Remorse shone in his gray eyes. Taking Ruth's hands, he gentled his voice. "The scriptures also speak of righteous anger, my love. Remember that our Lord was not so gentle with the money changers in the temple. Psalms 7:16 says 'His mischief shall return upon his head, and his violent dealing shall come down upon his pate.' Might be Ben just needs a little sermon, remindin' him of that passage."

Ruth took hold of her husband's arm again. "Then put that in this Sunday's sermon, Husband. Perhaps Ben and others could use the reminder that righteous anger and vengeance are not the same. " She turned a weak smile to Ginny. "We'll just keep our Ginny close until tempers cool. In the meantime, we will consider the meat a gift and roast it for supper."

Zeb hesitated but then gave in to his wife's insistent tugs as she towed him toward the cabin. While he went to work removing the carcass and butchering the deer, Ginny and Ruth heated water to wash the gore from the front step.

A sick feeling curdled in Ginny's stomach as she swiped her broom at the puddles of blood that Aunt Ruth had diluted with a bucket of steaming water. This was her fault. She'd brought this upon Aunt Ruth and Uncle Zeb. Ben and Esther Collins attended Uncle Zeb's church. If the Collinses persuaded others in the congregation to turn against Uncle Zeb, he could lose his church. Though Ginny had noticed angry looks from others in Underwood, so far, only Ben Collins had voiced his displeasure with her. If enough of their neighbors turned against Uncle Zeb and Aunt Ruth, they might even force them to leave Underwood. Aunt Ruth had said that she and Zeb would need to keep Ginny close to them. Was Ginny then to become a prisoner, kept inside her aunt and uncle's cabin? Her mind raced down myriad rabbit trails, none with a happy end.

Supper that evening proved a dismal affair. Ginny

could tell that Aunt Ruth tried her best to appear unaffected by the day's events, but the drawn lines in her face belied her placid demeanor. Uncle Zeb's attitude suggested a brooding anger, like a pot kept at a low boil. Ginny kept a tight rein on her tongue, afraid that a wrong word from her might cause him to bubble over again in fresh anger. Aunt Ruth seemed to sense the same, so an uneasy silence filled the room as the three sat around the table, scarcely touching the roasted haunch of venison.

When the silence became too oppressive, Ruth made a gallant attempt at conversation. "Ginny, I discovered a whole box full of rug rags I'd forgotten about." Her smile and the lilt in her voice were strained. "I think that you and I should spend the next several days making rugs."

Ginny took a bite of the venison and nodded. So Aunt Ruth planned to keep her within the walls of the cabin, out of sight of the neighbors. Her spirit shriveled at the thought.

That night, she lay on her buffalo hide bed before the glowing hearth. Upstairs, she could hear Uncle Zeb and Aunt Ruth talking. She could not make out the words, but their tones sounded argumentative. Tears stung Ginny's eyes. Never before had she heard the couple argue. It hurt to think that she was the cause of their discord, but after the day's events she could draw no other conclusion.

Later, when the house became quiet, she lay awake listening to the soft hissing and crackling sounds from the banked fire at her side. Her mind continued to roil, wrestling with the question of how to bring peace back to this home. Jeremiah had suggested that if she dressed like the white women, she might be accepted. The notion still irked, and despite her earlier decision this morning to do that very thing, defiance rose again in her chest. No! The people of Underwood would have to accept her as a Shawnee or not accept her at all.

She rolled her face against the soft nap of the buffalo rug to dry the tears that filled her eyes and slipped down her face. That Jeremiah joined those who would prefer to wipe every vestige of Shawnee from Ginny's appearance stung, but knowing he was right, hurt worse. Even though she now remembered her white parents who'd given her life, Ginny no longer belonged here. Bluelegs might be able to span both the white and Indian worlds, keeping a moccasin-clad foot solidly in each, but the blacksmith no longer had loved ones here to consider.

At the thought of Bluelegs, Ginny recalled his mention of the group of Shawnees heading down the river, Spelewathiipi. The notion of joining them sparked in her mind. She did not belong here. She had brought trouble and anguish upon herself as well as on her aunt and uncle.

The idea burst into flame, and she sat up, her growing resolve drying her tears. Bluelegs had also mentioned that a group of Shawnee in a village on Silver Creek, near the town of New Albany, planned to join the group when they docked at Louisville. Ginny could go with them back west, across the Mississippi, to live with other Shawnee where she belonged. But at the thought of sharing such plans with Uncle Zeb and Aunt Ruth, her excitement waned. Her aunt and uncle would doubtless oppose any notion of her leaving. Ginny's shoulders drooped in defeat. Her heart crimped at the thought of hurting them, and she feared her resolve would not bear an onslaught of Aunt Ruth's tears and Uncle Zeb's pleading. Far better to leave tonight and save everyone such a painful confrontation.

Ginny slipped on her moccasins and rolled up the buffalo rug. *And what of Jeremiah?* The question popped into her mind along with the vision of his handsome face. Her heart contracted painfully. New tears welled in her eyes to spill down her cheeks. The thought of never seeing him again felt like a hot knife twisting in her chest. Yes, she cared for him...*loved* him. And her throbbing heart told her he loved her, too. She squeezed her weeping eyes shut tight, trying to blot his likeness from her mind. Sniffing back tears, she hardened her heart with resolve and hurried to bind the rug with strips of leather. She and Jeremiah could never be together. She was foolish ever to have thought they could be. He was a Christian preacher, and she was a Shawnee medicine woman. Only if she gave up her Shawnee ways and, like Mother, embraced the God of Jeremiah's Bible book, could he accept her. But Mother had embraced Jesus moments before stepping from this world into the next. Unlike Ginny, she would no longer be practicing Shawnee medicine, something Ginny could not reconcile with the white man's Christian ways.

She wrapped her woolen blanket around her shoulders and headed for the door, but a nibbling at her conscience stopped her. She needed to leave tonight, but to leave without any message of good-bye contradicted the principles Painted Buck and Falling Leaf had instilled in her. For once, Ginny wished she'd asked Aunt Ruth to teach her to write the white man's words, but Shawnee symbols were the only way she knew to communicate in writing. She picked up a piece of charcoal and a slab of firewood from beside the stone hearth and began marking on the wood in hopes that Uncle Zeb would be able to decipher her message.

An hour later, Ginny left Underwood behind. Thankfully, the clear night allowed *Pooshkwiitha*, the Half Moon, to shine bright. Its pale light helped guide her along the narrow road that led outside the settlement. But now, the trail left the clearing and curved into the forest where it disappeared from sight.

Ginny shrugged, shifting the weight of the buffalo rug on her back. She'd deliberated whether to take the cumbersome hide. Without the extra weight she'd travel faster, but at some point she would need to stop and make camp. The buffalo hide would provide her a warm, dry spot on which to lie.

A sense of trepidation struck as she left the road. Her concern didn't spring from any fear of the woods or what might lurk there, for the forest and its animals were like family to her. But entering the thicket meant leaving the light of the moon and stars behind, making it far more difficult to determine her direction.

The canopy of new leaves blotted out the sky, plunging Ginny into darkness. She stood still among the trees, allowing her eyes to adjust to the lack of light. An owl called from its perch far above her. Ginny smiled into the dark mass of boughs. "Greetings, *Mea-the*. I am Shawnee medicine woman, Red Fawn. I hope you will welcome me to your home. The owl gave an answering *hoo-hoo,* which Ginny took as consent.

Without the moon or stars to chart her course, she decided to remain on the road. In the shroud of darkness, the southerly route would be safe, but at daybreak, she'd need to leave the road for the uncharted depths of the forest or risk being discovered by travelers—something she would rather avoid. Undoubtedly, Uncle Zeb would set out in search of her the moment he discovered she'd gone. Her heart pricked at the thought of the distress her leaving would cause her shee-tha and nik-kea, but leaving Underwood and returning to her Shawnee life would benefit everyone...including Jeremiah. A sharper stab at her heart this time, and she batted back the moisture welling in her eyes. With her gone, any affection Jeremiah had for her would wane, freeing his heart to find a white, Christian wife.

New tears forced Ginny to bat her eyes harder. Her thoughts had taken a path too painful to explore further.

Reining in her rogue thoughts, she focused harder on the path ahead and noticed the tiniest glimmer of light in the distance. Instinctively, she jumped to the side of the path and crouched behind a thicket, her heart pounding. Had she been mistaken about the road leading out of Underwood? Had it instead wound her back around to the settlement she thought she'd left behind?

Staying clear of the road, she carefully moved toward the light as quietly as the fawn for which she was named. As she drew nearer to the light, she could make out a clearing among the trees. The light was a campfire, and just beyond it, stood a wagon with a canvas covering.

Ginny's mind raced as it fought with itself. The firelight looked inviting in the chilly night. But to stroll into a campsite without knowing to whom it belonged could be dangerous, even deadly. The thought of being discovered in the dark forest by *hol-la-wich-kie* like those white hunters who'd killed Father, sent an icy squiggle of fear shooting through her.

Ginny inched closer, her eyes straining to peer beyond the flickering firelight. A shadowy figure moved behind the canvas covering the wagon and the wad of fear gathering in her chest jumped like a rabbit to her throat. She backed up, moving as soundlessly as possible. Better to keep warm by walking swiftly away from his place than to be lured into a deadly trap by the fire's warmth.

Ginny had taken only two steps backward when the figure of a bearded man with a long gun in his hands stepped from behind the wagon.

The man lifted the gun and pointed it directly at her. "Don't take another step."

23

Jeremiah woke to the warmth of the morning sun on his face. He squinted against the light shining through the cabin's window. Instead of cheering him, its brightness felt more like an aggravation, doing nothing to lift the dour mood that had settled over him since his argument with Ginny yesterday. When she ran away and left him standing in the road near the Pigeon Roost graveyard, Jeremiah had started after her. But with no idea of what he might say when he caught up with her, he'd let her go.

He slung off his coverlet with unnecessary ferocity and sat up in the bed, wishing he had something to punch. The bed's rope supports mimicked his groans as he swung his legs over the bedside and pressed his bare feet against the nubby rug on the floor—the rug Ginny had made for him.

Another groan.

Numerous times yesterday afternoon he'd considered going to Zeb and Ruth's cabin to speak with Ginny and try to make amends, but in the end, he'd decided to go back to helping Zeb with building the new church and seek his counsel before confronting Ginny again. But Zeb wasn't at the building site, and when he didn't return, Jeremiah released his frustrations by working alone, framing up the building's front door.

Sitting with his elbows on his thighs, he bowed his head and shoved his fingers through his hair. Defeat weighed down his shoulders like a stone. The warm relationship that had grown between him and Ginny over the past months had cooled after her visit to his parents' home in Deux Fleuves. He'd gone searching for her yesterday to warn her about Ben Collins and to try to mend any damage his brother-in-law had done at Mother's birthday dinner.

Before Rudd arrived at the house in Deux Fleuves, Jeremiah had found reason to hope. By all indications, Ginny had embraced his family, and they'd certainly embraced her. Her healing ministrations in caring for Isaac had won his family's affection and admiration. She'd even bowed her head and prayed with the family for Isaac's healing, buoying Jeremiah's hopes that Christ was working in Ginny's heart and that she, like Falling Leaf before her, was moving toward embracing Christianity. He had even sensed that his own relationship with Ginny was blossoming into something more than friendship. Then, with one tasteless comment, Rudd had wiped away all the progress Ginny seemed to have made in that direction.

At the memory, anger boiled inside Jeremiah. In an instant, his brother-in-law had destroyed the cordial atmosphere between not only Ginny and Jeremiah's family, but between Ginny and Jeremiah. On their trip back to Underwood, Jeremiah had noticed a distinct coolness in Ginny's attitude toward him. She'd seemed to intentionally avoid his gaze and scarcely spoke, allowing Lydia and Joel to fill the silence with their constant bickering.

Jeremiah balled his fists at his side. If Rudd were not his sister's husband and the father of Jeremiah's coming niece or nephew, Jeremiah would have given him a beating he'd not soon forget. Ginny's words from the deck of the steamboat months earlier echoed in his ears. *Do you plan to fight them all?*

Jeremiah's shoulders slumped, and he huffed out a weary sigh. No. As much as he'd like to, he couldn't fight every white man that disparaged Ginny because she chose to live as a Shawnee. Besides, what did the Good Book say about turning the other cheek? And what of Jeremiah's own prejudices? Was he, as Ginny had charged, a hypocrite in the matter? Was it truly for her safety that he'd urged her to adopt the white women's way of dressing or for the comfort of his own sensibilities?

Jeremiah rose and yanked on his shirt and britches as if his abrupt motions might shake off the troubling thought. He padded barefoot across the cabin's puncheon floor and opened the door. Breathing in the morning air, he hoped to clear his troubled mind and dispel his bad humor.

The spring morning sparkled with dew. The scents of freshly hewn wood, turned soil, and lilac blossoms tickled his nose. A robin perched on the branch of a seedling cottonwood, chirped a cheery song. The world seemed filled with the hope of new life, new beginnings. Its infectious optimism seeped into Jeremiah's breast and in spite of himself, he smiled. The words of the psalmist flew into his mind, encouraging his flagging spirit. *"Be strong and take heart, all you who hope in the Lord."* Every day, God made the world anew.

Would Jeremiah be more comfortable if Ginny were to abandon her brightly adorned black Shawnee skirt, calico blouse, and beaded moccasins and don a linsey-woolsey dress and bonnet and hard-soled shoes? Perhaps, but in the depths of his heart, he knew that his primary concern was securing her safety; both mortal and immortal.

And her love.

The thought drifted unbidden through his mind like the crisp breeze caressing his face. He'd won Ginny's affections before and, with God's help, he could do it again. Remembering Pa's advice in dealing with women, Jeremiah's smile turned to a grin. "If ever you should rile a lady, just remember that 'Love covereth all sins.' Just love it all away, and 'fore you can say Jack Sprat, you'll be back in your lady's good graces."

He turned back to the interior of the cabin. He'd boil some sassafras for tea then make his way over to Zeb's cabin and begin the work of mending the rift that had opened up between him and Ginny.

He'd just begun to prod the banked coals in the fireplace to life when Zeb's voice at the cabin's open door stopped him.

"Jeremiah, are you within?"

At the urgent tone in the older man's voice, Jeremiah's ready greeting died on his lips. "Come in, Zeb. Is something amiss?"

"Ginny's gone."

Jeremiah's jaw went slack as he struggled to make sense of Zeb's words. "Gone? What do you mean, gone?" All the breath left Jeremiah's lungs as if a mule had kicked him in the chest. He grasped the stone mantel above the fireplace to steady himself. Surely Zeb didn't mean... *No!* Jeremiah refused to believe that the woman he loved no longer lived. The searing ball of grief and fear twisting in his gut suddenly flashed to impatience, and he grabbed the other man by the arm. "Tell me, Zeb! What do you mean she's gone? She can't be...dead!" His voice withered with his heart on the last word.

Zeb shook his head, sending a *swoosh* of relief through Jeremiah. He put his hand on Jeremiah's shoulder. "No, no. Calm yourself, boy. I simply meant she has left the house, and we cannot find her."

Nearly felled by another wave of relief, Jeremiah fought to regain control of his emotions and equilibrium. He ran an unsteady hand over his brow, damp with beading sweat. "Maybe she's simply out gathering herbs or treating an ill neighbor."

Zeb shook his head again. "That's what Ruth thought at first, but the buffalo rug is gone, and we found some strange charcoal markings on a flat piece of beech wood." Alarm shone from his gray eyes. "You don't reckon she was...taken again, do you?" He pressed his hand to his mouth.

"By Shawnee?" Jeremiah could make no sense of the fantastic notion. "No. How could they have gotten in the house unheard? And besides, I've never heard of Shawnee, or any Indians, leaving behind any sort of message." He hated to admit it, but the truth seemed glaring. Ginny had left of her own accord. And Jeremiah felt at least partially at fault. He cleared his throat and glanced down to gather his thoughts, praying he could articulate his suspicions in a way that least hurt Zeb. "I think she left on her own, Zeb. My guess is she wants to go back to the Shawnee."

Zeb's attitude turned from distressed to angry. "Ben Collins did this! He scared our Ginny away."

"So she told you what happened over at the graveyard, yesterday?"

Zeb looked bewildered. "No. You mean over at Pigeon Roost? She never mentioned she was there. What happened?"

Jeremiah hesitated, unsure if he should divulge something Ginny might not have wanted shared with her uncle, but Zeb had a right to know that Collins had threatened Ginny. "Ginny and I were at the graveyard yesterday. She was...paying her respects to her ma and pa and brother." Jeremiah went on to tell of Collins's appearance and his threats to Ginny.

As he listened, Zeb nodded. "Somebody left a fawn with its throat slashed on our front step yesterday. My guess is it was Collins." He frowned, and his voice lowered to a near growl. "Liked to scared the life outta Ruth. Didn't seem to upset Ginny much, but like most Shawnee, she's good at hidin' her feelin's. Guess it scared her more than we thought." Zeb shook his head sadly. "If she wants to go back, Ruth and I won't stop her, but it's not safe for a girl to travel that distance alone." He looked squarely at Jeremiah. "We have to find her."

As Zeb talked, Jeremiah's minded raced, trying to guess in which direction Ginny had headed. Likely, she'd left in the middle of the night and already had several hours head start on them. "Show me what you found, Zeb. Maybe it'll give us a clue as to which direction she went."

When they entered the McLain cabin they found

Ruth sitting in her rocking chair, holding a piece of split birch log on her lap. She raised red-rimmed eyes to Jeremiah. "They took her, Jeremiah. They took our girl again." Her voice snagged on a sob, and she dabbed her wet face with her apron hem.

Jeremiah walked to her and took her hands in his. Of all the emotions he had felt concerning Ginny over the last twenty-four hours not until now, had he experienced anger. Surely, she had to know that her leaving would break her aunt's and uncle's hearts.

"I don't think anyone took Ginny, Ruth," he said as gently as he could.

"We think Ben Collins scared her off," Zeb said.

"Then Ginny did this?" Ruth held up the piece of wood with charcoal markings. "What do you think they mean?"

Jeremiah looked at the strange markings. The only one he could make heads or tails of was one that looked like a horse, but he had no idea what it meant. "I don't know, Ruth, but I think I know someone who might."

24

Ginny did as the man demanded and stood perfectly still. Standing tall, she met his hard stare with an unflinching gaze. If tonight the Creator called her to step into the land beyond the sunset, she would not dishonor herself or her parents by begging for another moment on earth.

The man, whose shaggy beard looked as fiery red as Ginny's own hair, narrowed his light eyes beneath the brim of his black hat and sighted down his gun barrel at her. "Who are you, girl, and why are you skulkin' around the woods at night dressed like an Injun?"

"I am Ginny Red Fawn McLain, a medicine woman of the Shawnee people. I am traveling to a Shawnee village on Silver Creek near a town called New Albany."

"A white Injun woman, alone?" His wary glance darted about the area surrounding Ginny before returning a skeptical look to her face. "How am I to know there ain't other Injuns lurkin' in the woods ready to scalp me an' mine?"

His words at once ignited anger in Ginny's chest and validated her reason for leaving Underwood. Because she was Shawnee, the whites would never believe her or trust her. She lifted her chin and squared her shoulders. "I am alone. The daughter of Painted Buck and Falling Leaf does not lie."

He snorted. "The McLain part I believe. Your hair's as red as mine. But somethin' tells me the woman that birthed you wasn't named for any kind of leaf."

Ginny fought to hold back the angry retort perched on the tip of her tongue. She owed this man no explanation. "The night is cool, and I saw your fire." For the first time, her voice wavered. She forced strength into it. "I mean you no harm Allow me to travel on my way, and I'll bother you no more."

He lowered the gun and cocked his head at her. "You say you're a medicine woman?"

"Yes. Like my mother, Falling Leaf." Ginny couldn't help emphasizing the word mother.

Once again, the man peered into the dark forest behind her. "Our young'un has turned sickly. If you can do somethin' for him, his ma and me would be glad to offer you some grub, a place by the fire to sleep, and maybe even a ride to New Albany."

Learning that the man had a wife and child gave Ginny a measure of relief. At least there were no other burly men about who might cause her harm. The thought of sleeping by a fire she didn't have to build and eating something more than the piece of dried venison in her medicine bag sounded tempting. "Show me the child."

"In the wagon." He nodded toward the canvas-covered conveyance.

Ginny stepped to the back of the wagon. She noticed that the man kept behind her.

"Judith. Judith, wake up," he called in hushed tones to the wagon's dark interior.

Ginny peered inside and could make out the forms of a sleeping woman and a boy of perhaps six winters. The child, covered in a wool blanket, lay wheezing and twitching in fitful sleep. His extra-rosy cheeks suggested a raging fever.

"Judith," the man called again, a little louder.

The woman stirred and then jerked awake. "W-what is it, Randolph," she mumbled, her tongue sounding heavy with sleep. Blinking, she sat up and seeing Ginny, her brown eyes flew open wide. She gasped, drawing in a sharp breath.

"This is Ginny Red Fawn McLain," Randolph said in answer to his wife's questioning stare. "Says she's a medicine woman. Thought mayhap she could take a look at our Davy."

Confusion, alarm, and consideration played in quick succession across the woman's haggard face. Pressing her hand to her mouth, she gazed with worry-filled eyes on her sleeping boy. Then she turned to Ginny. "Davy came down with a fever this mornin'. I dosed him with sassafras tea and wrapped him up good and warm, but he ain't got no better. If you can break the fever, we'd be much obliged." She moved aside in the wagon as if inviting Ginny to enter.

The man helped Ginny into the wagon. "We're Christian people, so don't be usin' no spells and such on my boy, or I'll toss you outta this wagon on your head!"

Ginny knelt beside the child and began searching

her medicine bag. "I use no spells, just the healing plants, leaves, berries, and bark my mother taught me." She handed the woman pieces of willow bark and offered an encouraging smile. "Brew these up in a tea for your son."

The woman looked at the bark in her hand, and her brow crimped in a frown. "You're sure this won't hurt my Davy?"

Judith's skepticism did not offend Ginny. From the Long Moon of winter until this Half Moon of Spring— five months in the way the white man counted time— Ginny had gained the trust of only a few of her Underwood neighbors. She couldn't expect a stranger like Judith to trust her without question, especially with her son's life. Giving the mother an understanding smile, she touched her arm. "I am a healer. I would do nothing to harm your child. What I gave you is the bark of the willow tree, which has been used by my people's healers to take fever from the body since the time before memory."

Judith's gaze studied Ginny's. At length, she nodded and left the wagon with the bark in hand.

When Judith had gone, Ginny touched the boy's forehead and frowned at the heat she felt. The boy's fever was strong. She could only hope that the power of the willow bark tea was stronger. She took the blanket from Davy and set it aside. The boy's body needed to release the heat burning him up not hold it near. She would never understand why whites seemed to think that air, especially cold air, carried sickness.

The boy stirred. "Mama. Ma." With his eyes closed tight, he knuckled a clenched fist against one eye.

"Shh," Ginny soothed, brushing Davy's blond curls from his feverish forehead. "Your mother is making tea that will take away your fever." As she gazed at the child, a sweet sorrow twanged deep in her chest. If she'd stayed at Underwood and she and Jeremiah had married, they might have one day had a son that looked much like Davy, with fair, freckled skin and blond curly hair tinged with red. The sad ache burrowed deeper, and she chased away the thought. She had no time for such useless feelings. She found herself in this wagon tonight, caring for this child, because she could not stay in Underwood. And Jeremiah and her growing affection for him was a large part of why she could not stay in Underwood.

A gentle movement of the wagon pulled Ginny from her thoughts.

"Here's the tea." Judith climbed into the wagon clutching a steaming metal cup.

Ginny stood and moved aside. "You give it to him. He will take it better from your hand."

With an understanding nod, Judith crouched beside her son. "Here, Davy. Mama's made you some nice warm tea." She slipped an arm around his back to help him sit up and put the cup to his lips.

To Ginny's satisfaction, the boy opened his eyes and sipped the tea then scrunched up his face. "This ain't sassafras, Ma. It tastes peculiar."

Judith lifted the cup back to his mouth. "Drink it down, Davy. It'll break your fever."

Davy wrapped his hands around the cup and looked up at Ginny. "Who's that, Ma?"

"That's Ginny. She's a Shawnee healer. She gave me the bark to make this tea that will make you feel better."

Davy's green eyes widened and then narrowed at Ginny. "How can you be an Injun? You've got red hair."

Ginny couldn't help smiling. "The Great Spirit gave me first to white parents but they died, so then He gave me to Shawnee parents." She could think of no better way explain to a child how she came to be Shawnee.

Davy's eyes grew wide again. "Will you tell me about the Injuns, how they scalp and all?"

At the boy's words the memory of Ma's screams echoed again in Ginny's head and stabbed painfully at her heart. She'd been about this boy's same age when the attack at Pigeon Roost happened, changing her life forever.

"Davy!" Judith's hushed tone sounded embarrassed. "Don't be askin' such questions."

Ginny mustered a weak smile. "I know nothing of scalping, but if you drink your willow tea and go to sleep, tomorrow, if your mother and father agree, I will tell you how my people make hunting tools."

Judith nodded and handed the cup to Davy, who finished off the tea with gusto. Then she stood and turned to Ginny. "You're welcome to sleep beneath the wagon tonight. Randolph tells me you're headed to New Albany. We'd be pleased to have you ride with us that far in trade for doctorin' Davy."

Ginny nodded. "I thank you." She needed to reach the Shawnee village on Silver Creek as soon as possible and riding in the Carroll's wagon would get her there at least a couple days quicker than traveling on foot.

Judith turned back to Davy. She took the empty cup from his hands and set it aside then started to spread the wool blanket back over him.

Ginny put her hand on Judith's shoulder. "Do not cover him, or the fever will grow stronger. You must trust me with this."

Judith's brow knit in deliberation. At last, she nodded. "Leavin' a sick person uncovered is agin' ever'thing I know about doctorin', but if I'm goin' to let you take care of my boy, I might as well start now."

~*~

"Can you make any sense of it?" Standing in the McLain's cabin with Zeb, Ruth, and Bluelegs, Jeremiah posed the question to the blacksmith while the older couple seemed to hold their breath.

Bluelegs studied the strange markings on the split piece of beech log and nodded. "Yes. She says she is going on a journey home." He looked at Zeb and Ruth who stood with their arms around one another and his voice gentled. "She calls you family and says that she loves you very much, but she doesn't belong here and she fears for your safety."

Ruth turned her face to her husband's chest, muffling a soft sob.

"I have to go after her," Zeb's said in a resolute tone. "There's no end to the number of hazards a young woman like Ginny could encounter between here and Missouri." He cleared the emotion from his throat. "If she's dead set on goin' back, me and Ruth wouldn't drag her back here to Underwood against her will, but I can't let her go all that way alone."

Jeremiah put his hand on Zeb's shoulder and gave it a squeeze. He didn't want to hurt the older man's feelings, but a man of Zeb's age shouldn't attempt such a trip alone. Such a venture required a man in his prime. He shook his head. "No, Zeb. You need to stay here and take care of Ruth. What if Ben or whoever left that slaughtered deer on your step decides to do more mischief? I'll go look for her."

Bluelegs set down the piece of wood. Crossing his arms over his chest, he leveled his gaze at Jeremiah. "Have you done much tracking, Jeremiah Dunbar?"

Jeremiah bristled at Cavanaugh's smug tone. He suspected the half Delaware man excelled at the art of tracking and guessed Jeremiah did not. It rankled to admit any inferiority to the man Jeremiah had long considered a rival for Ginny's affection. Pride lifted his chin as he returned the man's challenging gaze. "I've done some tracking."

Bluelegs huffed a half-laugh, and his lips tipped in a sardonic grin. "Finding and following the tracks of a Shawnee is far more difficult than tracking a rabbit or even a deer." His expression turned somber, and his dark gaze smoldered like burning coals. "I'd wager you wouldn't know where to begin looking for Red Fawn."

Anger sparked in Jeremiah's gut. Knowing Cavanaugh had supposed correctly, fanned his ire. "So where would *you* look?" His challenge dripped with scorn.

"Silver Creek near New Albany."

Jeremiah blinked. He hadn't expected an exact location.

"Why would you think she's there?" Ruth pulled away from her husband's embrace. "She knows no one in New Albany."

"We were talking yesterday, and I told her about a group of Shawnee coming down the Ohio River on their way to the Western lands." A look of remorse flashed across Bluelegs' chiseled features, and he emitted a soft groan. "I also mentioned that a group from the Shawnee village at Silver Creek planned to join the band of Ohio Shawnee when they docked at Louisville. I'd wager anything that she's headed to Silver Creek."

Jeremiah didn't know whether to hug the man or deck him. In the end, he did neither. "Then that's where I need to go."

Bluelegs laughed out loud. "You mean that's where *I* need to go." His expression turned grim. "An Indian does not need roads to travel, and there are many trails that lead from Underwood to New Albany." He uttered another, more derisive laugh. "It will take an Algonquin to find an Algonquin, Dunbar. You stay here and pray to your white God, preacher. I will go find Red Fawn and see that she gets safely to Louisville and on one of those Shawnee flatboats."

Jeremiah sizzled with fury, wanting nothing more at this moment than to give the pompous blacksmith the thrashing of his life. His pride rebelled against relinquishing the search for Ginny to Bluelegs. He didn't know which riled him most; the thought of putting Ginny's safety in the hands of someone else, or the image of Bluelegs tenderly seeing her off at Louisville. He wasn't about to allow either situation to happen.

Glowering, Jeremiah stalked to within two inches of the half-breed's face, his fists clenched. "If anyone is going after Ginny it's me, and if you want to argue about it, we can do that outside."

25

"The fever has broken." Relief and a good measure of satisfaction filled Ginny as she pressed her hand to Davy's face. The searing heat she'd felt on his skin last night had gone. From her kneeling position beside his bed, she smiled up at the boy's parents who crowded with her in the back of the wagon.

"Praise be to God." Judith Carroll pressed her hand to her chest and tears of relief shinned in her brown eyes. The morning sun's pale golden fingers poking through the back of the wagon revealed an easing of the lines on the woman's haggard face.

"Can't get out of work any longer, boy." Randolph's broad, bewhiskered face stretched wide as he beamed down at his son, but his voice sounded thick with emotion.

Last night, before coming upon the Carrolls' wagon, Ginny remembered crossing a creek. "I will search along the creek for willows. He should drink more willow bark tea today to make sure the fever doesn't return." She grinned at her young patient who screwed up his face at her pronouncement.

"That tea tastes bad." Davy wrinkled up his freckled nose. "I'd rather have sassafras tea with honey."

Judith smiled at her son, but her tone turned stern. "You can have some sassafras tea with breakfast, but you'll take your willow tea too, like Ginny says." She shifted her gaze to Ginny. "I'll help you gather that bark, Ginny. Then we'll make some breakfast."

"Good," Davy piped up, "'cause I'm hungry!" Scrambling from his pallet bed, he turned an eager face to his father while hooking his thumbs around his breeches straps and shrugging them onto his shoulders. "Can I help hitch Jack and Ike to the wagon, Pa?"

Randolph chuckled. "If you're feelin' up to it, son, I reckon I could use a hand."

While Randolph and Davy tended to the horses, Ginny and Judith headed through the woods in search of the nearby creek were Ginny suspected they'd find willows.

"You never said why you was headed south, Ginny." Judith's mood had turned relaxed as she and Ginny scuffed through the dead leaves and underbrush of the forest floor. As they walked, she gently swung the bucket she'd brought to fetch water from the creek. "Do you have kin south of here?"

"No. In a way." Ginny fell silent, unsure how to explain to Judith where she was going and why.

Judith stopped and gently grasped Ginny's arm. "Ginny, if you are in some kind of trouble, me and Randolph would like to help if we can."

Though she'd known Judith for only a few hours, she already felt like a friend. Ginny found herself pouring out the story of how she came to Underwood with Uncle Zeb and Jeremiah, and why she now felt the need to leave. "Many people around Underwood hate the Shawnee because of what happened at Pigeon Roost." Ginny blinked back the tears filling her eyes. She pressed her hand over her chest. "In my heart, I know I can become as good a healer as my Shawnee mother, Falling Leaf was." She searched for words that would convey her deep commitment to her life's calling. "I believe it is what the Shawnee call ka-tet—the will of the Great Spirit—that I be a healer of my people."

Judith touched Ginny's arm. "And you *are* a great healer. I'd done everything I knew to do to bring down Davy's fever, but nothing worked until your willow tea. If you hadn't come along..." Fear flashed across her brown eyes, and the tense lines from last night returned for an instant to her face before her countenance became peaceful again. Focusing back on Ginny, she cocked her head and her voice turned gentler. "I'm thinkin' maybe you left too soon. It sometimes takes folks awhile to get used to things that are not familiar to them."

Ginny couldn't help smiling. "You sound like Jeremiah."

A knowing look came over Judith's face, and Ginny knew she'd said too much. A little grin lifted the corner of the woman's mouth. "Would Jeremiah have somethin' to do with your leavin'?"

To cover her disconcertion, Ginny began walking again. The soft, musical sound of a running stream reached her ears, and she smelled the unmistakable scent of fresh water. A few more steps brought them to a sparkling stream meandering amid the ground's thick covering of dead leaves, and the willow trees Ginny had expected to find beside it. She began to peel bark from one of the trees while Judith dipped the bucket into the water. Judith didn't question Ginny any further, but at length, the urge to unburden her heart tugged too hard at Ginny, and her words tumbled out as if from a torn sack. "It is true. My heart has attached itself to Jeremiah." Ginny had to stop and swallow down a wad of tears. "But, like my Uncle Zeb, Jeremiah is a Christian preacher. He cannot have a wife who is a Shawnee healer, and if I become a Christian, I can no longer be a Shawnee healer."

Judith set down her bucket full of water and took Ginny by the hand. She towed her toward a fallen log. "I think we need to sit a spell and talk."

Ginny acquiesced. When they'd settled themselves on the log, Judith turned to Ginny. "Did Jeremiah or your aunt and uncle tell you that you can't be both a Christian and a Shawnee healer?"

Ginny shook her head. "No, they did not say the words, but if I became a Christian, would I not have to turn my back on all my Shawnee ways, even my Shawnee ways of healing?"

Judith shook her head. "I don't see any reason you should have to. Did your Shawnee ma tell you that you shouldn't become a Christian?"

"No." Ginny folded her hands in her lap and focused on her interlaced fingers. "Before my mother walked into the land of the sunset, she asked Jesus, the Son of the Great Spirit, to meet her there."

"Praise God," Judith whispered. She covered Ginny's hand with hers. "You called Jesus 'the Son of the Great Spirit.' Do you believe that Jesus Christ is the Son of God?"

Ginny nodded. She could not deny the belief that had put down strong roots in her heart. "The words of Jesus that Uncle Zeb and Jeremiah have read from the Bible book comfort my heart. 'Come unto Me, all ye that labour and are heavy laden, and I will give you rest.'" She lifted misting eyes to Judith. "Mother embraced the Son of the Great Spirit when she knew she was leaving this world and would no longer be doing the work of a Shawnee healer. If it does not please Jesus for me to be a Shawnee healer, I will have to do as my mother did and wait to embrace Jesus when I am ready to walk into the land of the sunset."

"*Pshaw!* That's hogwash!" Judith's surprising words and stern tone made Ginny blink. "Why, you said yourself that you think healin' folk is God's will for you, and I know for a fact that it is." Judith's voice softened as if she were speaking to Davy. "When Davy came down with the fever, I prayed to Jesus to heal my boy and He sent you. Now would you reckon Jesus would send you to heal Davy if He didn't approve of your way of healin'?"

Ginny blinked at the revelation, but Judith's words made sense. "I had not thought of it in that way." Jeremiah's parents had prayed for Isaac's healing when Ginny had appeared at their door with Jeremiah, Joel, and Lydia. Had the Great Spirit brought her to the Dunbar's home at just the moment her healing knowledge was needed? She met Judith's gaze. "You do not think the Son of the Great Spirit will turn His back on me because I am a Shawnee healer?"

Judith shook her head. "Of course not. If you accept Jesus as your Savior, He will accept you, whoever you are." Judith took her hand. "Look, Ginny, just like you said, you ain't usin' no spells or witchcraft to heal. You ain't callin' on no strange gods to do your biddin'. You're using herbs and flowers and willow bark and all sorts of things that the Lord Himself created. Ain't nothin' wrong with that. If you believe on Him, He'll accept you. It says so in the part of the Bible called Galatians 'For ye are all the children of God by faith in Christ Jesus.'"

Joy that she could belong to Jesus flooded Ginny's heart, but remembering the reality of her situation dampened that joy. "I do believe that Jesus is the Son of the Great Spirit and, like Uncle Zeb and Jeremiah have read from the Bible book, that He sacrificed Himself so we could be with Him and His Father, the Great Spirit, in the land beyond the sunset." She sighed and looked down at her laced fingers. "But even if Jesus *has* accepted me, many in Underwood have not, and my heart tells me they never will."

Judith stood and Ginny followed. Neither spoke for a moment, allowing the sounds of the running stream and the happy chirping of birds to fill the silence. At length, Judith spoke. "I reckon what happened at Pigeon Roost caused a world of pain, Ginny." Her voice took on a thoughtful quality, and her brown eyes gazed intently into Ginny's. "Seems to me, there's a powerful lot of healin' that still needs to happen there. I can't help thinkin' that God might have brought you back for just that purpose." Her eyes narrowed. "There's a place in the Bible where Jesus mentions a sayin' his people had. 'Physician, heal thyself.' I'm wonderin' if you're not so much runnin' away from the people of Underwood as runnin' away from what happened to you and yours at Pigeon Roost."

The notion struck Ginny like a felled tree. At Ma,

Pa, and Joe's graves, tears of grief that had remained dammed up inside Ginny for years had finally burst forth with the awful memories of that day twelve winters ago, and she'd wept until her heart had felt bruised.

Judith walked to the bucket of water. As she bent to grasp its rope handle, she cocked a sideways look up at Ginny. "Always be sure you're runnin' *to* somethin' and not *away* from somethin', Ginny."

As they began their trek back to the wagon, Judith turned a wizened smile at Ginny, reminding her very much of her mother. "Now that you're a child of God, be sure to pray over ever'thing you do. Mayhap, you b'long back with the Shawnee to take Christ's love to them, or it could be you should turn-tail and head back to your kin in Underwood." She shook her head. "I don't know, but God knows. Pray and ask Him, and He'll show you which way to go."

All day, as she traveled in the back of the Carrolls' wagon with Davy, Ginny pondered Judith's words. Was her decision to travel west with the Ohio Shawnee what the Great Spirit wanted her to do, or, as Judith had suggested, was Ginny simply running from the memories of what had happened to her family? That night, on her buffalo rug spread beneath the wagon, Ginny did as Judith had advised and whispered her petition to Jesus. "Jesus, Son of the Great Spirit, show me which way I should go: back to Underwood or west with my people, the Shawnee."

As her eyes closed, and she drifted off on her dream journey, the image of two women appeared before her. Somehow, she knew the vision came from the land beyond the sunset, and she knew the women; they were her two mothers, Carolyn McLain and

Falling Leaf, and they were holding hands. The sight filled Ginny with warmth and wrapped her spirit in a peace she'd not known. She woke with tears running down her face. The Great Spirit had spoken to her.

She rolled from her bed under the wagon and sat up in the dewy grass along the roadside where they'd made camp for the night. Her mother's parting words of nearly six moons ago echoed again in her ears. "You belong to the white man's world, too." Ginny pulled her knees to her chest and wrapped her arms around them as she gazed up into the dusky sky strewn with unnumbered sparkling stars. The full moon with its pale, shadowed face, beamed benevolently down upon her. Somewhere beyond the moon and the stars her two mothers walked in harmony in the land of the sunset with the Great Spirit and His Son, Jesus.

The dark sky and its heavenly lights misted before Ginny's eyes. Falling Leaf had been right. Ginny belonged to both the white man's world and the Shawnee world. Judith had said that Ginny should make sure she was running *to* something and not *away* from something. Traveling west with the Ohio Shawnee felt very much like running away. Smiling up at the sky, Ginny wiped the tears from her cheeks. "Mother. Ma. You both made me strong. I will try to have the courage to honor you, to bloom where the Great Spirit has put me, and make you both proud."

The next morning, Ginny crouched beside the campfire helping Judith make breakfast. She patted a corn cake from palm to palm until it grew wide and flat. As she plopped it into the pan of grease over the fire, she looked over at Judith. "I heard your husband say that we should reach New Albany today."

"Yes." Judith's smile seemed a little stiff as she

hung the coffeepot from the iron crane over the flames. "Reckon you'll be leavin' us when we get to Silver Creek." The lines around her smile softened, and sadness shined in her dark eyes. "It's been nice havin' the company of another woman. We'll be right sorry to see you go, Davy prob'ly most of all." She grinned. "The boy's took a real shine to you. He'll be lost not havin' you along to play checkers with him in the wagon."

Ginny glanced over to where Randolph and Davy worked to hitch the two horses to the wagon. At the sight of the curly-headed boy, sadness twanged in her chest. "I will miss him, too." She patted another cake between her hands. "I have thought much about what you said to me yesterday." Ginny told her about her dream after she'd prayed for guidance. "I believe the Great Spirit spoke to me in my dream. I believe He wants me to return to my Uncle Zeb and Aunt Ruth in Underwood."

Judith settled herself on a short stool. Her expression turned thoughtful and she nodded. "Many times in the Bible, God spoke to people in dreams. I reckon He still does, so I wouldn't argue with you about that." She grinned and a teasing twinkle glinted in her dark eyes. "And that feller, Jeremiah, you told me about, was there anything in your dream about him?"

Warmth not generated by the campfire leapt to Ginny's face. After making her decision last night to return to Underwood, thoughts of Jeremiah had held her mind and heart captive. Like Judith, Jeremiah might well feel that Ginny could, as a Christian, continue to practice as a Shawnee medicine woman. But for him to consider her for a wife was an altogether different matter. The notion of living in the same village with the man she loved but could not have caused Ginny's heart to quake far more than the thought of dealing with Ben Collins's hatred. At the same time, a longing to see Jeremiah again, to be near him, tugged at her as if their hearts were bound together by an unseen rope. "No, the Great Spirit did not speak of Jeremiah." She winced at the prick of disappointment in her chest but managed a forced smile. "I will continue to pray and ask His guidance in that."

Judith stood and walked over to Ginny. Smiling, she squeezed her hand. "Just trust the Lord, Ginny. Whatever happens, just remember what the scriptures say in Romans. 'And we know that all things work for good to them that love God, to them who are the called according to His purpose.'"

She patted Ginny's hand and then turned toward her husband and son. "I'll go tell Randolph that we'll be turnin' the wagon back south." She chuckled. "I don't expect him to be 'specially pleased about that, but for what it's worth, I think you're doin' the right thing."

Ginny plopped the second cake into the grease and hurried to grasp Judith by the arm. She shook her head. "It is not necessary that you delay your journey to Evansville to return me to Underwood."

Judith's eyes widened. "Well, we surely ain't gonna take off and leave you out here alone."

The woman's concern for Ginny touched her deeply, and she experienced another pang of sadness at the thought of parting from these kind people. She shook her head again. "I will go to the Shawnee village on Silver Creek as I had planned. It is the way of my people to provide shelter and care for any traveling Shawnee of another tribe or village. They will see me safely back to Underwood."

Two hours later, they came to a wide creek at the edge of a forest. The smell of wood smoke reached Ginny's nose, telling her they'd come within walking distance of the Shawnee village.

Randolph reined the horses to a stop and looked over his shoulder at Ginny inside the wagon. "Reckon we'll need to leave the wagon here and walk to the village. He turned back to look at the swift running creek beside the wagon road. "I'm a bit feared of drivin' this wagon over that rocky creek. Good way to bust a wheel, and I'm not keen on walkin' all the way into New Albany to find a wheelwright."

"I can find my way to the village from here." Ginny walked to the back of the wagon and climbed down, and the Carroll family joined her.

Randolph's blue eyes glistened as he gave Ginny an awkward hug. "Providence brought you to us, Ginny Red Fawn McLain" he said, his voice thick with emotion. "I truly believe that, and I believe your medicine saved our Davy's life. May God be with you and protect you, girl." Blinking, he cleared his throat, and turned away to look toward the forest.

Judith stepped up to give Ginny a warm hug then grasped her shoulders and held her at arm's length. Her brown eyes swam with unshed tears. "You're doin' God's work, Ginny. Don't ever let anyone tell you otherwise." Tears welled in her eyes and streamed down her face. "We'll be thinkin' of you and prayin' for you. Just keep trustin' in the Lord. He'll guide you right." She pulled Ginny to her, gave her another fierce hug, and whispered in her ear "I'll be prayin' that

Jeremiah feller o' yours has sense enough to see that you'd make him a wonderful wife."

Finally, Davy threw his little arms around Ginny's middle. "I surely do hate to see ya go, Ginny." The tears striping his dusty face flayed Ginny's heart. "Thanks for makin' me well. You have good medicine, even if it tastes bad." Turning Ginny loose, he dug into his pants pocket and then held out his open palm to her. In his hand lay a small red disk. Ginny recognized it as a piece of Davy's checkers game. "Here. I'd like you to keep this to remember me by."

Ginny took the piece from him, her own eyes now streaming with tears as she wrapped her arms around the little boy. "Thank you, Davy." She nestled her face against his head, drying her tears with his soft curls. "I will keep this always, and pray to the Great Spirit to keep you well." Blinking back new tears, she crouched down so she could look directly into the little boy's tear-filled eyes. "You taught me to play checkers well, Davy. Now when I go back to Underwood, I can win every game I play." She gave him another quick hug. "I pray that one day the Great Spirit will send me a son just like you."

With another quick hug all around, she bid the Carroll family good-bye and headed across the creek toward the Shawnee village. As she neared, she came upon a young woman carrying a baby on her back and harvesting dandelion greens.

Ginny quickened her pace and hallooed a greeting in Shawnee. "I am Ginny Red Fawn McLain, a Shawnee medicine woman in need of shelter."

The young woman rose from her work and turned to Ginny. Only a slight widening of her dark eyes showed her surprise at Ginny's appearance. She held out her hand. "Welcome, Ginny Red Fawn McLain. I am Morning Dew." When Ginny accepted her hand, Morning Dew gave it the customary quick shake. "I will take you to the lodge of my grandmother, Waits-by-the-Water. As an elder of the women's council, she will see to your needs."

"For what reason have you come to our village, Ginny Red Fawn?" Morning Dew's smile and friendly tone made Ginny feel at home. A longing for her own village back in Missouri rose up in her chest, tempting her to return to her original plan and join the group from this village on their journey west. But the memory of last night's dream returned, giving her the strength to hold fast to her decision to return to Underwood.

"I heard that a group from your village plan to travel to the town Louisville on the banks of Spelewathiipi to join a band of Ohio Shawnee on their way west. I had thought to join the group from your village, but the Great Spirit told me in a dream that I should stay here in Indiana."

Morning Dew nodded. "What you heard is true. There are men staying in our village who have traveled from beyond the big river, Mississippi, to guide the Ohio Shawnee on their journey west. My grandmother and I are among those here who are planning to go with them." She gave Ginny a wistful look. "I wish you were going with us. I would like having a medicine woman along if my son should become sick on the journey." She glanced down and her tone turned sad. "My husband died last winter from a fever after a cut on his leg became putrid." Morning Dew shrugged, shifting the cradle that held her sleeping infant on her back. "But I understand if you feel that the Great Spirit does not wish for you to go. Grandmother says we should always do as the Great Spirit guides us."

Ginny's heart ached for the young mother's grief, and she put her hand on Morning Dew's shoulder. "I wish I had been here to care for your husband during his illness."

They said no more until they entered the village. The sight of the bark-covered wigwams tugged hard on Ginny's heart, making her homesick.

"There is one of the men I spoke of." Morning Dew's voice lifted with excitement as she pointed toward a group of Shawnee men talking. "The one with the Eagle feathers tied to his scalplock. He is one of the men who will be guiding us west."

The man Morning Dew singled out turned toward them. Ginny jerked to a sudden stop and the air flew out of her lungs as if a horse had kicked her in the chest.

26

The look of surprise on Flying Hawk's face mimicked the astonishment that had frozen Ginny in place. For a long moment he stood still, his jaw slack and his mouth gaping open. At length, a broad smile stretched across his face, and he strode toward them.

Ginny's initial surprise at seeing Flying Hawk had rooted her feet to the ground. As the surprise ebbed, fear shot through her, sparking the instinct to run. She resisted, recognizing such an action as both futile and irrational. Flying Hawk meant her no harm. He'd come to guide the eastern Shawnee west, not to abduct her.

"Red Fawn." He took her hands in his. "*Melo' ka mi*, the one who sits where the sun rises and listens to the prayers of his grandchildren, has heard my prayers and brought you to me. Before I left our village on the White River, I sat before the sacred fire and burned tobacco and prayed to Melo' ka mi that I would find you here in Indiana." The joy on his face ripped at Ginny's conscience. Her mind raced, searching for a gentle way to tell him that she would not be going back with him to Missouri. Finding none, she remembered Morning Dew and turned to her. "Morning Dew has offered to take me to her grandmother's lodge."

Flying Hawk peered beyond her, his eyes searching. "Is your mother, Falling Leaf here? Is she going back with us, too?"

The pain of her loss stabbed again at Ginny's heart, and she winced. "Falling Leaf walked into the land of the sunset where the Pigeon Creek flows into Spelewathiipi."

For an instant, Ginny thought she glimpsed a look akin to relief cross Flying Hawk's eyes but dismissed the notion when his expression turned somber. "I am sorry for your grief. You honor your mother's memory." His face brightened again. "Tomorrow all in this village who are traveling west will meet together in the council house." He gazed into her eyes. In their dark depths, an intense emotion smoldered causing Ginny's insides to quake. Not love, but triumph gleamed in his eyes. "Soon after we return to our village, it will be the time of the Spring Bread Dance. There we will dance the last dance of the evening together, and this time I will not let you go until I say '*Ni haw-ku-nah-ga*. You are my wife,' and you answer *Ni-wy-she-an-a*. You are my husband.'"

A new burst of fear ignited and blazed in Ginny's belly. Flying Hawk's definitive tone left no question concerning his intention toward her or his understanding of what her returning to their village meant—Ginny agreeing to the marriage Flying Hawk's father had tried to force upon her before she left last fall.

Ginny didn't reply. Instead, she turned to Morning

Dew and asked to be taken to her grandmother's lodge.

Morning Dew nodded, seeming as eager as Ginny to leave Flying Hawk's presence. Her expression registered a mixture of embarrassment and dismay.

Anger joined the fear gnarling in Ginny's midsection as she walked with the now reticent Morning Dew. She hated that Flying Hawk's arrogant pronouncement had somehow dampened Ginny's budding friendship with the other Shawnee girl. "I am sorry that Flying Hawk caused you embarrassment, Morning Dew." She managed to quirk a half-hearted grin. "I fear that, too often, he thinks only of himself."

"You do not need to apologize. It is none of my concern." Though cordial, Morning Dew's easy friendliness had gone, and her tone sounded as brittle as a snapped dry twig. Her terse demeanor remained as she introduced Ginny to her grandmother then left, murmuring about needing to feed her son.

For the next hour, Ginny stayed inside the lodge of the old woman, Waits-by-the-Water. An inquisitive sort, Morning Dew's grandmother peppered Ginny with questions, reminding her of old Spotted Bird from her home village. Glad to be in the lodge and away from Flying Hawk, Ginny happily obliged Waits-by-the-Water's curiosity. Aside from stunning her, her chance meeting with her old suitor had complicated her plans to return to Underwood. Flying Hawk's parting words and the look of triumph in his eyes still made her insides clench. He clearly considered her his betrothed and would likely not take well to the news that Ginny wouldn't be returning with him to Missouri. He certainly wouldn't allow anyone to escort her back to Underwood. Her mind raced to formulate a plan of escape.

"You say there is much hunting in Missouri, Red Fawn." Waits-by-the-Water harrumphed as she sat by the fire chewing on a piece of doeskin she would later fashion into a moccasin. "But tell me, in the time of the Paw-paw Moon and the Wilted Moon, will I find in Missouri my paw-paws and persimmons? Are there many blackberry and raspberry bushes near the village?"

Ginny nodded as she sat cross-legged, sewing colored glass beads onto a soft piece of doeskin for the top of a moccasin. "Yes, you will find many paw-paws and persimmons as well as blackberries and raspberries in Missouri." For months, speaking English had felt awkward to Ginny, and she relished the chance to speak Shawnee again. "You will find that the land along Missouri's White River is much like the land here." She retrieved a red glass bead from her lap that had slipped out of her fingers.

Waits-by-the-Water scrunched up her wrinkled face and shot Ginny a critical glare. "Be careful not to lose any of those beads. My nephew, Laughing Fox, traded two beaver furs for those at a trading post in Louisville."

Ginny smiled. "Forgive my clumsiness, Waits-by-the-Water. These are beautiful beads. I can tell they are valuable. You will have a lovely pair of moccasins."

Waits-by-the-Water laughed, showing several vacant spaces among her yellowed teeth. "These moccasins will be far too fine for an old woman like me. I am making them for Morning Dew." Grinning, she gave Ginny a wink and lowered her voice to a conspiratorial tone. "By the time of the Spring Bread Dance, she will be ready to look for another husband.

These moccasins will help to entice a new husband for my granddaughter." Her grin widening, she leaned in and lowered her voice to a whisper, which seemed silly to Ginny since they were the only ones in the wigwam. "I think she has her eye on the man, Flying Hawk, from your home village." She fingered the doeskin in her hands, studying her work. "Perhaps you could encourage him to consider Morning Dew for a wife."

"Perhaps." Ginny mumbled the non-committal reply and focused on her sewing. The change in Morning Dew's attitude toward Ginny after their encounter with Flying Hawk began to make sense. A desire to warn the sweet Morning Dew of the many flaws in Flying Hawk's character pricked at Ginny's conscience. But after hearing Flying Hawk declare his intentions toward Ginny, Morning Dew would likely ignore Ginny's warning, considering it a ploy to discourage a rival for Flying Hawk's affection.

Ginny set aside her work. She needed to leave this village today and without Flying Hawk discovering she'd gone. Pasting as innocent a smile on her face as possible, she looked across the room at Waits-by-the-Water. "I would like to talk to Morning Dew. Where would I find her wigwam?"

The old woman grinned, and a knowing look twinkled in her dark eyes. "Ah, you are going to give my granddaughter advice on how to best win the affection of Flying Hawk." Her assumption seemed to require no reply. Craning her neck, she looked toward the opening in her own wigwam and pointed south. "The home of Morning Dew is a short walk south. There are but two wigwams between mine and hers." Her old brow wrinkled in a perturbed look. "After her husband, Spy Buck, died, I told her that she and her baby should live with me, but she was afraid the baby's crying would disturb my sleep—"

"How will I know her wigwam?" Ginny had quickly learned that, like old Spotted Bird, Waits-by-the-Water tended to ramble on in her talking, requiring Ginny to interrupt from time to time.

The old woman's brows shot up, and her eyes widened. "Did I not say?" She shook her head. "There are three white owl feathers over the door."

Without waiting for Waits-by-the-Water to expound upon the description, Ginny murmured a quick word of thanks and ducked out of the wigwam. She stopped and scanned the area to make sure Flying Hawk was nowhere in sight. Walking at a quick pace, she headed south. As she neared the wigwam with three white owl feathers over the door, she heard a baby's lusty crying and a woman's hushed singing and knew she'd found the home of Morning Dew.

Ginny bent and poked her head inside. "Morning Dew. May I come in?"

Morning Dew stopped her singing. "Red Fawn. Is there something you require that my grandmother cannot provide for you?" The girl's chilly tone saddened Ginny. Hopefully, Ginny's next words would thaw Morning Dew's attitude toward her.

"I do not wish to marry Flying Hawk. My heart is attached to someone else. Someone here in Indiana."

Morning Dew's wide-eyed reaction to Ginny's statement melted into a friendly smile. "Please come in and sit down." Still bouncing her fussing baby on her lap, she nodded toward a reed mat on the floor. "Why do you tell me this?"

Ginny settled herself on the mat opposite Morning Dew. "As I have told you, I no longer wish to return to

Missouri. But I know Flying Hawk well. He does not like to be denied of anything he wants. Now that he has found me, he will not willingly let me stay here in Indiana." She told Morning Dew of the agreement she and her mother made with Flying Hawk's father. "I fear that Flying Hawk will force me to go with him to Missouri."

Morning Dew's eyes narrowed as she rocked back and forth with her now sleeping baby in her arms. "Why do you tell *me* this?"

"Because I need you to help me leave this village without Flying Hawk knowing I have gone. I am not familiar with this area. I need you to tell me the quickest way back to Underwood." Ginny paused. She hated to ask the young widow for provisions, but if she didn't have to stop and hunt for food, she could get back home much sooner. "If you have any dried meat you could spare, it would help me on my journey home."

Morning Dew rose and gently placed her sleeping baby on a blanket-covered bed of pine boughs then went to crouch beside one of the many baskets scattered about the wigwam. She reached into the basket and pulled out a handful of dried meat, which she handed to Ginny. "This should be enough to sustain you until you get to Underwood," she said, smiling.

Ginny put the meat into her medicine bag and hugged the other girl. "Thank you, Morning Dew. I wish you and your son well. I will pray that the Great Spirit will grant you both safe travels and happy lives." Knowing she would likely never see Morning Dew again made Ginny sad. She could easily imagine the two of them becoming great friends.

As Ginny turned to leave, Morning Dew grasped her arm and a concerned frown etched her delicate brows. "Tell me, Red Fawn, is Flying Hawk a bad man?"

The question took Ginny by surprise. How she answered could well affect the rest of the girl's life, and that knowledge pressed heavily on her heart. She answered truthfully. "No, Morning Dew. Flying Hawk is not a bad man. I have known him since we were children, and I have seen the kindness the Creator has put in his heart." She tapped her finger against her chest. "But for many years his father, Great Hawk, has spoiled him, and Flying Hawk became used to getting his way." Remembering his drunken tirades, she frowned. "I have only seen him act cruel when he is full of the white man's strong drink." She touched Morning Dew's shoulder and gave her an encouraging smile. "I have long thought that with the right woman for a wife, Flying Hawk could become a fine man and a fine husband. But I am not that woman, and any woman who would consider Flying Hawk for a husband must insist that he never drinks the white man's liquor again."

Smiling, Morning Dew nodded and embraced Ginny. "Thank you, Red Fawn. I will remember your words." She then gave Ginny detailed directions back to Underwood by following Silver Creek and its tributaries northward. "Two days travel should bring you to the place called Underwood."

Ginny gave Morning Dew a parting embrace and left the girl's wigwam, hoping to sneak out of the village without Flying Hawk learning of her departure.

Outside the village, the forest opened to a clearing. As she left the forest behind, the tension twisting

Ginny's insides like a grapevine relaxed a bit. She'd seen no signs that any of the other villagers had noticed her leaving. Fear had dried her mouth and throat, so she knelt beside the creek to scoop up handfuls of water to slake her thirst for the journey ahead. As she dipped her cupped hands into the water, hard fingers gripped into her shoulder. Jerking, she whipped around.

"Where are you going, Red Fawn?" Anger smoldered in Flying Hawk's eyes.

Rising, Ginny pushed down the fear that had jumped to her throat like a ferocious animal. She must practice the advice Father gave her as a child: "Never show fear to your enemy." With all the composure she could muster, she met his glare and raised her chin. "I have been directed by Jesus, the Son of the Great Spirit, not to go back to Missouri but to return to the home of my uncle."

His lips twisted in a sneer, and he gave a derisive snort. "I do not believe in the white man's Jesus." He gripped her arm, his strong fingers biting into her skin. "I believe it is the will of the Great Spirit that you come back with me to our village and become my wife. That is what I believe, and that is what you will do." Tugging on her arm, he began towing her toward the forest.

27

An anxious knot formed in Jeremiah's chest as he and Bluelegs guided their mounts across a narrow section of Silver Creek. According to Bluelegs, they should be nearing the Shawnee village where the blacksmith suspected Ginny had gone. Glancing at the stoic expression on his traveling companion's face, Jeremiah managed to restrain his urge to kick his horse into a gallop. Not for the first time, Jeremiah experienced a feeling of respect for the man riding next to him as well as gratitude for Bluelegs's company.

Thankfully, Zeb's cool head and diplomatic skills had defused the fight that had threatened to erupt between Jeremiah and Bluelegs two days ago. Under Zeb's calming influence, Jeremiah and Bluelegs had agreed that working together would prove far more productive in finding Ginny than wasting time and energy battling one another. Jeremiah had to concede that Bluelegs's tracking skills far exceeded his own. While he couldn't exactly call the man a friend, their relationship had at least grown cordial. However,

Jeremiah hadn't managed to deduce the extent of Bluelegs's feelings for Ginny or his intentions toward her.

Bluelegs reined his pinto to a stop. Peering ahead, he nodded. "The village is just over that ridge. I can smell the smoke from the lodges' cooking fires."

"Then let's go." Jeremiah allowed his horse to prance in place. The chestnut sorrel seemed as eager as its rider to hurry on to the Shawnee village. From the moment Jeremiah and Bluelegs left Underwood, Jeremiah's desire to see Ginny again had grown with each passing mile. The thought of never seeing her again had caused a deep ache inside him that throbbed with his every heartbeat. But what he might say to her when he found her—if he found her—continued to elude him. Like Zeb, if Ginny was dead set on going back to Missouri, he wouldn't stop her, but before she left, she at least needed to know of his feelings for her.

At his next thought, a sharp pain jabbed at his heart. Perhaps it wouldn't be Jeremiah's feelings, but those of his traveling companion that would prove more effective in convincing Ginny to stay in Indiana. Looking at Bluelegs, jealousy curdled in Jeremiah's gut followed by a wave of remorse. He, Zeb, and Ruth had all put Ginny in God's hands, and God had blessed them with Bluelegs's help. Unlike Jacob of old, Jeremiah wouldn't wrestle with God. *Your will be done, Lord. Your will be done.*

Bluelegs shook his head. "We must move with caution. We cannot go galloping into the village, demanding to see Red Fawn. When we get near the forest, we must dismount and lead our horses to the edge of the village. There I will request permission for us to enter."

Jeremiah nodded. Since Bluelegs spoke both Delaware and Shawnee, Jeremiah had left all dealings with the local Indians to him and so far, that strategy had served them well. Yesterday, they'd learned from an old Delaware woman that someone fitting Ginny's description had been seen traveling south in a Conestoga wagon with a white family. The news had filled Jeremiah with both hope and relief. If true, it meant that Ginny wasn't traveling alone.

Following Bluelegs' lead, Jeremiah urged his horse up a gentle rise where a flat, grassy meadow stretched for some distance before them to a forest line. Within those woods, according to Bluelegs, they'd find the Shawnee village and, hopefully, Ginny.

As they crested the hill, the distant sound of voices met Jeremiah's ears. Venturing nearer, the figures of a man and woman who looked to be arguing came into view. And the woman had red hair.

Jeremiah's heart raced. Not waiting for Bluelegs' blessing, he kicked his horse into a gallop. The closer he came to the pair, the harder his heart pounded. Ginny. His lips mouthed her name, but his lungs couldn't find sufficient air to give it voice. He shifted his attention from her to the man and pulled his horse up short. The man with whom Ginny tussled looked remarkably like Flying Hawk, the man Jeremiah had bested in the tomahawk-throwing contest back in the Missouri village.

Jeremiah sat still in his saddle, frozen with astonishment. Out of the corner of his eye he noticed Bluelegs dismount and stride toward the couple. As Bluelegs walked, he addressed the man in an Algonquin language. His voice sounded calm, but stern.

Jeremiah dismounted and followed Bluelegs. "Ginny!" He found his voice, and her name exploded from his lips as he quickened his pace toward her through the shin-high grass. "Ginny, Ginny!"

Surprise and relief shone from Ginny's widening eyes as she looked at Jeremiah and Bluelegs. She continued to struggle in the grasp of the man Jeremiah now identified without a doubt as Flying Hawk. With her adversary distracted in an animated conversation with Bluelegs, she broke free from Flying Hawk's grasp and ran into Jeremiah's waiting arms.

"Ginny. Praise God. Praise the Lord you're safe." Holding her tight, he nuzzled his face against her hair, scarcely able to believe she stood safely in his arms.

The conversation between Bluelegs and Flying Hawk grew louder and more argumentative. Rage contorted Flying Hawk's features, and he waved his arms in furious gestures as he shouted at Bluelegs.

Standing back and watching the proceedings felt frustrating to Jeremiah. A strong desire to insert himself into the argument tugged hard at him. But such an action could inflame the situation rather than defuse it. He'd best leave the negotiations to Bluelegs, who knew the man's language and customs.

In contrast to Flying Hawk's wild rage, Bluelegs exhibited a more conciliatory demeanor. At length, Flying Hawk seemed to calm, and Jeremiah relaxed a bit. Hopefully, the Delaware blacksmith had managed to broker some sort of deal that would allow all parties to part peacefully. Bluelegs held up his hands, palms forward, took two steps back, and then turned and started to walk toward Jeremiah and Ginny.

With lightning speed, Flying Hawk pulled a war club from his belt and struck Bluelegs on the back of the head, felling the blacksmith.

Ginny gasped and ran to Bluelegs's crumpled figure and fell to her knees in the grass beside him. Flying Hawk strode to the pair. With murder in his eyes, he stood over them, screaming and brandishing the war club.

At the horror before him, Jeremiah's mind went blank at the same moment his feet took flight. Bounding through the tall grass, he plowed head-first into Flying Hawk, knocking him and his menacing war club away from Ginny and Bluelegs.

~*~

Cradling Bluelegs's bloody head in her lap, Ginny sat in shock watching Jeremiah and Flying Hawk battle a few feet away. Her emotions reeled while her mind struggled to process all she'd experienced within such a short span of time: the terror of being discovered by Flying Hawk, the relief of seeing Jeremiah and Bluelegs, the bliss of feeling Jeremiah's arms around her, and the horror of witnessing Flying Hawk's attack on Bluelegs. It all left her numb.

The grunts and flailing arms of the battling men before her seemed like something from a dream. *Jesus, help! Protect Jeremiah. Save Bluelegs.* Somewhere from deep within her, the prayer lifted up and a calming peace came over her.

Jeremiah sprang up and away from Flying Hawk who lay face-up on the grass, blood streaming from his nose. Jeremiah held the hunting knife he always wore on a belt around his waist.

Flying Hawk reared his head back, exposing his throat. "Kill me, Dunbar. Why do you wait? You have earned the right."

Ginny held her breath. While she didn't particularly like Flying Hawk, the thought of seeing Jeremiah plunge his knife into the man and having that image burned into her mind, horrified her.

"Get up." Jeremiah reached down with his free hand, grasped Flying Hawk's arm, and pulled the man to his feet. "I serve a merciful God who commands that I not kill without cause, but if you put your hands on Ginny again, I just might take that as cause. Ginny," he called without taking his eyes off Flying Hawk, "tell me. Do you want to go back to the village with this man or not?"

"No. I left the village to return to Underwood." Later Ginny would tell Jeremiah all that had taken place since she left her uncle's home but, for the moment, the short answer would suffice.

Jeremiah kept the knife's point pressed against Flying Hawk's throat. "And this man was taking you back against your will?"

"Yes."

Flying Hawk's dark gaze turned steely as it shifted between Jeremiah and Ginny. "Dunbar, you were there when my father, Great Hawk, made the deal with Red Fawn and her mother Falling Leaf. When they left our village, they were never to return." His gaze slid to Ginny and fastened on her face, and his voice turned petulant. "Tell Dunbar the laws of our people, Red Fawn. Ka-tet, the will of the Great Spirit, brought us together again at this place. We both know it is the will of the Great Spirit that you return with me to our village in Missouri and become my wife." He pressed forward against the knife's point, causing a crimson trickle to slip down his neck.

Jeremiah pulled the knife from Flying Hawk's throat but kept it pointed at him. "The God I know gives people free will to make their own decisions, and if Ginny ever planned to go back with you to Missouri, she changed her mind."

"You would ignore ka-tet and stay here in Indiana, Red Fawn?" Pain flashed in Flying Hawk's eyes.

For the first time, Ginny felt sorry for the spoiled child who'd always gotten his way and now suffered the consequences of his indulgent upbringing. She gentled her voice as if she were reasoning with a child. "I am not ignoring ka-tet, Flying Hawk. I do believe that the will of the Great Spirit brought us both to this village. And I believe you will find your wife here, but it is not me." She looked toward the forest. "It is my belief that there is someone here who will love you, and who will need your love and protection." A smile tugged at her mouth. "And when you find her, you will be glad I did not return with you."

Bluelegs groaned and rolled his head in Ginny's lap, drawing her attention back to him. To her relief, his eyes fluttered open, and he struggled to sit up. She helped him into a sitting position. The sizable gash on the back of his head along with the considerable amount of blood loss suggested he'd suffered a serious wound. If he had any hope of surviving his injury, they'd need to get him back to the village where she could better care for him.

Flying Hawk didn't reply to Ginny. Instead, he narrowed a glare at Jeremiah. "You are outside of the village now. So go, and take Red Fawn and your half-breed Lenape dog with you. But if you return, we will fight again, and the next time, I will win, and Red Fawn will be my prize." He turned and walked back to the forest, disappearing into the shadows.

Jeremiah crossed to where Ginny and Bluelegs sat. He reached down and helped her up then bent and grasped Bluelegs's arm and started to tug him to his feet.

Ginny put her hand on Jeremiah's. "No, he cannot ride. I doubt he can even walk. We have to get him back to the village."

A look of frustration wrinkled Jeremiah's brow. "You heard Flying Hawk. We can't go back." He took off his hat and shoved his fingers through his pale hair. "I can't promise I'll be able to beat Flying Hawk a second time."

Ginny had no doubt that Flying Hawk meant his words and would make good on his threat, but she looked down at Bluelegs's bowed and bloodied head and her heart crimped. "If we don't get Bluelegs back to the village, he will die."

28

"Help me up. I can ride." Though his voice slurred, Bluelegs sounded strong and determined. He struggled to stand, and Jeremiah gained a greater respect for the man.

"Take it easy, friend." He grasped one of Bluelegs's arms while Ginny took hold of the other, and they hauled the big blacksmith to his wobbly feet.

Bluelegs took a couple of unsteady steps toward the spot where the two horses stood grazing. He let off a surprisingly strong whistle that brought the pinto trotting to him with the sorrel following behind. Bluelegs reached up and grasped a handful of the pinto's mane in his right hand while he fisted the saddle pummel with his left. "Help me up on the horse, and I can ride. I think I can make it as far as Charlestown. I don't know all that happened, but if we don't go now, Flying Hawk will come back with others, and we will have to fight."

Bluelegs was right. They needed to get as far away from Flying Hawk and this Shawnee village as quickly as possible, but Jeremiah doubted Bluelegs could ride the twenty miles to Charlestown. He shook his head. "Don't know if you can make it to Charlestown. Might be best if we head for Clarksville instead."

Bluelegs's jaw clenched, suggesting the severity of his pain. Swallowing hard, he met Jeremiah's gaze with a determined look. "If I am to die, I want to do it in Charlestown where my parents are buried."

Ginny put her hand on Jeremiah's arm. "Jeremiah, we must try to get him to Charlestown." She sounded as resolute as Bluelegs.

"Then we'd better get going." Jeremiah helped the blacksmith situate his foot in the stirrup and with Ginny's help, hoisted the man into the saddle. Then he turned to Ginny. "You'll need to ride behind him to keep him steady."

Ginny nodded and Jeremiah lifted her up onto the pinto's rump.

Taking hold of the pinto's reins, Jeremiah mounted the sorrel and headed northeast. He prayed that Bluelegs would be able to stay on his mount until they were out of sight of the forest line in case Flying Hawk changed his mind and decided to come after them with a group of friends.

Glancing back at Bluelegs slumped over his horse's mane, doubt gnawed at Jeremiah's conscience. If Bluelegs didn't survive the ride to Charlestown, would Ginny ever forgive him for not taking the man back to the Shawnee village? The worried look on her face as she wrapped her arms around her injured friend caused the doubt to gnaw harder. *Lord, we need Your help. Keep Bluelegs alive until we can get to Charlestown.*

By the time they reached Charlestown, the sun had

vanished, leaving only streaks of purple and scarlet to light the slate-gray sky behind them. Only once, a few miles outside Clarksville, had Bluelegs agreed to stop and rest. There, they'd refreshed themselves with creek water and Ginny's handful of dried venison.

Jeremiah's body ached, and his stomach ground with hunger as he urged his horse down Charlestown's main street toward the livery. As bad as his discomfort was, he suspected that Ginny and Bluelegs suffered far more.

At the livery, Jeremiah dismounted and banged on the building's closed door.

"I'm comin'. I'm comin'! No need to wake the dead." The surly male voice on the other side of the door sounded like music to Jeremiah's ears. *Thank You, Lord!*

When the doors finally creaked open, Jeremiah recognized the stableman whom he, Ginny, and Zeb had met last fall.

"I have a hurt man outside that needs a place to lie down. You know him. Bluelegs Cavanaugh."

At Bluelegs's name, the man perked up. He poked his head out of the building to peer into the dusky evening. "Bluelegs? Bluelegs is hurt, you say?" Working a wad of tobacco in his jaw, he scurried to the pinto as fast as his halting gait allowed. "Aw, Bluelegs. What's happened to ya, boy? It's me, Mose. Mose Barnes."

Jeremiah helped Ginny down then, and with Mose's help, they dragged Bluelegs from the horse's back. As he and Mose half-carried Bluelegs into the livery, Jeremiah gave the stableman a quick account of the day's events.

"Lucky you got away with yer scalps," Mose said

between grunts as he helped Jeremiah settle Bluelegs in a stall on a bed of clean straw." He turned and shot a stream of brown spittle into the stall behind him. "I'll git my grandson, Toby, to fetch you some grub and somethin' to drink." With that he shuffled off toward the other end of the livery, barking the boy's name.

A half-hour or so later, a tow-headed youngster of about twelve years of age appeared with a wonderful smelling, linen-covered basket. "Squirrel stew and cornbread," Toby said, plunking down the basket. "Ma makes real good squirrel stew."

The appetizing smells coming from the basket made Jeremiah's mouth water. Accepting the basket, he gave the boy a big smile. "Thanks, Toby, and tell your ma we thank her, too." Jeremiah dug into his pocket. "I don't have any coin for trade, but here's a right nice piece of quartz that catches the light real pretty."

Grinning, Toby took the rough, yellow stone in his grimy hand and loped away.

Ginny turned from tending to Bluelegs's wound. The blacksmith continued to go in and out of consciousness causing Jeremiah to fear he might not survive the night.

"How is he?" Jeremiah removed the square of linen from the basket, revealing the promised crock of stew and tin of cornbread, along with a jug of water.

"He is sleeping. His injury is severe, but he is strong." She glanced over to where Bluelegs slept while covered with the buffalo rug Ginny had carried on her back. "Now, he needs rest more than he needs food. I will wait until he wakes again to feed him."

Jeremiah handed Ginny a plate of stew and cornbread then fixed a plate for himself. "You look done-in. Sure appreciate Toby bringing us this food." Shoveling in a forkful of the stew, he grinned. "Wish I had more than the quartz to give him in payment."

Ginny smiled around a bite of cornbread. "Toby reminds me of Davy Carroll, only older."

"Who's Davy Carroll?" Jeremiah took a sip of the water and then passed the jug to Ginny.

"The son of the people I met on my journey to Silver Creek."

"The people in the Conestoga?" Jeremiah said, telling her of the information they'd gleaned from the old Delaware woman.

Ginny nodded. "Yes." She told him how she'd treated the boy's fever, and how his parents had befriended her. "I liked them very much, especially Judith." Her expression turned pensive as she took another bite of stew. "Judith told me that the Bible book says I can be a healer of my people and a Christian, that it says so in the part of the book called Gala...Gala—"

"Galatians?"

Ginny's words at once surprised Jeremiah and sparked hope in his chest. Could Ginny be considering accepting Christ as her savior?

Ginny nodded. "Judith said if I believe that Jesus is the Son of the Great Spirit, I can be a Christian. She said it does not matter who I am. Do you believe that to be true?" Her look both challenged and questioned.

"Yes, it is true. I thought you knew that." Jeremiah groaned as remorse smote his heart. He'd failed her. And, in their own way, perhaps Zeb and Ruth had failed her as well.

The tears glistening in Ginny's eyes slashed at his heart. "No, I did not know that. And why would I think such a thing when many of the whites in Underwood call me a heathen. They were happy to have me heal their sick children, but they were ashamed to let anyone know that it was me that healed them. Ben Collins called me evil and warned me to stop using the healing knowledge my mother, Falling Leaf, taught me. Then someone, maybe Collins, left a dead fawn in front of my shee-tha's home to frighten me away."

"I'm sorry, Ginny. Zeb told me about the fawn." It hurt to think she had felt so alone, scared, and unprotected that she'd felt forced to leave home. "You didn't need to run away. Surely, you knew that your uncle and I would protect you from the likes of Ben Collins."

The tears welling in her eyes slipped down her face. Her chin lifted in a defiant tilt and her voice turned angry. "I did not run away because I was afraid of the man, Collins. I ran away because I would never be accepted by the white Christians in Underwood, the people who sit and listen to you and my shee-tha preach to them from the Bible book. Even if I did love Jesus and His words and believe Him to be the Son of the Great Spirit, I would still be looked on as a heathen because I choose to dress as a Shawnee and practice my people's healing ways."

Her tone turned accusing. "I saw the hate in the eyes of your sister's husband when he looked at me, and even *you* told me to stop practicing my healing and to wear the white women's clothes." She looked down at her plate of food and her voice lowered, turning sad. "It hurt my heart to leave behind the ones I love in Underwood, but the hate there withered my spirit. I felt the need to go where my spirit can bloom, where I can be what I am—a proud Shawnee medicine woman."

She couldn't have crushed Jeremiah more if she'd taken a war club to his head like Flying Hawk had done to Bluelegs. He, and a member of his own family, had contributed to her pain. But worse, they'd acted as stumbling blocks, preventing her from entering Christ's fold. How long had she desired to accept Jesus into her heart but had resisted because she thought she would need to give up practicing her healing methods?

He covered her hand with his. "I'm so sorry, Ginny. I'm sorry for the way you were treated, but mostly I'm sorry—and ashamed—that I did not try harder to teach you of Jesus' love and acceptance." Guilt seared his conscience. "In my desire to keep you safe, I shamed you, and for that, I am heartily sorry and heartily ashamed." His voice lifted with his growing fervor. Now he had the chance to make up for his failings. "Judith is right. You *can* be a Shawnee healer and a Christian. Galatians 3:28 says 'There is neither Jew nor Greek, there is neither bond nor free, there is neither male nor female: for ye are all one in Christ Jesus.'" He gazed into her eyes, hope and joy blooming in his heart. "And do you believe that Jesus is the Christ, the Son of the living God?"

"Yes." Ginny gave a somber nod. "I told Judith, and she said I was a Christian."

Joy filled Jeremiah until the emotion flooded his eyes, threatening to stream down his face and embarrass him. Embracing her, he pulled her to him and pressed his face against her hair. "Praise God. And God bless Judith Carroll."

Pushing away, he gazed into her lovely eyes. The temptation to kiss her lips became overwhelming, so he let go of her and picked up his plate of food again. He needed to focus on helping her grow in her newfound faith. "So was it finding Flying Hawk in the village on Silver Creek that made you decide to head back to Underwood?"

"No." She took a long swig of water from the jug. "Judith told me to be sure I was running *to* something and not *away* from something. She told me to pray to Jesus and ask Him to guide me."

The lovely smile he'd missed so much returned to Ginny's lips.

"Last night I prayed and asked Jesus to tell me what I should do. Later, on my dream journey, I saw both my mothers, Falling Leaf and Carolyn McLain, standing together and smiling at me from the land beyond the sunset. I remembered my mother Falling Leaf's words before she died. She said that I am both white and Shawnee, and that I must embrace both worlds. I knew I needed to return. When I parted with the Carrolls, I went to the Shawnee village looking for help in my journey back to Underwood."

"But instead you found Flying Hawk."

She set her plate aside and nodded. "He had come to guide the Ohio Shawnee west."

A groan sounded from the buffalo rug. Bluelegs stirred and then sat up. Ginny hurried to his side. Watching the tender attention she gave to Bluelegs sparked a flame of jealousy in Jeremiah's middle. Ginny may have given her heart to Christ, but that did not assure Jeremiah that she'd give Jeremiah her heart as well.

He watched her smiling and conversing in Shawnee with Bluelegs as she tenderly fed the injured man, and the jealous flame inside Jeremiah blazed hotter. Moments ago, when he learned that Ginny had accepted Christ into her heart, the temptation to ask her to marry him had tugged hard. Thankfully, he'd resisted that temptation. Even if she agreed to such a proposal, the odds of her living a happy life with him seemed remote. More likely, such a union would bring more pain into her life. In truth, she had far more in common with Bluelegs than with Jeremiah.

His appetite gone, Jeremiah set his plate of stew on the straw covered ground beside him and bowed his head. *Dear Lord, You know I love Ginny, but if we should not marry then show me, and give me the strength to let her go.*

In the corner of the stall, Ginny and Bluelegs shared a private laugh. The pleasant sound ripped at Jeremiah's heart. He seemed to have his answer.

29

"Are you sure you are strong enough to travel?" Concern coursed through Ginny as she examined the wound on the back of Bluelegs's head. The blood had dried to a crusty scab, and she found no sign of pus, which eased her concern.

Grasping the wood planks of the barn stall, he pulled himself to his feet. "If now was my time to join my ancestors, I would have done so last night. Besides, Mose needs the stall, and I have a smithy in Underwood that needs tending."

Not fully agreeing with his assessment, Ginny held on to his arm to steady him. "The road to Underwood has many ruts. I will tell Mose to put much straw in the back of the wagon he has given us for the journey."

Bluelegs grinned down at her. "You are a good medicine woman, my little fawn. You do honor to your people."

Nodding her thanks at his compliment, Ginny slipped her arm around his waist to help steady his steps out of the livery. Again, she wished she could feel something more for Bluelegs than a sisterly fondness. Last night she'd enjoyed conversing with him in Shawnee as they shared memories of Shawnee and Lenape celebrations, but despite how hard she tried, she could not force her heart to twine around Bluelegs anymore than she could disentangle it from Jeremiah.

Witnessing Jeremiah's joy at learning that she'd embraced Jesus and hearing his remorse for any imagined pain he'd caused her, had made her want to weep. When he wrapped her in his arms, her heart had sung. For a blissful moment she'd closed her eyes, expecting to feel his lips on hers. When that didn't happen and he let her go, her joy had melted into a puddle of disappointment.

Disappointment again, jabbed at her heart as she watched him drive the borrowed wagon and team of horses to the front of the livery. His now-distant attitude confused and pained her, leaving her spirit feeling darkened as if storm clouds had shut out the sun's rays.

Mose shuffled out of the livery to join them beside the wagon. He patted Bluelegs on the shoulder. "Glad you're feelin' better, boy. You take it easy now, ya hear?" His gruff voice thickened with emotion.

Bluelegs reached out his hand and gave Mose's hand a quick shake. "Thank you, Mose. I am in your debt."

Mose shook his head, his faded blue eyes turning watery. "You don't owe me nothin'. He turned to Ginny and gave her a wink. "You take care of my boy, here, missy."

Smiling, Ginny nodded. Her smile faded at the

granite-hard expression on Jeremiah's face as he walked toward them.

Offering the stableman a tepid smile, Jeremiah shook his hand. "We thank you and your kin for all you did for us, Mr. Barnes. I'll be back tomorrow to return your team and wagon and get our saddle horses. I'll settle up with you then."

With another round of parting handshakes, Ginny climbed in the back of the wagon with Bluelegs and Jeremiah headed the horses down the road toward Underwood.

The three engaged in scant conversation during the trip back to Underwood. Bluelegs mostly slept while Jeremiah focused on driving and dodging as many ruts in the road as possible. Left to her own thoughts, Ginny couldn't decide what bothered her more, Bluelegs's sleeping or Jeremiah's reticence.

When Jeremiah finally brought the wagon to a stop beside Uncle Zeb and Aunt Ruth's cabin, the sun had slipped low in the sky. Ginny's stomach knotted at the thought of facing her kin, making her glad she hadn't eaten since her meager breakfast of flapjacks and sorghum molasses hours ago. Guilt skinned her conscience. How would they react? At least she'd learned from Bluelegs that he'd deciphered the message she'd left for them in Shawnee symbols on the piece of Birchwood.

"Ginny! Ginny, girl!" A beaming Uncle Zeb raced out of the cabin with Aunt Ruth close behind, drying tears from her face with her apron hem.

After the anguish Ginny's leaving must have put them through, her aunt's and uncle's joy and excitement in seeing her again felt like a briar branch whipped across her heart. She scrambled down from the wagon as quickly as she could.

Strong hands encircled her waist, lifting her gently to the ground. She turned, expecting to fall into her uncle's embrace. Instead, she looked up to find Jeremiah's face inches from hers. She melted against him and, for one glorious instant, their hearts beat as one. His warm breath caressed her ear as his whispered voice caressed her heart. "Ginny. Oh, Ginny."

Her arms slipped around him, and she stood in his embrace, wishing she could remain there forever. But the next moment, he shifted her to the waiting arms of Uncle Zeb and Aunt Ruth.

Once again, Ginny's remorse tumbled down on her like a pile of logs. "I am sorry, Uncle Zeb. Aunt Ruth. I am so sorry for the pain I caused you. I have dishonored you and my parents." Her words dissolved into sobs.

"No, no Ginny, girl. You've done no such thing," Uncle Zeb said as he and Aunt Ruth both wrapped their arms around her. "We just praise God for protecting you and bringing you back safe to us."

Bluelegs popped up to peer over the side of the wagon, blinking. "Are we in Underwood?"

Ginny smiled up at him from her family's embrace. "Yes. We are at the home of my aunt and uncle." She and Jeremiah took turns recounting to Uncle Zeb and Aunt Ruth what had happened outside the Shawnee village on Silver Creek.

Aunt Ruth gasped and pressed both hands to her mouth as Jeremiah told how Flying Hawk had clubbed Bluelegs on the head. She lifted compassionate eyes to Bluelegs. "You poor thing. Praise be to God it was not a fatal blow!"

Bluelegs gave her a crooked grin. "The Creator is not yet ready to have me back, I think."

"There is still much healing that must happen," Ginny said. She'd seen her mother treat people with head injuries. Some seemed to recover quickly and go back to living as normal then suddenly, without warning, they would die. "I do not think he will be healed until the beginning of the Strawberry Moon. Until then, he should not work at the smithy."

"Then you'll be staying here with us, young man." Aunt Ruth's pronouncement broached no dissent. "Zeb will fix you up a bed in the loom room and that's that." She gave Ginny another hug and, with her arm still around her, guided her toward the cabin. "The important thing is you are home safe, and we can get back to the way things were."

But for Ginny, things were not as they were before. Though their daily lives soon slipped back into normalcy—with the exception of Bluelegs's presence— Ginny knew that her journey to Silver Creek had changed her life forever. Her decision to embrace Jesus brought her closer to her aunt and uncle. They both wept at the news and, like Jeremiah, they praised God for bringing the Carroll family into Ginny's life. Ginny now joined Zeb and Ruth in their daily Bible reading which not only pleased her aunt and uncle, but also soothed Ginny's troubled heart at the stark change in Jeremiah's attitude toward her. In the two weeks since their return to Underwood, he hadn't visited her once.

At first, Ginny attributed Jeremiah's absence to Bluelegs's presence. But the restless blacksmith had returned to his smithy a week ago, and still Jeremiah stayed away.

Thoughts of Jeremiah pressed hard on Ginny's

heart as she crouched at the hearth and prodded the glowing embers to life with the iron poker. He ruled her waking hours and stalked her dreams. Every night, she prayed for Jesus to either restore Jeremiah's affection for her or to take away her love for him that left her heart bruised and her spirit weak, but her prayers went unanswered.

Her heart throbbed painfully as her mind went back to the tender moments when Jeremiah had held her, kissed her. Tears filled her eyes, blurring the orange flames licking up the stone fireplace. In those moments, she'd felt his affection as surely as she now felt the warmth of the blaze before her. His avoidance of her made no sense. He'd traveled for two days to find her, and now that she was home, he seemed not to care. Since they first met in her Missouri village during the time of the Long Moon, he'd worked to convince her to embrace Jesus as the Son of the Great Spirit and now that she had, he seemed to have turned his back on her.

The only reasonable answer to why Jeremiah continued to avoid her crept from the recesses of her mind to whisper its hateful taunt. He didn't love her. At least not enough to ask her to be his wife. The cheerful crackling fire and popping sparks mocked her pain. She sniffed away her tears, glad that Uncle Zeb had gone to work on the new church building and Aunt Ruth had returned to her rug-making in the loom room.

A rapping at the front door pulled Ginny from her melancholy muse. She rose and opened the door to find Esther Collins on the front step weeping and wringing her hands.

"My twin girls have come down with a fever. I've

tried ever'thin' and nothin' I've done has brought down their fevers." Worry and exhaustion had carved deep lines in the woman's face, making her almost unrecognizable. "I'm at the end of my rope. Ben would kill me if he knew I was here, but you've got to come and see if there is anythin' you can do for my girls."

~*~

"You goin' somewhere?"

At the sound of Zeb's voice, Jeremiah turned from saddling his horse. "Back home to Jackson County," he said, turning back to finish tightening the saddle's cinch strap. He hadn't relished his planned stop at Zeb's cabin to say his good-byes, so maybe it was best this way.

"Somethin' wrong at home?" Zeb's concerned tone touched Jeremiah.

"No." Jeremiah turned to face Zeb. "Something is wrong here."

"Does that 'somethin' have to do with Ginny?" Zeb moseyed over to the cabin and settled himself on the stone step beneath the door.

Jeremiah gave a soft chuckle. "Guess it was more obvious than I thought." He'd dreaded this conversation. Might as well have done with it. With a sigh of surrender, he walked over and sat beside Zeb.

Zeb's laugh sent a squiggle of irritation through Jeremiah. "You two have been sweet on each other since before we left Missouri." He snorted. "A half-blind man could see that." His tone turned harder, scolding now. "Ginny's been mopin' around since you come back from Silver Creek. Bein' the closest thing she has to a pa, I think I have the right to know what's goin' on."

"I figured she'd be happy as a lark with Bluelegs close at hand." Jeremiah couldn't keep the bitterness from his voice.

"Ah, I wondered if jealousy was at play here." Zeb leaned back and rubbed the tops of his thighs. He paused for a long moment before he turned a stern face to Jeremiah. "I never saw nothin' but friendship between Ginny and Bluelegs. It's you she keeps askin' about, pinin' for." He narrowed his gaze at Jeremiah. "If you don't have any feelin's fer the girl, tell her so she can turn her eyes in another direction, but I don't think that's the case."

Jeremiah heaved another sigh, deeper this time. Resting his forearms on his knees, he hung his head. "No, it's not the case. I love Ginny with all my heart." He quirked a sad grin at Zeb. "But you already know that, don't you?"

"I do. So why are you leavin'? You love her. She loves you, and Ginny's a Christian now with as strong a love for the Lord as you and me." Zeb's gray eyes turned watery. "It like to broke my heart the other evenin' when she asked me to read her Scriptures that give comfort to those who are sad. I had a good mind to tromp over here and take you by the shirt front and give you a right smart shake!"

Jeremiah winced at the thought of causing Ginny heartache. At the same time, his heart thrilled at the knowledge that she cared enough about him to feel that way. He cocked his head toward Zeb. He needed to make the man understand. "Can't you see, Zeb? A life with me would only bring her pain." Frustration filling him, he threw out his arm in a futile gesture. "Shoot, you've seen how some people around here treat her, even some in your own congregation. How much worse do you think it would be if she were the wife of a preacher?" He hung his head again as the weight of his despair pushed down on him.

Zeb sighed and put his hand on Jeremiah's shoulder. "You're afraid you can't protect her from all the nasty looks and comments of ignorant people, is that it?"

Jeremiah turned and looked straight at Zeb. "You couldn't, and I can't either. In the livery in Charlestown, she told me she ran away because she knew she'd never be accepted here, and she's right." Jeremiah's voice lowered in defeat. "Maybe it would have been better if she'd gone back west with the Ohio Shawnee, after all."

"Jeremiah, God had a reason for us to find Ginny last fall. What kinda odds would you put on such a thing, us travelin' all those miles away and endin' up at the very Shawnee village where Ginny lived? She didn't want to come back, but God worked it out where she had to." Zeb rose slowly with a soft grunt and then patted Jeremiah's bent back. "Ginny finally come to the understandin' that bein' here is God's will for her." He smiled. "Even the Shawnee have a word for it: ka-tet. And I believe you're a part of that. Don't do what Ginny did and try to run away from God's will." He sighed. "You can't protect her from every hurt, boy, but you don't need to hurt her either...or yourself."

Jeremiah bristled at Zeb's scold and sought solace in a pity-wallow. "And what makes you think God didn't bring her here to be the wife of Bluelegs?"

Zeb grinned. "Because God put in her heart a love for you, not for our blacksmith friend."

"Zeb! Jeremiah!" Ruth came racing toward them, her eyes wide with fear. "Ginny went to treat the Collins girls," she blurted, gasping for breath. "And Ben's gone on a tear, threatenin' to kill folk over it!"

30

"You git outta my house this minute, you dirty little savage!" Ben Collins raised his hand as if to strike Ginny while his wife sat weeping at the bedside of their sick daughters.

Though quaking inside, Ginny stood tall in the Collins's cabin, her chin lifted in a defiant tilt. "Your wife asked me to come and treat your children. You can let me try to save them, or you can let them die."

"Well this is my cabin, and I'm tellin' you to leave!"

"Please, Ben. Pleaaase." Sobbing, Esther fell to her knees and lifted her clasped hands to her irate husband. "I've done all I can for our Mary and Jane. They're gonna die if Ginny can't help them. Please let her do...something!" She sank to the floor, dissolving in a heap of tears.

Ben's eyes blazed with rage, and his face turned an even deeper purple. "More like, she'll put some kind of evil Injun spell on them and us!"

"Ben Collins, you lay a finger on Ginny, and it will

be the last thing you ever do." Jeremiah's low, menacing voice from the cabin's open door sent a wave of relief washing through Ginny.

Ben shook his fist at Jeremiah. "Git outta my house, Dunbar! You, too, McLain." He glared past Jeremiah to Uncle Zeb. "I'm not gonna let this savage kill my girls!"

Esther sprang to her feet. The despair vanished from her haggard face, replaced by a rage that equaled her husband's. "It's *you* that's killin' them, Ben! I brought Ginny here to doctor our babies. You can kill me for it if you want to, but she's gonna get the chance to save our Mary and Jane!"

A stunned expression replaced the one of rage on Ben's face. His eyes welled with tears and, for a moment, his shoulders sagged as a look of defeat came over him. "Do what you will." His anger returned, seeming to bolster him, and he turned a murderous glare on Ginny. "You shoulda died with your kin and mine back at Pigeon Roost, you little heathen." Pointing his forefinger at Ginny, he stabbed the air in front of her face. "But I promise you this, if my girls die at your hand, you and yours won't draw an easy breath from this day forward!" With that, he stalked out of the cabin, shoving his way past Zeb and Jeremiah, who came in, followed by Ruth.

Esther turned a tender look down at her little daughters who lay sleeping together on the bed, a patchwork quilt pulled up to their chins and their yellow hair splayed out over a calico-covered pillow. Ginny guessed their ages to be about five winters. That they'd continued to sleep through their father's ranting both surprised and troubled her. Their too rosy cheeks and cracked lips troubled her even more.

When Esther turned back to Ginny, her demeanor had changed. Her eyes looked clear now, and her worry-worn countenance grew strong and determined. "What do you need to heal my girls?"

Ginny stepped over to the girls' sickbed and touched their faces. Their fevers burned much hotter than Davy Carroll's had. Willow bark might help, but it wouldn't save them. "I will need bark from the dogwood tree to make a tea." She fixed Esther with as serious a look as she could muster, praying the woman wouldn't reject her next demand out of hand. "This kind of fever will not be healed with medicine alone. It will only leave their bodies by sweat. We must put them in a sweat lodge."

To Esther's credit, she met Ginny's look squarely. "Whatever you have to do, do it."

Ginny turned to Jeremiah. "You must build a sweat lodge outside." She described how to build the lodge with willow sapling poles and dig a hole in the center of the space in which to place hot rocks. "You will need to cover the lodge with blankets, or whatever material you can find so the steam will not escape. Then you must build a fire a short distance from the lodge. There, you will heat rocks this big." Spacing her hands apart, she indicated the size of rocks needed. "You will need three times as many hot rocks as the fingers on your hands."

Jeremiah nodded and headed out the door. Under her breath, Ginny whispered a prayer of thanks for his presence, which both calmed and reassured her.

Over the next hour, no hands remained still. Esther and Ruth went to search for dogwood bark while Zeb and Jeremiah worked to construct the sweat lodge. Ginny removed the quilt from her young patients and opened the cabin's window to allow the cool, spring breezes to waft over them.

Thankfully, Ben Collins stayed away, seeming to want nothing to do with the proceedings. As she worked with Esther and Ruth to dose the girls with the dogwood tea, Ginny prayed for the children's recovery and that their father would cause no more trouble. She'd rather not contemplate on what actions Ben Collins might take if his daughters died.

An hour later, Jeremiah stepped into the cabin, his shirtsleeves rolled up to his elbows. "The lodge is ready, and the rocks are red hot and ready to be put in the pit we dug in the center of the lodge."

Ginny nodded. "You and Zeb must carry Mary and Jane in first and lay them on blankets near the pit. Then fill the pit with the hot rocks and pour cold water over them to make the steam."

Jeremiah turned as if to leave. Then he stopped, turned back, and took her hand in his. His soft gaze caressed her face. "You are the most remarkable woman I've ever known, Ginny Red Fawn McLain." The tender look in his blue eyes took away Ginny's breath and released a flutter of butterflies in her middle. Still smiling, he crossed the cabin to the sickbed and gently lifted little Mary in his arms. Zeb picked up Jane and carried her out first.

For the next two hours, Jeremiah and Zeb worked to keep the lodge filled with steam, continually reheating the hot rocks and pouring cold water over them. Ginny, Esther, and Ruth took turns tending to the girls who, now awake, coughed and fussed in the steamy lodge.

Inside the lodge, Ginny sat amid a cloud of stifling vapor, praying over the sick children. Against her will, the hateful words of their father muscled their way into her thoughts. *You shoulda died with your kin and mine at Pigeon Roost.*

The question that had lain silent inside Ginny, putrefying over the past twelve winters of her life finally surfaced, demanding she give it voice. The words left her throat in a tortured groan. "Tell me, Jesus. Why *was* I spared? Why did Missilemotaw and his men not kill me when they killed Ma and Pa, and Joe?" In the quiet of the lodge, the answer came like a whisper to her heart. *It was for this, you were saved.* Judith Carroll's words came back to Ginny's mind. *Seems to me, there's a powerful lot of healin' that still needs to happen there. I can't help thinkin' that God might have brought you back for just that purpose.*

Many times, Ginny's mother, Falling Leaf, had told of how the Great Spirit speaks to those who seek His wisdom. Suddenly, the understanding that had eluded Ginny for twelve winters smacked her in the face. All the hidden guilt she'd carried for surviving what her parents and brother had not washed away, leaving her spirit feeling cleansed, light, and unencumbered.

She buried her face in her hands and sobbed. Judith was right. The Great Spirit had saved her and given her to Painted Buck and Falling Leaf so she could learn the Shawnee ways of healing. Perhaps it was for the sake of Jeremiah's brother, Isaac, or for Davy Carroll. Or perhaps it was for this moment, so she could help heal the children of the man who hated her.

Snuffing back her tears, Ginny turned her focus again to her young patients. She reached over and touched Mary's face. Though damp from the steam, the child's skin felt cool now, sending relief like a waterfall sluicing over Ginny. Pressing her hand to Jane's forehead, she found the same. The children's fevers had broken. Ginny bent her head, her joyful tears mingling with the sweat trickling down her face. "Thank You, Jesus. Thank You for saving them. Thank You for saving me," she murmured.

Eager to share the good news, she crawled out of the lodge, drenched in happiness and her own sweat. "The fever is gone. They will live," she announced to the others who sat resting outside the lodge.

"Praise be to God!" Esther let out a happy sob and immediately disappeared inside the lodge. Rejoicing, Zeb and Ruth fell into each other arms, weeping, laughing, and praising God.

Ginny felt the strength that had sustained her all day seep away with the releasing tension. Her legs grew wobbly beneath her and she might have collapsed to the ground, but Jeremiah wrapped a strong arm around her and guided her to a grassy spot in the shade of a sycamore tree.

"Sit here." He gently lowered her to the grass. "You must be exhausted." He sat down beside her and took her hands in his. "You didn't have to come, Ginny. Knowing how Ben feels about you, no one would have blamed you if you'd refused Esther."

Ginny drew in a refreshing breath of air and lifted her face to the cooling breeze drying her wet hair plastered with sweat to her forehead. Untarnished joy like she hadn't experienced since early childhood filled her along with a desire to share the amazing revelation the Great Spirit had just given her. "I am a healer, Jeremiah. I had to be here. It is ka-tet."

Jeremiah gave her a sweet smile. "After today no one, not even Ben Collins, can doubt you are a skilled healer."

"No. No, that is not what I mean!" She shook her head. She had to make him understand what Jesus had revealed to her. She gripped his hands, unable to hold back the joy bubbling up inside her as happy tears flooded down her face. "You do not understand. While I was in the sweat lodge, I prayed to Jesus to tell me why my life was spared those many years ago at Pigeon Roost, and He spoke to me, Jeremiah." A fresh deluge of tears coursed down her face. She tapped her chest. "He spoke to me here, in my heart. He told me that it was for this moment that I was saved."

The smile left Jeremiah's face and a look of awe came over his features. Without another word, he slipped his arms around her. For a long moment, he gazed into her eyes as if he could peer into the very depths of her soul. Then his eyes closed and his face leaned in to hers. When their lips met, Ginny's heart lifted, soaring higher than any eagle could fly. At once, time and her heart seemed to stand still as she luxuriated in his kiss, returning his caresses with equal passion and tenderness.

When he finally lifted his head, his eyes, glistening with welling tears, once again searched the depths of hers. Taking her hands, he folded them warmly in his. "Ginny, Red Fawn McLain, will you do me the great honor of becoming my wife? Because I don't think I could manage to live the rest of my life without you."

Giggling, Ginny gazed at his dear face through a veil of happy tears. "I have to, my darling Jeremiah. It is ka-tet."

A Devotional Moment

Dear friends, I urge you, as foreigners and exiles, to abstain from sinful desires, which wage war against your soul. Live such good lives among the pagans that, though they accuse you of doing wrong, they may see your good deeds and glorify God on the day he visits us. ~ 1 Peter 2: 11-12

It is difficult to be among strangers and to practice our special relationship with God. We may be concerned about offending, or perhaps being mocked for our beliefs. Ironically, we often do the same thing to those who don't believe as we do. But we are to act as Christians no matter where we are, so that the light of Jesus shines through us. Doing good works and praising God will help others to consider their choices, too. They may even be encouraged to ask about Jesus, and be willing to receive the Good News.

In **The Time for Healing**, the protagonist was taken as a child into a foreign culture, and she has embraced some of that culture. When her adopted mother insists that she comply with a promise made long before, she returns to her people, but her foreign ways are censured and misunderstood, even though they are kind and helpful acts that would not offend Christ.

Have you ever been so caught up in your own Christianity that you failed to see the goodness in others. Non-Christians are loved by God equally as much as Christians, and we are to be the light of Christ. That means being able to see the goodness in others and to understand the difference between those beliefs that would offend Christ and those that are simply different. The next time you are tempted to condemn someone for their lack of faith, take a breath. Remember a time when you were misjudged, put on the spot or ridiculed. Did that behaviour help you to agree with those who were abusive, or did you turn a hurt, blind eye? The adage is true; we catch more bees with honey. Be firm in your faith, but be understanding, also.

LORD, WHEN FOREIGNERS ARE AMONG US, HELP ME TO ACT WITH THE LIGHT OF JESUS AND DISCERN WELL THEIR HEART AND INTENTIONS. HELP ME TO KNOW HOW YOU WOULD WANT ME TO ACT SO THEY CAN BE ENCOURAGED TO ACCEPT YOUR LOVE. IN JESUS' NAME I PRAY, AMEN.

Thank you

We appreciate you reading this White Rose Publishing title. For other inspirational stories, please visit our on-line bookstore at www.pelicanbookgroup.com.

For questions or more information, contact us at customer@pelicanbookgroup.com.

White Rose Publishing
Where Faith is the Cornerstone of Love™
an imprint of Pelican Book Group
www.PelicanBookGroup.com

Connect with Us
www.facebook.com/Pelicanbookgroup
www.twitter.com/pelicanbookgrp

To receive news and specials, subscribe to our bulletin
http://pelink.us/bulletin

May God's glory shine through
this inspirational work of fiction.

AMDG

You Can Help!

At Pelican Book Group it is our mission to entertain readers with fiction that uplifts the Gospel. It is our privilege to spend time with you awhile as you read our stories.

We believe you can help us to bring Christ into the lives of people across the globe. And you don't have to open your wallet or even leave your house!

Here are 3 simple things you can do to help us bring illuminating fiction™ to people everywhere.

1) If you enjoyed this book, write a positive review. Post it at online retailers and websites where readers gather. And share your review with us at reviews@pelicanbookgroup.com (this does give us permission to reprint your review in whole or in part.)

2) If you enjoyed this book, recommend it to a friend in person, at a book club or on social media.

3) If you have suggestions on how we can improve or expand our selection, let us know. We value your opinion. Use the contact form on our web site or e-mail us at customer@pelicanbookgroup.com

God Can Help!

Are you in need? The Almighty can do great things for you. Holy is His Name! He has mercy in every generation. He can lift up the lowly and accomplish all things. Reach out today.

Do not fear: I am with you; do not be anxious: I am your God. I will strengthen you, I will help you, I will uphold you with my victorious right hand.
~Isaiah 41:10 (NAB)

We pray daily, and we especially pray for everyone connected to Pelican Book Group—that includes you! If you have a specific need, we welcome the opportunity to pray for you. Share your needs or praise reports at http://pelink.us/pray4us

Free Book Offer

We're looking for booklovers like you to partner with us! Join our team of influencers today and periodically receive free eBooks and exclusive offers.

For more information
Visit http://pelicanbookgroup.com/booklovers